Blue HORIZONS

a Horizons novel

KATHRYN ANDREWS

Copyright © 2015 Kathryn Andrews
Published by Kathryn Andrews, LLC
www.kandrewsauthor.com

Cover design by Indie Solutions by Murphy Rae
Formatting by JT Formatting

First Edition: October 2015
Library of Congress Cataloging-in-Publication Data
Andrews, Kathryn
Blue Horizons (a Horizons novel) – 1st ed
ISBN-13: 978-1517601416

Dedication

To My Husband . . .
Thank you for always dreaming about what's beyond the blue horizons. Our life together has been and is an amazing adventure, and I can't wait to see what happens next. I love you.

Chapter ONE

WILL ASHTON

SWEAT DRIPS OUT from underneath my black Stetson and rolls down the side of my face. My eyes squint to see through the blinding stage lights and past the crowd. It's almost eleven thirty, and I know the stars are out there somewhere, but between the lights and the heat, one would never know.

Taking a deep breath, the smell of damp dirt and cattle slams into me, and my stomach rolls. For months, we've been following the pro rodeo across the country, closing down their last night in each city with sold out shows, and tonight I can't help but think this is mine. My last night.

The truth of the matter is, I just don't care anymore. All I ever wanted was to be somebody. Somebody to someone and somebody to myself, and ten years later, I feel more lost than found.

Lost.

Just the thought sends an overwhelming sadness coursing through me. No one would understand. After all, over the last five years, we've had three albums go double platinum, won seven Grammy's, continue to sell out sixty thousand-plus stadiums, and are now considered to be one of country music's greatest bands—The Will Ashton Band.

I hate this name.

Yes, it's my name. But naming the band after me implies that the music is all about me, and it's not. Originally we were called Blue Horizons, but since it's my voice—and only my voice—the change was required to sign with the label. Not a day goes by that I don't regret this and feel bad for Clay, my best friend and lead guitarist, and the others who put so much of their heart and soul into it.

Stepping back from the microphone, I pull on the worn leather of my guitar strap and force it to swing around and abruptly land on my back. I wince from the impact, not because of any pain inflicted, but because out of everything around me—the stage, the set, the equipment—the only thing that holds any value to me is this old acoustic guitar.

Realization hits me like a Mack truck, and it feels true. Nothing about this life or this dream holds any meaning anymore. Is it possible to love something so much, for so long, that one day you wake up and realize you don't love it at all? No, right? So, what's happening to me?

Vaguely, I hear the familiar riff that is my cue, reach for the microphone, and just a beat too late miss the opening bar. I glance over to Clay, and although I can't see his eyes behind the aviators he's wearing, I can read his concerned and pissed look all the same. Lucky bastard to have those sunglasses on . . . what I wouldn't give for a pair myself right now.

Clay takes a step toward me and I shake my head, halting him. Quickly recovering from my mistake, he turns back to the audience and walks to the stage edge to, one, appease the fans and, two, give me a little more time. Hands fly up into the air to touch him—he plays this part so well. I'd rather be on the receiving end of a thoroughbred's hoof to the groin than be touched by so many people. You'd think I'd be used to it by now, immune, but I'm not. Wanting to be touched, hugged, or felt up just because I'm well-known is weird, and has always been my least favorite part in all of this.

Walking back to his place on stage, he glances at me one more time. He's known that I've been off for the last couple of months, but we've never talked about just how off. This is going to affect him too, and as much as that causes my gut to ache with guilt . . . he'll just have to get over it. I hope he can understand. No, I need him to understand.

Without thinking, I pull my hat off and lift my shirt to wipe the sweat from my face. The volume of the crowd moves to a deafening level and my heart sinks. When did getting a glimpse of skin become just as exciting as the music? It's supposed to be about the music, dammit.

Sucking in more air, my lungs feel like they're on fire, and the flames are ripping through my insides, scorching my throat. I've poured myself into this show more than any other to try and regain that lost feeling . . . but nothing. I feel empty except for the rawness that has become my voice.

The band circles back to the intro and I remind myself that this is the last song. With that reminder, a familiar kick of adrenaline hits my chest and I smile. It's a feeling I once basked in when I walked on stage, to now only have it return when I've finally made the decision to walk off.

A rueful chuckle escapes me as I think about the repercussions of this, but I just don't give a shit. For years, I've laughed at those in the industry who caved under the pressure . . . and now, I'm no different.

Or maybe I am.

I don't feel pressure so much as I feel unease. The thrill and the passion, it's all gone. I used to think I was born for this. I craved it with every fiber of my being. Music has always been what fed my soul. But now, I just don't know . . .

I lean forward and grab the mic. My eyes drift shut as I place my bottom lip against the cool metal like I have a thousand times. I can do this. Just one more song . . . One last time.

Chapter TWO

WILL ASHTON

TWO LOUD KNOCKS hit the front door startling me. Whiskey lets out a warning bark and then it swings open. Clay leans against the door frame, toes off his shoes, and barges in, slamming the door shut behind him. He spots me immediately, scowls, and I can't help the smile that splits across my face. I'm surprised it took him this long, but seeing him here, man, have I missed him.

"You d-d-do know that everyone, and I do mean everyone is looking for you," he says as he shoulders past, glaring at me. He's more upset than I thought he would be, and hearing the stutter catch makes me feel like shit. It only comes out when he's feeling extreme emotions, and he hates it.

He drops his bag next to the couch and turns to face me. I've been avoiding his calls, so I can completely understand his irritation. It's been two months since I walked away from him after that last show and went into hiding. Hiding from life, hiding from responsibilities, hiding from myself. It was desperately needed and felt so good.

I drag my hand back and forth through my hair, suddenly noticing how long and shaggy it's gotten. Dark brown pieces fall over my eyes and I push them off. "I figured as much. Good thing we never told anyone about this place." I eye him suspiciously, crossing my arms over my chest. I've known him for so long that I'll immediately be able to tell if he lies to me.

His frown deepens as Whiskey runs over and rams his head into Clay's leg. Clay grunts, but bends down to give him a good petting. Whiskey is just as much his as he is mine, and I'm elated the three of us are together again. Living on the tour bus and being on the road, I had forgotten what it was like to live by myself. Growing up as an only child, there's more silence than there is noise, and in a way, that silence is equal parts comfort and loneliness. But the day I met Clay, the silence vanished. He became my best friend and the brother I never had.

Letting out a sigh, he makes his way into the kitchen and grabs a beer from the refrigerator. Clay's never been much for words, but even through the unspoken, I've always heard him loud and clear. He leans back against the counter, and I feel him watch me as I move away from him and drop into a large leather chair in the living room. I'm still smiling and he's still frowning.

For the last five years, Clay and I have been trekking around the U.S. with barely any breaks between tours. This last tour, *The Roundup,* we hit twenty different cities in four months. We are constantly on the go, and lately, the only thing I've wanted to do is stop. Now, I'm not gonna lie and say it's all bad, but there are a lot of moving parts to this job that just outright suck.

The label assembles most of the band. It's easy for them to find the talent; what's hard is getting them to stay committed and focused when none of us have any personal connection. We all work tirelessly to make this unified sound, but if one person is off, it affects everyone. Between finding rehearsal space, getting equipment, being on the road, and making sure everyone stays motivated, it's a twenty-four seven job to lead this group. There is no down time. I've spent more nights than I care to admit worrying that someone will flake and not show, and by the time we hit Phoenix, I was mentally spent and just over it. Yes, walking off was a dick move, and all my preaching about loyalty was discredited in a flash. I can own that it was an incredibly irresponsible thing to do, but sometimes a man can only take so much before he cracks.

Guilt hits me as I take in Clay's appearance, my smile slipping. He runs a hand through his blonde hair, stress lines on his face. Clay never frowns. Me shutting him out at the end of the tour has hit him harder than I thought it would. I hate that I've disappointed him, but at the time, I just didn't know what else to do.

Taking a bow, I raise my guitar with one hand and wave toward the guys in the band with the other. The crowd is wild and has begun chanting, "More, more, more . . ." But I just don't have any more left in me. Brian, our manager, is standing off to the right enthusiastically rocking back and forth—

heel to toe—and sheer joy is radiating off of him. I know this show was probably the best of the tour, but damn, if it wasn't completely draining. I left it all out there. I have nothing.

With one more wave, I brush past Clay and walk off the stage. Immediately, I'm surrounded by crew and security. After our last show in Flagstaff, I had asked for more security coverage. I swear, with each show the fans have been getting crazier and crazier.

"Hey, Will, over here!" a shout comes from my left.

"Oh my God, it's Will Ashton!" comes from my right.

"Will!"

"Will!"

"Will!"

All around me, people are shouting my name and trying to reach through security to touch me. The noise turns into a buzz and the people turn into a blur. I'm hot, my head is pounding behind my eyes, and I just need out of here. I pull my hat down a little lower over my face and focus on walking.

I miss the days of the small town bar. People came out because they enjoyed the quaintness and realness of listening to original live music. The people here at these concerts? I'm not so sure. The piercing screaming of the girls night after night has drilled into the base of my skull, giving me a headache that can only be relieved by a six-pack in dead silence, along with some ibuprofen and sleep.

I weave my way past those who've somehow managed a backstage pass. Rudely, I don't stop for any of them, and I just don't care. That seems to be my motto tonight, not caring. Whatever. Clay and the other guys will handle them.

Out of nowhere, a tiny blonde girl steps in front of me, forcing me to stop.

"Great show tonight, Will." She draws out my name,

looking at the ground and then back up through her eyelashes. If I've seen this look once, I've seen it a thousand times.

I look her over from head to toe and can't help but smirk at her in disgust. Sure, she's cute and all, but at this point, they all look exactly the same, and easy girls have never been my thing.

My eyes shift to Frank, the head of my security team, and he knows I want her gone. Moving past her, she grabs on to my arm to stop me. Frank immediately pulls her off.

"Hey, aren't you going to say anything?" She sounds desperate. How did she get back here and out from behind the barricades anyway? I glance behind her and see Brian, our self-appointed ass monitor. Why this guy thinks he knows what I need and want, I'll never know. I glare at him with complete loathing and he takes a step backward.

Gritting my teeth, I walk straight past the rest of the guys from the stage crew and out to the tour bus. I'm done with this shit. No more lights, no more screaming, just no more.

By the time I have my bag packed, I already know where I'm headed. Grabbing the Gibson, and with Whiskey by my side, we hop off the bus and start walking.

"Ash!" Clay's voice echoes from behind me.

I close my eyes for a brief second before turning around to face him. I shake my head at him, and we stare at each other from across the parking lot. His eyes are locked onto mine and he sees the desperation. He knows not to come any closer and understanding widens the space between us. No words are said—they aren't needed. He understands. Instead he lifts his head and throws me a cocky grin. That's his way of saying, "I'll see you soon."

Clay clears his throat and I'm pulled from the memory. "You look like shit," he says, eyeing me from head to toe.

My hand automatically goes to my chin, and I rub the full beard that's grown in. I haven't bothered to shave or even brush my hair really. I stocked up on groceries on the drive in and I've only gone out a few other times. I haven't seen anyone; there's been no need.

My tongue rakes across my teeth—yep, at least I remembered to brush them today—and my smile grows bigger. I'm so freaking excited to see him. I didn't realize how much I missed him. I'm trying to think of another time when we've been apart this long, and I can't come up with anything.

Clay and I met the summer I turned thirteen, just after my grandfather died.

Up until then, my grandfather raised me. I have no idea what happened to my parents, and he refused to talk about them. I don't remember them at all, but I don't miss them either. Can't miss something you never had, right? Out of curiosity, I asked him once, and a pained expression crossed his face before one of anger. He looked right at me and said, "Do you see them here?" I shook my head no. "Exactly, so no point in talking about what doesn't exist." I hated making him upset, mad, or whatever—he was always so happy—and I never wanted to see him like that again. So I let it go.

I ended up in foster care when he died, and bless the day I was assigned to Clay's family. The first few months after losing the one and only constant I ever had in my life was devastating, unbearable. To me, my grandfather was larger than life. I idolized him in every way, and felt so lost and scared without him. But I got lucky. Instead of ending up another foster care horror story, Clay became my best friend, and his family eventually became mine.

"So?" he finally asks, breaking the silence, his eyebrows raised in annoyance. What he really wants to know is, "Are you at least going to tell *me* what's going on?" and honestly, I'm not sure.

I love being a musician, but something's got to give. I miss the quiet days Clay and I used to have when we were writing music and just being ourselves. The originality, the level of talent, and the heart that poured out of us was what I lived for. Not this. On our last album, of the fourteen songs, only two of them were ours, and they were so patched together I didn't even want them. They were forced by the label, and that lack of control has also been eating me up.

"So, what?" I smirk at him. Whiskey circles around the room and then curls up at my feet.

His eyes narrow. "Really?" But what I actually hear is, "After all these years, that's *all* you're gonna say?"

Looking away from him, I pick up the guitar pick that's lying on the table next to me—it's an old one from the days of Blue Horizons—and I begin to roll it up and down over my knuckles. "Honestly, I'm trying to figure it out. At the end of the show in Phoenix, at that moment, I was so over it and couldn't think of anything but getting out. God, we've been going at it for five years. I'm tired; aren't you?"

I look back to him, his eyebrows furrowed while he considers what I've said. Shrugging his shoulders, he walks over to the large floor-to-ceiling living room windows and resumes drinking his beer. The sun has dropped behind the mountains, but it's still dusk, leaving a gorgeous view across the lake. A good ten minutes pass before he finally turns back around to me.

"This last tour has been rough," he concedes, letting out a sigh and then moving to flop down on the couch. Fireflies have started to rise up out of the grass, and together we watch them float by and into the trees. "Are we done then?" he asks quietly. He doesn't look at me, but continues to stare out the window.

I'm sure it's a hard question for him to ask and I can see the disappointment forming on his face. He doesn't want to be done yet. Clay has always loved this. He loves the music just as much as I do, but he loves the crazy crowds too, whereas I for damn sure could do without.

"No, dude, not done. I don't think we'll ever be done. I just . . ." Silence. I don't know how to finish my sentence, and I'm pleading with my eyes for him to keep understanding a little longer. He studies me and then his expression relaxes. That's all I needed to see, and I breathe a sigh of relief.

"Say no more. I'm staying this weekend and then I'll head back to Nashville on Monday to do some more damage control." He tips the bottle and drains the beer.

"Thanks, man. Believe it or not, this time away has been good. I think I'm finding my way back; I just need a little more time." The relief is evident in my tone.

Years of friendship and understanding flash across his face and are then replaced by cockiness. "Well, I just need a steak. I'm starving and you're cooking." He pats his stomach and stretches out a little more on the couch. He's never been one to stay mad long, and that's one of the qualities I've always admired the most about him. He's easygoing and takes things as they come. Me, on the other hand, I need time to process.

I narrow my eyes at him. "What makes you think I have steaks lying around?"

"When do you not?" he chuckles. He does know me so very well.

I bust out laughing and the tension in the room dissipates. Whiskey feels the energy change and his tail starts thumping on the floor. "Whatever you say, dear. Anything else?" I ask as I get up.

He quirks a smile at me and holds up his bottle. I just shake my head at him. Man, is it good to see him.

"Juliet is worried about you," he says as I head out the kitchen door to turn on the grill.

"She worries about everything." A twinge of guilt slips under my skin. I hate that I'm making her worry.

"You disappeared and haven't called her either." His tone is slightly accusatory, and I can't say that I blame him.

"I haven't called anyone, but I'll call her soon." Just like with Clay, I hadn't known what to say. If I had everything figured out, I'd have called her . . . but I don't. Hopefully, she'll understand.

Pulling a steak from the refrigerator, I toss him a beer and head back outside.

"Tomorrow night, we're going out," Clay says just before he flips on the TV. That's smart of him—he knows I'll argue, and this way he can't hear me.

I groan at the thought of being surrounded by a crowd of people. What if someone recognizes me? I'm just not ready to be outed. This cabin here on the lake is my sanctuary.

"You owe me," he calls out.

13

I know I do. I can only imagine how angry the label has been.

Flipping over his steak, a shiver runs through me. I hadn't realized the temperature had already dropped so significantly since I arrived. Fall is in full swing and I'm loving every minute of it. In a way, I'm grateful for that last concert. If I hadn't reached my breaking point, I wouldn't be here, and being here in this house, on this lake, it grounds me. I've needed this time to remind myself of who I am and what I love, without the lights, the fans, and the show.

Chapter THREE

Ava Layne

COLD AIR SLIPS through the windows, and as the curtains sway back and forth, the morning sunlight dances across my room. I crack my eyes open and a huge smile creeps onto my face as I stretch and remember where I am. It was late when we pulled in last night, and other than the moonlight shimmering on the lake, we were surrounded by darkness. Throwing back the covers, I slip on a sweatshirt and slide open the glass doors that lead out to the back deck. Tank, my dog, jumps off the bed and follows me.

I've been counting down the days until we arrived, and now that we're here, a calm settles over me. I'm a Midwestern girl, born and raised, and although it's peaceful with its rolling fields and farmland, nothing beats the smell or view of the mountains.

Nestled high up in the southern part of the Blue Ridge

Mountains lies Horizons Valley. The valley is small, mostly hidden, and contains a quaint town, a lake on the southern end, a large orchard, a few small cattle ranches, and several resorts. It's fair to say that this town is equal parts vacationers and locals. In the summer, people go hiking, rafting, and horseback riding, and in the winter, skiing. I think it's idyllic and a little slice of heaven.

The house belongs to Emma's parents, a vacation home conveniently three hours from their lives in Atlanta. I'd met Emma on our first day of college. She's petite with thick, wavy, brown hair, and is the epitome of a Southern belle. In front of others, she's poised and polite, but behind closed doors, she's spunky and funny. She was just what I needed after that last summer at my parent's house, and after that first trip here during our fall break, I've been coming with her ever since. Spring, summer, and fall, I live for the days when we'll be here relaxing, and out of the noise and fast pace of the city.

I'm not sure what it is, but the wide open space with the mountains surrounding us makes this one of my favorite places in the world. Maybe it's time I think about buying a place of my own. There's no question that I plan on spending endless amounts of time here, and then I would be able to come whenever I wanted.

Emma's parents' home is on the southern end of the lake, so every morning we get to see the sunrise and every evening the sunset. Living in New York City, I rarely get to see either, so whenever I'm here, I make it a point not to miss them. I should go for a run, but all I want to do is sit here, enjoy this serene morning, and slow my mind down to match my surroundings.

"Av! We know you're up; we heard you wander outside. Coffee's made; come get some." Emma's voice echoes through the trees as she calls out to me.

"I'll be right down," I holler, just needing a few more minutes here.

Leaning against the railing, I breathe in the crisp, clean air. The sky is golden with the morning sun, and the leaves on the trees have begun to change, speckling the mountainside with shades of yellow, orange, and red. The lake is covered in a quiet peace. Ripples from a kayaker gently break the smooth, glassy water, and a low-lying fog hovers just above the surface. The only sound is of the leaves rustling in the trees that surround the house and the lake. It's all so beautiful.

A purple finch flies by and lands on top of the feeder hanging on the corner of the deck. A fast warbling song of fourteen notes hits my ears. It's an up and down cadence that lets me know it's a male. Male birds sing so handsomely, and I'm always fascinated by the timbre, tonality, and assertiveness of their songs.

Music is my life. I eat, sleep, and breathe it. It's all I've ever known. Everywhere I go and with everything I do, I focus in on the sounds around me. I've been given the gift of perfect pitch—a rare auditory phenomenon that gives me the ability to identify or recreate musical notes without the help of a reference tone. If I'm asked what the pitch is of a particular chord in a song or a note played on an instrument, I know it . . . and I'm never wrong. Some say it's a learned thing, but as far as I know, I've always had it. Chords and melodies can come from just about anywhere. Being able to open my ears and listen, it calms me, and I love the challenge of finding sounds and matching them. The simplest things can inspire me . . . like the birds or the rustling of the leaves.

Poems, screenplays, novels, they are the art of words.

KATHRYN ANDREWS

People marvel at how twenty-six simple letters can create such brilliant works as the great classics and today's contemporaries, but what about the art of music? Music is created with only seven notes, A through G. Sure those notes can be played sharp, flat, or in a different octave, but letters can change as well. Take 'read'—it sounds different pronounced in the past or present tense. Or take the letter 'c'—it sounds different from mic to mice. In the end, I'm in awe of what can be made by seven little notes. The beauty that comes from the harmony and the emotions that it can evoke, it's all fascinating, and the people who compose the music even more so.

Another finch flies by and lands on the feeder. Tank sees them, sprints across the deck, and jumps. She'll never reach the tiny birds, but bless her for trying. I make a mental note to add sunflower seeds to the grocery list.

"Come on, Tank. Let's go get some coffee and I'll let you out." She jumps again and runs around my legs. This little dog has so much energy.

Taking the deck stairs, I head down a level toward the kitchen. Emma and Cora are sitting in the rocking chairs drinking coffee and eating cupcakes. There's a comfortable silence and a contentment floating around them that makes my heart smile. They're both relaxed and the cool mountain air looks good on them.

"Where did those come from?" I'm unable to hide my excitement.

Emma stuffs the last of her cupcake into her mouth and Cora grins at me. "Oh, I may have snuck them into my carry-on yesterday before we left," she says smugly.

"Really?! How did I not know this?" I walk through the French doors that lead to the kitchen, and there on the table is a box from Kelly's Kupcakes. I've died and gone to heaven.

18

"And this is why I love you the most." Reaching into the box, I pull out a chocolate cupcake with maple-buttercream icing and bacon sprinkles.

"Hey!" says Emma. "I was with her too."

I sink my teeth into the delicious cake and moan in delight. So good.

Emma and I met Cora right before graduating. She is two years older than us, and although she had attended the same school, we didn't cross paths early on. Everyone knew of her though. She was born and raised on the Upper East Side of New York City, her family is extremely wealthy, and their name is repeatedly recognized for their generous donations to different annual school campaigns. But the night we saw her play at Talents, we knew she was meant to be with us.

Emma and I had gone out for our usual mid-week escape at Talents, a bar near school, where every night is open mic night, and anything goes. We went for two reasons: One, because we related to the people who were performing, and two, you never knew what you were going to see or hear. The diversity of the performances ranged from poetry slams, Broadway monologues, dance routines, original written music, cover artist music, you name it . . . if it can be performed, it's allowed. Even though sometimes the performances were awful, some were amazing. It was the only place in the city I felt comfortable. I connected to those who stepped onto the stage because some were trying to conquer their fears, and others were trying to set their souls free.

One minute Emma and I were lost in conversation, and then suddenly we heard "Like I'm Gonna Love You," by Megan Trainer on the cello. The place silenced as every jaw dropped at the girl on the stage. We were captivated and moved by the enormous feeling and passion pouring out of her.

Her! Cora Rhodes.

What we were witnessing was a complete contradiction to the girl we knew. The Cora from school was trained in the classics and carried herself like the socialite she is. Her hair is always styled and the perfect blonde, her figure and her face have been tweaked to match her pedigree, and she wears diamonds instead of pearls. She's refined with an air of sophistication about her that says "I am way out of your league," but watching her that night up on the stage, with her hair loose, wearing casual skinny jeans, we knew she wanted more. More out of life, more than what she was entitled to, and more of who she longed to be and less of what she was expected to be.

Emma and I took one look at each other, abandoned our seats, and followed her off the stage. Instantly, she became a new best friend, we became a trio, and the three of us never looked back.

"Okay then, I take it back. I love you both," I say, while licking off some of the icing. No one loves cupcakes more than I do. I love to bake them and I sure love to eat them.

"So, Av, what are your plans today?" Emma asks me.

"My plans are to do nothing." I grin at her, set my coffee cup on the ground, and take my seat in the rocking chair on her other side.

"I think we're going to head into town, do a little shopping. Wanna go?" She already knows I'm going to say no, but I appreciate that she still asks anyway. The thought of being crowded in the little shops has me tensing.

"No, thanks. My Kindle and I are going to spend most of the day in the hammock down by the lake." I glance down toward to dock to make sure that the hammock is still there. In the past, Emma's parents have started to pack up the house for the winter when they come for Columbus Day weekend. But there it is, hanging off to the side, just waiting for me. I spot the kayaker again and my eyes are drawn to the fluid way he paddles. Even from here, the strength in his arms is impressive.

"Okay, well, make sure you rest up because we're going out tonight," Cora says, smiling at me, letting me know she's up for the challenge if I choose to argue.

"Oh," I groan, frowning at her. I hate going out and they both know this.

"It'll be fun. Besides, you never know who you'll meet there." Emma takes a big sip of her coffee to hide her face. She's been pushing me lately to try and meet a guy. She says it's not normal for a twenty-five-year-old to not have had a boyfriend or two by now. But what she seems to be forgetting is that I *have* had one, and he was enough to last a lifetime. I don't want another one, not now, maybe not ever. That may not be normal, but I'm not normal, and I'm okay with that.

"Yeah, try no one. I don't *want* to meet anyone." We've had this conversation so many times. My relaxed mood shifts and now I'm feeling slightly attacked by my friends.

"One of these days, when you least expect it, someone is going to sweep you off your feet, just like in all those romance novels you read." She winks at me and grins like she's in on some big secret. Whatever. I've got news for her . . . no way. It's not that I'm opposed to love—I actually love the idea of falling and being in love. It's all the other stuff that comes with it—the fear, pain, and uncertainty. Very few people understand what my relationship to Chris did to me, and I plan on never repeating that mistake again.

21

"I highly doubt it." My tone comes across sharp.

"Mmm hmm," she mumbles.

"So listen," Cora changes the subject, "I've got a few chords floating around in my head, and I think it's time to put them down."

"Really? That's awesome. How long have you been working on this?" I look past Emma to see Cora grinning. She's excited, which makes me excited.

"Not long, but this one came on fast."

Emma, Cora, and I love to write music together. Although we can each play a broad range of instruments, my heart lies with the piano, Emma's the violin, and Cora's the cello. I imagine to most, our little jam sessions would seem odd, considering their classical nature, but to us, nothing beats the creative cohesiveness that comes alive. Half the time, it doesn't turn into anything more than us having an awesome afternoon together, but during the other half, magic is made.

"Well, you just tell me when and I'm there." Understanding our love for music, Emma's parents helped us change the downstairs basement from a game room to a permanent music room. Everything we could ever need or want is there waiting for us.

"Perfect! After shopping and before we go out," Emma chimes in, grinning.

I can't help but groan at the reminder.

Chapter FOUR

WILL ASHTON

AT TEN, WE walk into Smokey's, and I instantly feel as if I have walked back in time. Clay and I haven't been to this place for years, and a rush of nostalgia takes over. True to its country roots, the wood floors are polished, the decorations are rustic, and the whiskey barrel bar tables have held up nicely. It appears as if not much has changed, and I wish I could say the same for us. As of late, all I seem to be longing for are more of the days we played at Smokey's and less of the days at large arenas.

The music pumping through the speakers is from the current pop country top forties, and as much as I love the place, I suddenly feel too old to be here. Even if tomorrow is my birthday and I'm only turning thirty, all I see are a bunch of college kids, a few locals, and a lot of young professionals playing up one of the last few weekends Smokey's will be open until the spring. I'm over this scene. I should have just stayed home tonight.

"Dude! The eye candy is out tonight. Seriously, there is more sk-skin in this place than clothing!" I look over at Clay and he's grinning from ear to ear. All he's ever needed to make his night is a beer in one hand with a pretty girl by his side. I, however, prefer a glass of Scotch neat and a bar stool in a quiet dive. Maybe some things haven't changed after all.

"Whatever, man. I'm gonna head to the bar and grab a drink."

"Yeah, get me one too. I'm gonna take a look around and then I'll meet you over there," he shouts after me as I walk away. Pulling my hat down over my face a little more, I push through the crowd, keeping to the perimeter of the room. I'm hoping no one recognizes me tonight. I really don't need any more bullshit in my life.

There's an empty seat at the end of the bar and it's perfect. It's a little darker in the corner, and it gives me a chance to sit back and look around. Images of us playing on the stage, laughing together, flash before my eyes. Things were simpler, and even though we still had the dream of making it big, we got to be ourselves.

Smokey's is where it all started for us. It's where we got our first gig and where we fell in love with performing. Weekend after weekend, we would empty our hearts, leave it all on the stage, and it felt invigorating. Now, I'm still leaving it all on the stage, but I walk away feeling drained and exhausted. Remembering how good it felt to perform here, my blood hums, and I find myself smiling.

Tapping the bar, I catch the bartender's attention as his back is to me. "Hey, man, can I get two local IPA drafts?"

"Sure, coming right up." The bartender strolls down to the far end, grabs two frosty pint glasses, and pulls the drafts. He glances at me and I see his eyes spark. It only took ten minutes to get recognized, but then again, he would—there was a time we saw each other every weekend.

As he walks my way, a smile stretches across his face and he begins shaking his head. "Holy shit. Will, I almost didn't recognize you." He leans across the bar and gives me a one-armed hug.

"Yeah, well, I'm hoping that's how tonight plays out." Maybe I should have kept the beard. I glance around to see if anyone just caught our exchange, and they didn't. I relax a little on the stool.

"How the hell are you?" he asks. I look Rich over and can't help but smile. His familiarity feels like home.

"Good, man. Tour's over for now, so just getting a little R&R in. How's business?" Rich is in his late fifties and part owner of this place.

"Not the same since you left." He winks at me.

A chuckle breaks free as I take a sip of the beer. I know this place has run just fine without us.

"So, how long are you in town for?" He picks up a rag from behind the bar and wipes down the space in front of me.

"A while, I think. I always did like it up here." I don't want to tell him that I bought a house. For some reason, it just feels like it's my secret place to hide without having to share it with the world. No one except for Clay and Juliet knows about it.

"Well, anytime you want to come back in and do your thing . . . door's always open."

I smile at him again. He genuinely means this. "Thanks, man."

Three girls push up to the bar right next to me. I can't see the face of the one closest to me, but I've been invaded by blonde, curly hair. It's brushing up against my arm and my senses are flooded by the strawberry scent left lingering from her shampoo.

"Hey, Rich, can we get another round?" one of them asks, putting an end to our conversation.

"Sure thing, doll. I'll be right back." He smiles at her, nods his head at me, and sets off to make their drinks.

I swivel around, silently enjoying the whiff of strawberry surrounding me, and scan the room for Clay. The girls are giggling, and as much as I try to not hear their conversation, the music just isn't loud enough.

"Oh my God, please tell me you got a good look at that blonde guy standing over by the front door. He's so freaking hot." The smallest of the three is jumping up and down and grinning from ear to ear. None of them looks to be young, but then, I don't have a clue about girls these days.

"Seriously? He may be good-looking, but the lines he was feeding you could have filled the stomachs of a small village," says the girl closest to me.

A sharp laugh escapes me and her back immediately stiffens. Speaking of lines, that was one of the best I've ever heard. A moment of silence passes between the girls, and slowly the blonde turns around to acknowledge me. The softness of her hair slides across my arm, strangely sensual and comforting at the same time. The other two peek around her, and all three stare at me like I'm an eavesdropping pervert.

Shock ricochets through me and stalls everything around us. My heart hits my stomach, bottoming out, and the world shifts. I'm face to face with the most beautiful girl I've ever seen in my entire life. I'm rendered speechless as our eyes lock, and I begin to drown in blue stormy eyes surrounded by long eyelashes, flawless ivory skin that's flushed pink in the cheeks, and perfectly glossed lips. I've stopped breathing and for the life of me can't remember how to start again. Her eyebrows pop up as her gaze scans over my face and she proceeds to give me a look that asks, "Are you stupid or something?" All I can do is shake my head no, and hope she understands.

Pull it together, Ash; she's waiting for you to say something.

Say something.

Say something!

"Ah, I'm sitting right here, so I can't help but overhear you, and I'm not going to apologize, because what you said was funny."

Something crosses in her eyes, but then it quickly goes away and a look of disregard replaces it. It wasn't there long enough for me to name the emotion, and for a split second I panicked that she recognized me, but nope. And I'm glad. Dealing with fangirls is not something I can handle tonight, no matter how incredibly beautiful she is. With a look of annoyed indifference, she turns back around to her friends, and her hair takes its place back on my arm.

The three of them immediately go back to ignoring me. Rich brings their drinks over and the little brunette throws down her credit card.

I can't move. I also can't decide if what just happened is tragic or exhilarating. I'm so acutely aware of everything about this girl, from how she's shifted her weight, how stiff her back is, to the way she tilts her head. Even though she's trying to play off indifference, her posture tells me she's affected too.

"I don't care if he thinks he's charming and witty . . . just look at him. Besides, I could put those lips to better use than

27

having to listen to him, if you know what I mean." The voice is coming from the brunette.

The three of them laugh and turn to walk off. The blonde takes one quick glance back at me and our eyes lock again—her blue eyes to mine, blue to blue. Her face is completely devoid of any emotion, but her eyes are so penetrating that my heart skips a beat and I feel frozen.

Who is this girl? And can't she see what she's doing to me?

She spins around, they blend into the crowd, and they're gone.

What the hell just happened?

I've never given much creed to the idea of instalove or soulmates, but damn if I didn't just feel something instinctual about her in the deepest part of me. It's crazy. My heart is thundering through my ears, not because it's interested in her, but because it feels like it knows her.

Turning back to my beer, I take a deep breath as a warm flush spreads up my neck and into my face. Rich is staring at me with a knowing grin on his face.

"What?" I ask him, annoyed, wiping my hands across the top of my thighs. They're sweating and I didn't even realize it. His grin turns into a smirk.

"Well, can't say I've ever seen one get to you like that before." He knows I was never one of those guys that was looking for female company. I enjoyed my friends and I enjoyed the music.

"I don't know what you're talking about." I turn and look back over the crowd of people, pulling my hat down lower. That's the benefit of the wide, flat brim on a cowboy hat—it hides and shades what's underneath.

"Whatever," Rich mumbles.

I spot Clay's hat as he pushes through the crowd. He's smiling from ear to ear and looks like a freaking kid in a candy shop. His eyes swing past me and spot Rich, lighting up immediately.

"Hey, Rich, nice to see you, man." Clay leans across the bar and wraps him in a bear hug. Clay has always been more hands on than I have and people are drawn to him.

"You too, kid, although you look less like a kid now and more like an old man."

"Old man? That's funny coming from you. What's it been, like five years?"

"Something like that." Rich pats him on the shoulder and steps back.

"It's really good to see you." Other patrons have begun tapping on the bar and yelling his name, trying to get Rich's attention.

"You too! Duty calls." He glances back down the bar.

Clay turns to face me and his smile is back in full force. "Bro! The girls here tonight are smokin' hot! I talked to this one little brown-haired girl—she's small, reminds me of a pixie, but I bet she'd be a fire pistol in the sack though. Speaking of which, am I allowed to be escorted home?" He looks at me with hopeful eyes.

"No. Sorry, man, I don't need everyone knowing about the new house yet, just let it go. Head to her house and you do the walk of shame." Clay talks a big game, but hooking up with girls is a rarity for him. He's enjoys their company when we're out, but he's always been more of the "wine and dine" them type of guy versus one-night stands.

"If I get to be so lucky in doing her, trust me, there will be no shame." He grins, takes a big swallow of his beer, and then wanders off back toward the dance floor.

Four guys walk out onto the stage and begin to mess around with their instruments. The singer approaches the mic, the front stage lights kick on, and my heart jumpstarts with a forgotten familiarity. Adrenaline instantly courses through me, and my body falls in sync with the movements happening on-stage. I've missed this feeling and I realize I've missed the music.

"Hey, everybody . . . how's it going tonight?" The lead singer pushes his cowboy hat back up off his face a little, smiles, and the crowd lets off a cheer. "We're The Storm Chasers and we'll be your entertainment for tonight. Mostly cover songs, but a few of ours will be mixed in as well. We do take requests, so feel free to drop them in the jar." He fingers the guitar pick up and down his knuckles, grabs it with his thumb, and rips out the first chord. The vibrations pulse through me, something about that sound that gets me every time. Peace washes over me and I settle into my spot. This is home.

Chapter FIVE

Ava Layne

HROUGHOUT THE NIGHT, I find my eyes wandering back to the quiet guy sitting at the bar. I don't know why I am so intrigued by him, but I am. Unlike most of the people here, he doesn't seem to be into the night crowd and having fun, but instead keeps his eyes shielded under his hat and his body angled to where he can watch the band. Occasionally, he leans over and talks to Rich. The two of them interact like they know each other pretty well, which makes me wonder if he's local.

I find myself liking the fact that his eyes aren't wandering over every single girl here. Maybe he has a girlfriend . . . he must have a girlfriend. This thought suddenly saddens me—I don't know why; it's not like he'd ever be interested in me anyway. But if he does, I hope she realizes how lucky she is.

My mind drifts to his eyes. When I turned around and

mine connected with his, every hair on my arms stood up. It's dark in here and they were shaded by his hat, but even so, they were so bright, clear, and blue. I was certain that he recognized me by the way his eyes scanned over my face, but it felt like more than recognition. And then he smiled. It was slow, lopsided, and dimples pierced his cheeks. As my heart fluttered in my chest, I quickly catalogued every detail—from his build, the clean smell of his cologne, to the crispness of his shirt—and then pulled myself together. I couldn't let him know he affected me, couldn't give him any reason to believe that I was interested, but for the first time in a long time, I wished I was normal.

"You're staring at him, you know?" Emma slides up next to me and bumps me in the shoulder. She's spent most of her evening flirting with the guy we met when we walked in, Clay, and I'm glad. Justin, her on and off again boyfriend, has been a little more off lately, and it's been hard on her.

"I know," I say, letting out a sigh. "There's something about him. I can't put my finger on it, but he looks familiar." Both of us look his way—he's talking to Rich again and something said between the two of them causes him to laugh. Even from across the crowded room and past the loud atmosphere, I remember exactly what his laugh and voice sounded like.

When he'd chuckled, the smooth and deep baritone timbre of his voice sent every nerve-ending in my body firing. People's voices don't generally strike a particular melodic chord one way or another, but being an expert on tone and pitch, I understand that some are more appealing than others. But I swear, it's as if the sound of his voice was made just for me, and I could not only hear it, but feel it.

"Yeah, he kind of does, but it could just be that tall, dark, and handsome in a cowboy hat look he's got going on."

I laugh at her assessment of him and realize she's probably right.

"You should go back over there, order another drink, and talk to him." She gently shoves me in the arm, forcing me to break my stare.

I glance over to her; she's smirking at me, and I'll never tell her this, but the way she pushes all the time irritates me and hurts my feelings. "No, I can't." She knows this too.

"Yes, you can." Her tone is more encouraging and compassionate than it is antagonizing, and that makes me feel even worse. I know she thinks it's way past time for me to let go and move on, and one day I might, but today is not that day.

"When was the last time you tried to talk to a guy?" she asks. My heart sinks, she knows the answer to this and I hate that she's still pushing.

"You know when," I snap back, crossing my arms over my chest. "Besides, he hasn't talked to anyone all night except for Rich. He has to be here with someone, right? I mean, if he came here by himself, that's kind of weird."

"Why is that weird? And who cares if he's here by himself? Dude obviously wanted to go out tonight instead of sitting at home in front of his television, and he isn't trying to hit up every girl in here. He's easy on the eyes, so why not go talk to him?"

She glances back to look at him and something stirs in the bottom of my stomach. I don't want her looking at him, and I don't want her to think he's easy on the eyes.

"You're right. He isn't trying to meet anyone. A guy like that screams 'girlfriend.'"

Emma lets out a sigh and looks at me with sadness. I hate that look.

"Tell me about Clay." I've had enough about me and it's time to turn the tables. Her cheeks redden as she smiles.

"Not much to tell. He hasn't really talked that much, but when he does, he's funny. I haven't stopped laughing all night." Her eyes are bright; she's happy.

"Cora and I noticed. We also noticed he can't keep his hands off of you." Relaxing a little, I uncross my arms and tuck my hands in my back pockets.

"Oh my God, his hands. The boy doesn't even need to talk, his hands do enough for him . . . whew." She takes a step back, starts fanning herself, and then her eyes light up as she glances over my shoulder. "Speak of the devil, we were just talking about you."

"Oh yeah?" He grins at both of us, handing Emma a drink.

"Yep," Emma says, scooting a little closer to him. Clay pushes the brim of his hat, tipping it up, and looks down at her adoringly. His features are lighter than that of the guy at the bar who has that rugged, handsome appeal to him; Clay seems more like the boy next door. His eyes are light, his skin coloring is more golden, youthful, with blonde hair curling around the collar of his shirt. His shirt is light blue and inviting, whereas mystery bar guy is wearing black.

My phone vibrates under my hand in my back pocket, and I'm thankful for the interruption. Standing next to the two of them as they stare at each other—no, thanks. Pulling it out, there's a text from Mona.

Mona: Just got an interesting email. When you're up, call me.
Me: I'm up, give me five.
Mona: Okay.

"Hey, this is Mona, I'm going to take a step out and call her." Both of them look at me and surprise flashes on Emma's face.

"It's so late; I wonder what she wants?" Emma asks.

"Well, I'm about to find out. I'll be right back," and I step past them, looking around the bar for a way out.

"Who's Mona?" Clay asks Emma, and I pause to hear what she says.

"Oh, we work for her." The perfect answer.

It's a lot more crowded than I thought, and I realize there's a good possibility of a line out front. If not, then there are certainly people lingering around the entrance, and that's not good. I spot the red glowing exit sign and head for the hallway. I hate going out the back door, but this conversation can then be private.

Stepping out the door, I shiver from the cold and laugh at myself as I stare out at the darkness of the trees directly in front of me. I hate being in the dark, and I'm thankful there's a floodlight on so the back is somewhat illuminated.

Dialing Mona's number, she picks up on the first ring.

"Well, aren't you out a little late this evening?" she says mischievously. I lean back against the door to settle into the call.

"Tell me about it. Emma dragged us out to Smokey's." I scan the back area to see if there is any movement, but there isn't. Just a couple of dumpsters and a few chairs lined up against the back of the building.

"How's the talent there tonight? Any good?"

"They're all right. They don't even come close to the band that used to play here." I look down and realize my fingers are tapping against my leg. I guess I'm more nervous back here than I thought. But then, it *does* have that murder-scene-from-every-horror-movie kind of vibe.

"Well, speaking of playing, what are you doing on Black Friday?"

Her question catches me off guard and I can't help but laugh. "Shopping."

She snorts. "You know what I mean. Are you going home or will you be in the city?"

"City." She knows that I never go home unless forced. My relationship with my parents all but ended when I was eighteen, and the thought that I might accidentally run into *him* is more than I can handle.

"Talk to the girls—a job was offered I think you'll want. It's in Nashville."

"Nashville!" I jerk up off the door. "We haven't been there in years. Sounds good to me . . . I'll run it by them and let you know."

"Thanks. I'll send the details. Hope you girls are having a good time."

"We are; it was needed." I run my free hand through my hair and let out a deep breath. A white cloud forms in front of me and I shiver.

"I hear ya. I could use a little getaway myself. Keep in touch and I'll talk to you soon."

"Perfect. Bye, Mona."

She clicks off the phone and I look down at mine. Mona loves spending the holidays with her family, so if she wants to do this, then it must be good. I also love Nashville. If she'd said L.A., I might have hesitated, but I'll always go to Nashville.

Chapter SIX

WILL ASHTON

TWO AND A half hours have flown by. Rich kept pouring and I just sat back and enjoyed the music. I've heard better, but I've definitely heard worse too. But what I realize is it's been a long time since I've just sat and listened to someone else play.

I've always found it interesting to listen to the way people play. Some play because they can, and others play because it's the way they speak. The originals that the band performs are good and could have real potential, but then again I shouldn't be surprised—Rich did bring them in. He's always had a gift for spotting talent.

Sometime around one, I decide to call it a night and make my way over to Clay. He's probably not ready to leave yet, but he'll get back to the house whenever he's ready. He always does.

I find him on the other side of the room talking to two of

the three girls from the beginning of the evening. The blonde isn't with them, and a wave of disappointment washes over me. I spent most of the evening thinking about her and cursing myself for not seeking her out, and there was a huge part of me that hoped she would come back and order another drink, but she never did. And then on the walk to Clay, I scan the room hoping to see her one more time, but nope. Lots of blonde hair, but none curly like hers.

Damn, well, that sucks.

Clay, the brunette, and another blonde are laughing as I join their circle. By the way he's looking at the little brown-haired one, he's more interested than I thought. Maybe she'll be his challenge, even after this evening is over, and I can't help but smile. Clay likes girls, but rarely does he allow himself to open up. He's guarded, understandably so, but between the two of us, he's always been the one to want a relationship.

"Hey, man," Clay says, smiling at me. The two girls turn and stare. The brunette's eyes get big as she remembers what I overheard, and I give her a knowing smirk.

"Lips, huh?" She looks thoroughly embarrassed and drops her gaze to the ground.

"What are you talking about?" Clay asks as he looks from me to her, and then back to me.

"Nothing. Listen, I'm out." I grab his shoulder and squeeze.

Clay looks down at his watch and just shakes his head at me. "Something is better than nothing I guess. Thanks for coming out . . . it's been a while." He wraps his arm around mine and squeezes my shoulder in return.

"You good to get back?" I ask.

"Always." His eyes flicker over to the little brown-haired girl.

"All right, I'll see you later." I nod at the girls, and head for the back door. We've always used the back door—I guess old habits die hard—but really this exit seems safer for me to avoid being noticed.

Pushing open the door, it smacks right into the girl with the curly blonde hair and I watch as she stumbles backward. Her eyes grow wide as we both realize she's going to fall. In what feels like slow motion, I reach out and grab her arm, pulling her toward me. The girl and her smell crash into me, and at that moment, all I can think about are strawberries and snow. My other arm wraps around her waist as her head slides perfectly under my chin. Heat from her impact scorches my skin under my clothes, and before I even realize what's happening, her knee rams full force into my groin.

Pain.

Shooting. Nauseating. Excruciating.

My knees take aim and become one with the dirt as I drop straight down and double over. The door slams shut behind me and I moan out in agony.

"Oh my God, I am so sorry. I really didn't mean to do that. You startled me and my instincts just kind of took over. Are you okay?" The pretty blonde hovers over me, runs her hands all over my back, and tries to pull me up. Unbearable sensations are radiating through my stomach, back, and junk. I feel like an electric shock has gone straight through the middle of my chest and I can't breathe.

What the hell?

Anger bleeds and blends in with the pain. Am I okay? Is she kidding? Pissed is a good word for how I'm feeling.

"Instincts? Are you kidding me? What did you think was going to happen, I was going to kidnap you or something? I was trying to keep you from falling and hurting yourself." I suck air in through my nose, my eyes and mouth watering. "*Shit* . . ." I groan in pain. Glancing up at her, I pause. Her hair is hanging all around her face and her eyes are filled with fear and remorse. Such a strange combination of emotions to have at the same time, and that's when I feel that her hands on my arm are shaking. Instantly, I feel bad.

"Whatever, don't worry about it, okay? I'll be fine in a minute." I pull my eyes from her and squeeze them tight.

"I'm so sorry. Can you stand up?" The pressure from her fingertips strengthens and my mind gets stuck on the fact that she's touching me.

"Just give me a minute." Waves of nausea are rolling through me and I moan again. Still breathing in through my nose, I try to focus on her smell and on her fingers.

"What are you doing out here?" she asks. I can't answer her. Why does she insist on talking to me now, at this moment? I would have loved to have talked to her inside. I really just need this pain in my stomach to go away. Throwing up in front of her is not high on my to-do list.

"Me? I was going home! What are you doing out here?" I look around to see if there are any other people out here with her. Nope, no one.

"I had to take a call." I glance down and see her cell phone lying at her feet. She bends over to pick it up and grips it like it's her lifeline.

"At one in the morning?" I ask her.

"Yes." Her tone is sharp. Whatever, it isn't any of my business anyway. Maybe she was talking to her boyfriend.

Putting one hand on the ground, I look back up to her and she takes a step back. My heart rate speeds up. I feel like I know this girl, but I don't know why. I've never seen her before; I would have remembered someone as beautiful as her.

The music from inside picks up its tempo and the cold sweat that had broken out across my back chills in the night air. My hand rubs across my stomach to try and ease the pain as I suck in a few more breaths.

She starts pacing back and forth in front of me, and my eyes lock on to brown cowgirl boots and bare legs. Her legs are lean but look muscular and strong. In another time and another place, what I wouldn't give to run my hands up them.

She stops in front of me. "Where are you staying? I can drive you if you need me to. I mean, I came with my friends, but I can drive your car and they can follow me." She's rambling and sounds unsure of herself, her nerves are coming through, but it's still nice that she offers.

"Oh, off of Lake Horizons Road, but no, thanks, I'll really be fine in a minute." Maybe I should take her up on her offer. It would give me more time with her.

"Are you here by yourself?" she asks.

Peeking back up at her, she's turned toward the parking lot, scanning it for something.

"No, I'm here with my friend, Clay." Breathing in another breath, I let go of my stomach, brace my hand against the door, and attempt to stand up straight. "He's staying a little while longer."

She lets out a little laugh, and it's as if the first chord of the guitar has strummed all over again. It zaps my heart.

"It's got to be the same Clay hitting on my friend then." She smiles and my zapped heart stops beating.

"He is. I saw them on the way out." I turn to face her finally and her eyes lock on mine. There is something so striking about her that I can't put my finger on it, and her eyes are so blue and clear, I feel like I'm falling into them. Blue to blue comes to mind again. They're beautiful. She's beautiful.

"Lake Horizons Road, that's where we're staying." So she isn't local; she's vacationing. That answers that question.

"Maybe we're neighbors then." I offer her a small smile and that's when I see it. "You're wearing a Blue Horizons t-shirt. Where did you get that?" I'm shocked. I haven't seen one of these t-shirts in years. At least, not one that isn't in my closet.

She looks down at her clothes and runs her hands down the sides of her skirt like she wants to make it longer.

"Oh, I got it years ago. They were a local band that used to play here."

"Yeah, I know. Did you ever see them play?" My curiosity is evident and she looks back up at me peculiarly.

"Yes, a couple of times actually. I guess you could say I was a fan. I even have two of their albums. I take it you've heard of them?" She gives me a small smile.

How do I answer that? This beautiful girl was a fan? She saw the band play, but yet she doesn't recognize me? I feel as if I'm having an out of body experience. I'm already attracted to this girl because of her looks, and now it seems as if her taste in music is exceptional as well.

"I have. Clay and I have been coming here for years. Do you live around here?" I need to know more about her. Why? I don't know . . . but for some reason I do.

"No, New York City." She wraps her arms around her middle. It's a defense mechanism—she clearly doesn't want to talk about herself—and I have to pull my eyes away from the way she's pushed up her chest. She's a thin girl, but based on this move, there's definitely a good handful. Forcing my eyes back to her face, that's when I see the moonlight reflect off of the tiny diamond stud in her nose. Internally, I groan. That piercing is hot. Everything about this girl is hot.

"Forgive me for asking, but how old are you? You don't seem old enough to know them. They stopped playing like five years ago."

"I'll take that as a compliment, I think. And I'm twenty-five." She shifts her weight from side to side.

Silence fills the space between us and she glances towards the door.

"So where on Horizons Road are you staying?" I don't want her to leave. I want to keep her talking. I want to learn as much as I can about her before she disappears.

"Oh, I can't remember the exact address. Cross the bridge, turn left, and it's the fifth house on the right." I can't help but smile at her; those directions are almost identical to the ones I gave Clay last year. "Why are you smiling?"

"Because I'm the eighth house on the right."

She drops her gaze, smiles, and then looks back up at me. "I guess that does make us neighbors."

"I guess so." I continue to watch her and she shifts her weight from side to side. A shiver runs through her and it dawns on me she must be cold. The fingers on her left hand begin to twitch, and although I'm not sure why, it's as if she's suddenly gotten nervous.

"Listen, I'm gonna go." I point my thumb towards the parking lot.

"Can I go with you?" she blurts.

My eyebrows shoot up and I watch her expression turn to horror as she realizes how that sounded. "I mean, do you mind dropping me off on your way home?"

I start laughing and then so does she. There's that sound

again. I could get used to hearing that. Wait! What am I thinking? I don't want to get used to that. Getting to know this girl means having to tell her who I am. Reality sinks in and I look at her speculatively. She's probably no different than all the others. She sees the shift in my mood and takes a step back.

"Never mind, my friends will be ready soon enough. I'm sorry again for what happened." She moves past me and grabs the door handle to go back inside. Ugh. I don't want her to go back inside.

I reach out for her arm. "No, I don't mind. It's not a problem." She jerks her arm away from me and the fear returns to her eyes.

Whoa. This girl seriously does not like to be touched. I hold my hand up so she can see I meant nothing by the move.

The only sound around us is the muffled music coming from inside. Her uncertainty lingers between us and then she straightens her back.

"Okay, great. Which one is yours?" She lets go of the door and starts walking toward the parking lot. I'm thankful we came out the back door; last thing I need is someone flashing a picture of the two of us together. I walk behind her and notice that she drops her head so her hair hides her face as we approach a few people.

"The black one-fifty in the back." She slows down, looks at me hesitantly, and then loosely loops her arm through mine, still keeping her face down. I'm beginning to wonder who this girl is because only people who are followed or watched regularly behave this way.

I pull my keys out of my pocket, unclick the locks, open her door for her, and she quickly slides in. As I walk around the front of the truck, I feel her eyes on me.

Shutting my door, I see her jump out of the corner of my

eye. Tension fills the truck. I toss my hat onto the backseat, run my hand through my hair, and turn to look at her; she's gripping the door like she wants to escape. "You sure you're ready to go?"

"Yep." She gives me a small smile. Well, okay then.

As soon as I turn the truck on, music blares from the speakers, and I inwardly cringe. Her gaze jerks over to me and she starts laughing.

"I can't believe you're listening to Blue Horizons! What are the odds? No wonder you asked me about my shirt." Her eyes are sparkling and my breath catches in my throat. I really want to freeze this moment. I go to turn the sound down, but she stops me by placing her hand on top of mine. Warmth radiates across my skin. I'm so affected by this girl, it's insane.

"Nah-uh . . . leave it loud!"

I don't drop my arm; I don't make a move. The tension in the truck turns to electricity, and her chest starts rising a little faster the longer we look at each other. I could look at her forever. She blinks and licks her bottom lip—what I wouldn't give to do that for her. A few seconds pass, but that's all it takes. I'm determined to find out more about her. Even if she doesn't tell me tonight, Clay will know something from her friend.

She moves her hand and the moment is over. We both let out a sigh at the same time and I grin at her.

As I pull out of the parking lot, she shoots her friends a text letting them know she left. The song changes and she relaxes. Rolling down her window, she sinks into the seat, and slightly leans her head out as the wind whips across her face and through her hair. I open up the sun roof and my window as well. The stars are out and it's a perfect night.

We ride in silence as the tracks change from one to another. I look over at this girl with the wild blonde curls and the tiny nose piercing, and it occurs to me, I don't even know her name. Her eyes are closed and she looks completely content. I'm trying to think back to when was the last time I felt that way, when she starts to sing along with the song. My mind goes blank. Here I'm thinking that the sound of her laughter is the most beautiful thing I have ever heard . . . man, was I wrong. My heart is actually fluttering in my chest.

Propping my left elbow up in the window, I run my hand through my hair. As we drive down the road and head back toward the lake, I stick my hand out the window to feel the wind like she is and for the first time in a long time, I feel free. It's then that I decide to take the long route home.

Chapter SEVEN

Ava Layne

I CAN'T BELIEVE he's currently listening to Blue Horizons. I was so nervous about getting in the truck with him—after all, I don't know him—but as soon as I heard the lyrics to "That Place in Time" echo throughout the truck cab, all of the uneasiness just melted away. Inwardly smiling, I'm proud of myself for trying to let go and do things that a normal twenty-five-year-old would. He's a good-looking guy, he's been kind to me, and my creep radar isn't going off. Catching a ride home just seems nice and normal.

I don't remember the last time I was in a truck, but his is really comfortable. The dark leather seats quickly warm, and without thinking, I roll down the window and let my hair whip out into the cool breeze. The air has a scent to it that is a mixture of clover and grass; it smells clean, sweet, not at all like the city. It reminds me of my childhood home, and a familiar ache washes over me. It's then that I realize I'm remembering a good time and not a bad one. My eyes close with contentment and that inward smile breaks free.

The song changes to "Why Can't the Future Be Now," and I begin to sing along. I've only seen this band play three times, but it's their two albums containing all of their own original pieces that I love. On stage, they sang covers of other bands to keep the crowd entertained, but it was when the lights dimmed and they sang their own work I felt internally moved. I've written songs my entire life, but I don't feel as if I've ever written any as soulful as those. Their songs speak to me, and as strange as it sounds, I have always felt like they were written for me. Whoever thought of mixing the blues with rock was a genius. Toss in an acoustic guitar, it gives off that country feel, and it's a unique sound that was only theirs. It's a shame they never went on to pursue something bigger. The talent was incredible.

Time passes as the truck coasts down the road. There's a comfortable silence between us and I'm grateful that he isn't being inquisitive for the sake of useless small talk. Enjoying this time, I keep my eyes shut because I don't want to see him watching me. Maybe he isn't, but right now, I feel at peace. Something I haven't felt in a long time. I have no obligations to be anywhere or anything to someone else, no assistant calling, no emails to be checking, and no flights to be boarding. It's times like this I wish I could quit and just be me.

The truck slows and turns. The tires crunch along the rock driveway of Emma's parents' house and my heart sinks knowing the drive is over. He puts the truck in park, the inside light brightens the cab, and I look over at him. His gaze collides with mine and my breath lodges in my throat. Wow, he really *is* a good-looking guy. His dark brown hair is mussed up from being under his hat all night, the line of his jaw looks smooth with just the hint of a five o'clock shadow, and his lips are full, but it's his eyes that capture me, just like at the bar. They are pale blue—lighter than mine—soft and kind. Heat floods my cheeks. It's been so long since I've been under the obvious perusal of a guy. I blink several times to regain my composure.

I can always tell a person's character by looking them straight in the eyes. It doesn't matter what they say or how their body language is perceived, the eyes will tell you everything. I've looked into so many sets of eyes in my short lifetime, I've seen it all: excitement, contentment, love, kindness, greed, fear, sadness, anger, disgust, lies, lust, hatred, evil, and guilt. If I look long enough, the truth will always be glaring right back at me, and with this guy I see a gentleness mixed with curiosity.

Glancing over at the house, I notice there are several lights shining through the windows. I'm so glad, because if the house had been dark, I'm not sure I would've been able to go in it. With this thought, anxiety trickles into my veins and my heart starts beating faster. Why didn't I think of that before when I asked him to bring me home? At the time, I saw an opportunity and just wanted to leave. The bar was officially packed full, I'd put my time in so Emma and Cora were happy, and I was ready to leave. I can't handle people putting their hands on me, and if I had stayed, with the crowds, it would have been inevitable. I chance another glance at him; he's probably wondering why I'm not getting out of the car. I close my eyes, take a deep breath, and count backward from five to one as I exhale, willing my heart to slow down.

Peeking over at him, he's still looking at me; he hasn't

moved. "So, I hate to ask you to do something else for me . . ." My fingers are tapping quickly against my leg, a nervous tic I'm sure he's noticed and I'm thankful he hasn't asked. "But I was wondering if you would mind coming in and just looking around for a sec before you head home." I stretch my fingers to get them to stop, my hands starting to sweat at the possibility he'll say no.

"What do you mean?" He blinks, looking at me curiously. Oh my, does he think I'm trying to invite him in for something more? Instead of calming, the anxiety flourishes and thousands of little nerves race through my chest and down my arms, my fingers clamping down on my leg.

"Let's just say I've seen one too many scary movies and I never go into an empty house by myself." I give him a small smile hoping to ease the strain that had quickly formed between us.

Slowly, the corners of his eyes crinkle as one side of his mouth lifts to a grin. That little dimple makes its appearance just before he chuckles. He's assessing me—that would definitely be the word—and he isn't sure what to think of me.

Looking back toward the house, he runs his hand through his hair. "Sure, come on." He turns off the truck and we both climb out.

"You know if you were looking for a little . . . fun . . . tonight, you could've just come out and asked." He looks over his shoulder, his eyes drop down to my legs, and he smirks at me as he walks ahead.

What?!

Oh my God.

I'm sure he's just trying to be playful, but I can't tell and on the off chance that he's not, his words seep under my skin, freezing me on the steps heading up to the front porch. What was I thinking asking him to go into the house? Of course he would read between the lines and interpret my question differently. I mean, look at him—he's gorgeous! Girls probably throw themselves his way all the time, but that's not who I am. What am I supposed to do now? I can't go into this house with him. I can't believe I put myself in this situation.

He realizes that I'm not following him up the stairs and turns to look at me. Just a couple of steps separate us, but I can't be this close to him. I can't. Desperate for escape, I spin around quickly and start walking toward the road to put distance between us. I don't know where I'm going, but at this point, it doesn't even matter. I have to get away. Now. My arms are wrapped around my stomach and I'm squeezing my ribs as hard as I can, but the panic won't stop.

Don't go in the house! Get away from the house!

My skin is on fire, my eyes have blurred, my ears are ringing, and my chest is so tight I'm afraid I might pass out.

I'm being irrational, but I just can't help myself.

I hear and feel the thudding of his footsteps as he comes up behind me, *that sound.* From when I was running down the dark hallway away from *him.* There's a deep murmuring—he's talking to me—but the noise is so loud in my ears I can't hear him.

A light sprinkling of rain settles on the windshield as he puts the car in park, and we sit in the driveway of my parents'

home. I never should have gone out with him tonight. As much as it breaks my heart, I've been trying to pull away from him, but he doesn't seem to be catching on. When he asks me out, I tell him I have homework. When he tries to hold my hand at school, I shift my books so he can't touch me. And last week after he won his wrestling match and drove us to the water tower hoping to "relieve some stress," I told him I had my period. At what point does he lose interest in me and start looking for someone else?

Chris and I have been together forever. Literally, since the day I was born. Our fathers were fraternity brothers, both married their college sweethearts, and after law school decided to open a practice together. Chris is two months older than me and one of my first baby pictures is of the two of us together in the hospital after I was born.

Every memory I have, he's in it. He was my childhood friend turned middle school best friend, and when I was fifteen, he kissed me for the first time. From holidays to vacations, cotillions to prom king and queen, he has always been with me and me with him. Up until a year ago, I thought he was my forever too. Now, I know he's not, I just don't know how to get out of it. We are the golden couple of Kensington County and we are expected to last.

I begged and pleaded with my parents to let me stay home tonight, but they insisted I accompany him to the annual Memorial Day dinner at the country club.

"People won't understand," she says. "They expect to see the both of you, together. You know how proud everyone is of the two of you. Kensington's very own All-American couple."

I'm so sick of this nickname. I don't want to be an "All-American couple," and I didn't want to see him, but they don't understand. I've tried confiding in my mother, and I think she believes me, but she's never been one to rock the boat, and in the end told me I was overthinking things. If dark fingerprint bruises scattered across the tops of my arms is me "overthinking," I shudder at the thought of what an actual eye-opening cause for change would be.

Chris turns the car off, pulling me from my train of thought, and I know it's now or never. Letting out a deep sigh, I look straight out the windshield, tightly clasp my hands together on my lap, and say the words I've dreamed of saying for months now. "Chris, we are over. I don't want to be with you anymore, and if you would stop and think about it, you don't want to be with me either." Silence fills the car and instead of feeling relief, I'm both heartbroken for the end of what we once were and frozen with fear.

"What?" he says a little too calmly for me. "Do you hear what you're saying? You're out of your damn mind if you ever think for one second that I will let you walk away from me. I know that things have been a little off between us, but you'll come around. You are *mine*. You always have been and you always will be."

My heart falls. He isn't taking me seriously. I didn't think this conversation was going to be an easy one, but I've prayed nightly that he would be relieved and agree with me.

"No, Chris, you're wrong. I might have been yours at one time, but I'm not anymore. I don't know who you are, but I do know this . . . I don't like the person that you've become. Obviously, our families are close and I hope that we'll still be friends, but I can't be your girlfriend anymore."

His eyes narrow into slits and his jaw ticks from grinding his teeth. His skin flushes as his evident anger surfaces, I know I need to get out of the car soon and go inside.

"Did you really just give me the 'We can still be friends' line? We've never *been* just friends and we'll never *be* just friends. Is there someone else? There better not be. Do you have any idea what I'll do to him—and you—if I find out there is? Jesus, Avery, you are making me angry and you know how I get when I'm angry." His fingers squeeze the steering wheel and his knuckles strain white.

Fear slithers in under my skin leaving goosebumps in its wake.

"Of course there's not anyone else. When would I have time for that? Unlike you, I've been one hundred percent faithful." Disgust slices through me at the memory.

Over spring break, he had gone to Florida with his friends and thought it was okay to experience a little "once in a lifetime fun," as he called it. I never would have known if I hadn't seen a text come in to his phone that said, "Thanks again, Chris. You were awesome in and out of bed. Next time you're in Florida look me up." I was devastated.

His nostrils flare at the reminder. Like any self-respecting person who thinks they deserve better, I'd tried to end it then, and that was the first time he hit me. Being hit by someone you love and cherish was so degrading. It wasn't the physical pain, but the emotional pain that was so excruciating. It was as if at that exact second the dream of us had died. Yes, things weren't ideal between us before that moment, but that hit had been the exclamation point I needed to finally say, "No more." Every girl in this type of relationship fanaticizes that the other person will change—see how hurtful they are being. After all, something changed to make them this way, but after I realized the behavior wasn't going to stop, there was no going back.

"Why do you always have to get angry? Why do you have to hurt me? Why can't you just talk to me like you used too? I don't understand what's happening to you, Chris." I've tried to have this conversation with him before, but each time he just blew me off or talked down to me. I used to know him so well. We laughed, joked, shared secrets, and finished each other's sentences. We used to be so happy.

He tilts his head as he mulls over my words. "What's happened to me? Are you serious right now? I'll tell you what's happened to me . . . I am God around these parts. I was expected to be the town hero and that's what I became. Perfect grades, perfect football, perfect wrestling, perfect college acceptance, perfect family, and perfect girlfriend. Although you don't seem to be holding up your end of the deal." I've always recognized the pressure he felt to be perfect, but I had thought we were in this together . . . stupid me.

"What deal?"

"That you belong to me! Where I go, you go. What I do, you do. What part of this have you forgotten?"

"No." My voice comes out in a whisper as I shake my head. For quite some time now, I've known that I am not going with him. Once it's time to leave Kensington, I will be going by myself and not to Northwestern where he thinks we're going. I've secretly made my own plans.

"YES!" He pounds the steering wheel. "Why won't you just do as you are told and shut up?! I swear, the older we get, the dumber you get! It's really not that hard of a fucking concept!" My heart clinches at how easy it is for him to talk down to me. I've spent so much time loving him, and now it just feels wasted.

His hands start rubbing the steering wheel, back and forth, and it reminds me of that children's game where you give Indian burns. It's only a matter of time before his hands are on me mimicking the action. He's not thinking clearly. I need to get out of the car and into the house as quickly as possible.

Opening the door, I put one foot out when I'm suddenly jerked back into the car. My hip hits the seat belt connector and pain streaks down into my thigh.

"Where do you think you are going?" he snarls through his teeth.

"It's been a long day. I'm ready to go to bed," I say quietly to try and calm him.

His fingers loosen on my arm and I rush to get out of the car and close the door. Mist covers my face and I wrap my coat more tightly around me as I start walking. *Get inside, lock the door. Get inside, lock the door.* If I can just get inside, everything will be fine.

"You know what?" His voice comes up from behind me and slithers under my skin. "I think that sounds like a great idea—let's go to bed." His hands wrap around my arms and he squeezes, pushing me forward. Tears blur my eyes at the pain, and fear strikes my heart over and over like the pendulum of a grandfather clock.

Why is he doing this to me?

Dark hair flashes before my eyes and I'm instantly brought back to the present. Chris has blonde hair—he's not here, he's not chasing me. The guy moves to stand right in front of me and I jerk to the left to go around him, but he holds his hands up to stop me. All I can do is look at the ground. I can't breathe and I just know he's going to touch me . . . *please don't touch me.* He puts one finger under my chin and pushes it up so he can look me straight in the eyes. His other hand is holding up the number two and he begins to slowly wave his fingers back and forth between our eyes. He's asking me to keep eye contact with him. He removes his finger from under my chin and steps closer to me, but he still isn't touching me. *Please don't touch me.* Slowly, he bends down where his eyes are level with mine and pries my hand off of my stomach and places it on his chest. He lets go of my hand and with perfect clarity I hear him say, "Breathe with me."

I can't take my eyes off of his. It's too dark out to see their color, but the wrinkles between his eyes on his forehead show concern for me. Concern! He isn't upset with me, he isn't freaking out over my behavior, and . . . he doesn't want to hurt me.

My hand registers his heartbeat. It's smooth, steady, and I focus on the gentle cadence as it thumps against my hand. Warmth from his skin pushes past his shirt and drifts over my hand and up my arm. There's an inner strength that's radiating off of him and he's passing it to me. Whoever this guy is, he's slowly taking control of the situation and me. I hate feeling out of control, and I never want another person to hold control over me again, but there is something about him in this moment that makes me feel safe and makes my heart slow. If only I had had this feeling about five minutes ago, maybe none of this humiliation would be happening.

"Breathe with me." He repeats this a few more times and I begin to mimic his deep breathing.

The noise in my ears quiets and the pressure on my chest gradually begins to relax. Being overwhelmed by the situation,

I look around when he brings back up the two fingers and waves them between us again. My eyes lock back on his and tears pool in my eyes. I don't know if these tears are leftover from the adrenaline, the relief that this is passing, or from embarrassment. A breeze passes and feels like it's pushing me into him. Leaning forward, I lay my forehead on the middle of his chest. He doesn't move and makes no attempt to touch me, but the steady rhythm of his heart welcomes me.

"I'm so sorry I said that to you." His voice is quiet and remorseful. "I was trying to be funny, and I didn't mean to make you feel uncomfortable. I'm sorry."

I don't say anything back to him. I mean, what would I say? Besides, I certainly do not want to get into a conversation as to why this episode of mine happened in the first place.

I'm not sure how long we actually stand in the driveway, but eventually I step a little closer to him. His hand comes up and cradles my head, almost like one would a child. His fingers slip into my hair and my eyes close at the sensation. I can't remember the last time that I was this close to a guy. My heart is still pounding a little harder than normal, but I'm starting to think that it's for a different reason and not out of fear. The scent of his cologne from earlier has faded, but he smells just like what I think a guy should smell like . . . clean, a combination of fresh laundry, citrus, and a musk scent. It isn't overpowering and the scent of him combined with the air from the fall night is intoxicating.

Letting out a deep sigh, I relax against him, and slowly, he reaches down and grabs one of my fingers with one of his.

"Come on, let's get you inside." He takes a step back from me, his eyes scanning my face, and then he pulls my finger and together we walk back up the steps and to the front door.

Chapter EIGHT

WILL ASHTON

WHAT. THE. HELL. Just. Happened.

I made a one-off flirtatious remark, and by the way she reacted, you would think I was threatening to tie her up and physically harm her. I mean, *shit*, that was stressful.

I've never seen someone have a panic attack before. The poor girl could barely breathe, she was shaking all over, and she was frantic to get out of here. No way, sweetheart. I wasn't letting her go anywhere.

The first few weeks after my grandfather died, Clay's mom would find me in the closet hiding and crying, and she used to put my hand on her chest to calm me down. It worked then, and it was the only thing I could think of to reassure her that I was here with her and not going to hurt her. I've known her for thirty minutes, but all it took was five for me to understand she doesn't like to be touched. So this way, her hand was on me, not the other way around. The power was in her hands, not mine.

Seriously, what the hell happened to this girl? I can't wrap my head around it. She's beautiful and has the voice of an angel, but when her eyes locked onto mine, they were so wide with fear, I wanted to wrap my arms around her to protect her and at the same time kill whoever made her this way.

Shit.

I need to calm down and remain that way. If I get upset, she might get upset, and I don't ever want to see that happen to her again.

As the front door closes behind us, I take a few deep breaths before turning to face her. Giving her another once over, I check to make sure she's all right. I'm confused and she's embarrassed, so I'm certainly not going to start firing questions at her, but damn, if I don't want to.

She looks down at the ground and another tear slips out. Now that she's calm, I can't help myself, I need physical contact with her. Moving a little closer, I wrap my hand around her face and use my thumb to wipe away the tears. Her face is blotchy from crying, big, watery blue eyes stare up at me, and her lips are swollen with emotion. God, she's gorgeous. My gaze shifts to her mouth—what I wouldn't give to kiss all of this away, make her forget what happened on the driveway, and replace it with a memory of us that's worth remembering.

"Stay here while I check the house out and turn on a few more lights." I squeeze her finger and then drop it. Walking into the kitchen, I can feel her eyes following me. She still hasn't said anything and I wish that I was a funny guy who could make her laugh, but I'm not. I mean, look what happened at the last joke I tried on her.

Pulling open the refrigerator door, there's a six-pack of cider beer sitting on the top shelf. I grab two, one for her and one for me. Walking back over, I hold it out and she takes it.

"I thought you might need this." I give her a small smile and turn to take a look around the downstairs floor. The home looks really nice, from what I can see of it. Mine just has the basics, but this one looks like it's been lived in for a while. I check the garage, the laundry room, the master bedroom, and the living room. I don't know what I'm looking for, but if wandering around the house is making her feel better, I'll wander all night.

"So, this level is all clear and I just got a text from Clay that he's headed back with your friends. I'm going to go sit outside on the back porch and wait for him, if that's all right." Her face relaxes and the relief in me staying here with her is evident.

"I'm sorry about earlier." Her voice is hoarse and throaty. She doesn't mean it to be, but it's sexy and could rival her singing voice any day. I hate that she feels the need to apologize. I shake my head no, not wanting her to continue.

"Don't." There's a pause in our conversation and she watches as I lift the bottle to my lips and take a swallow. Her eyes on me make me feel good.

"I appreciate you offering to stay, but you really don't have to." Her arms wrap back around her center and my eyes are drawn again to her chest and the Blue Horizons t-shirt. I'm captivated by her and even after this, I still want to know more about her.

"I know, but they'll be here soon and then I can take Clay with me." Half of my mouth curves upward in a smile and her eyes drop. Looking at my mouth, she smiles in return, but it doesn't reach her eyes. She's still cautious of me, and based on whatever's happened in her past, she has good reason.

A stretch of silence makes this moment officially more awkward than it already is.

Giving her a small smile, it's time to say goodnight. "All right, well, I guess I'll see you around. Come lock the door behind me." She nods her head, and I turn and walk through the middle of the house. Just like before, I can feel her watching me as I pull the sliding glass door open and shut it quietly behind me.

Dropping down into one of the Adirondack chairs on the back deck, it's completely dark outside except for the moon and the stars. The moon is reflecting off of the lake and it makes the water appear silver. Looking to the right, I try to get a glimpse of my house. With the curve of the lake, I thought it might be possible, but it's pretty well hidden by the trees.

My mind races as I think back over the episode she had out in the driveway. Seeing that much fear in her eyes, it tears at my soul and makes me want to pound my chest like a caveman at the same time. It's the same fear I saw outside of Smokey's, only there she was able to contain it, whereas here she just couldn't. I don't know who put it there, but they better hope they never cross me in a dark alley.

I feel awful for trying to joke around with her, but I didn't know, and now I do. Speaking of knowing, it occurs to me that not once did I introduce myself to her. And I still don't know her name.

After a while, the crunching sound of gravel lets me know the girls and Clay have pulled in. The car turns off and giggling hits my ears. Such a different ending to their night than mine and the girl's upstairs.

The glass door behind me slides open and Clay walks out with the girls following right behind.

"Hey, man. This worked out perfect. Thanks for waiting

for me." He doesn't know the real reason I'm here. My text just mentioned I would stick around until he got here. I'm sure he thought it was for other reasons, whatever, I don't even care. All I know is that I wasn't leaving her here by herself.

"No worries." I get up and face the three of them.

The two girls are standing slightly behind Clay, and while he is smiling, the two of them are glaring at me. How he can be oblivious to the tension radiating off of them?

"You two got home all right?" the little brunette asks me.

"Yep." I walk over to their patio table and place the empty bottle on it. Her forehead wrinkles a little in confusion and she tries to process my clipped answer. I'm not going to tell her what happened on the driveway, that's between the girl and me. She glances over to the other blonde who shrugs her shoulders, and then they both look back at me.

"Soooo . . ." Clay drags out. His smile has dropped a little as he watches our exchange. "The girls are here for one more day and invited us over for a barbeque tomorrow. What do you think?"

The unease that has been coursing through my veins for the last forty-five minutes dissipates. I wanted to see her again, I just didn't have a reason to, and now I do.

"Sounds good. What time should we come over?" I shove my hands in my front pockets and grab my keys.

"How about any time after lunch? Clay volunteered you to do the grilling," the blonde says innocently.

Clay smirks and I just shake my head. "Of course you did."

"What?" he shrugs. "You're much better at grilling than I am."

"Well, that's the truth." I rattle my keys and Clay takes

63

that as his cue.

"Th-thanks for bringing me home," he addresses the little brown-haired girl. "We'll see y'all tomorrow."

"Looking forward to it," she responds. My eyebrows shoot up at the suggestiveness in her tone.

The blonde and I watch as the two of them smile at each other. Clay blushes. Man, he's got it bad.

The air is cold this morning, more so than last night, so I grab an extra layer to throw on and an ear band. It's my thirtieth birthday and I can't think of a better way to start my day than on the lake.

Years ago, Clay and I were driving by a yard sale, and out front there were two single-person kayaks. We stopped, the seller gave us a great price, and we never looked back. We immediately drove to the lake, dropped them in, and with one stroke, I fell in love with flat-water kayaking. It calms me; it's my therapy.

After I walked out in Phoenix, it was here in the middle of the lake on the calm waters that I truly began to ask myself the tough questions. I had spent the last however many weeks brooding, becoming more asocial, and all around just a pain in the ass. I needed to sort my shit out, and here was the place to do it.

It's easy to have self-reflection when you are surrounded by the solitude, the quiet, and the impossibility of escaping what's in your own head. It makes you realize how awful things have become and that it's time for change. With a tightness in my chest, I confronted what I had been avoiding: Is it possible to love what you do so much that in the end you don't love it at all? And if I don't love it anymore, what do I love? What do I do? Music is all I know, it's all I've ever wanted, so if not that, what?

Dragging the kayak into the water, I step in, use my paddle to launch off the shore, and float into the freeness that comes with leaving the world behind on dry land. The feeling I still get each time is indescribable and invigorating.

Paddling across the water, I easily fall into the routine of alternating the strokes from toes to hip and then right to left. Twisting my hips, there's a symmetry between me, the paddle, and the water that is almost hypnotizing, and often times I find myself so relaxed in the repetitive movements, that I'll end up on the other side of the lake but won't remember the journey.

Consciously, I track the number of houses I pass and slow down as I approach where the girls are staying. I went to bed last night thinking about the beautiful blonde and I woke up this morning thinking about her too. The house is quiet and I can't help but wonder if she's still asleep. Thoughts of her in bed with those gorgeous legs and full lips, every fiber of my being tightens and I let out a groan. I still say there's something about her that feels eerily familiar. Maybe I'll be able to figure out what it is later.

Switching to high-angle paddling, the stroke pulls closer to the boat and my speed picks back up. I've made this trip around the lake no less than two hundred times and I love it as much now as I did the first time.

I had been reluctant to go out last night, and Clay doesn't even realize what he did for me, but it turned out to be just what I needed. It's like they say, "When you least expect it is exactly when you'll find it." For quite some time now, I've been lost, confused, and not really sure what direction to go. It makes sense to go back to where it all started. Back to the roots. If I hadn't been so adamant about hiding, I should have come up with this on my own.

In many ways, last night I felt like a fly on the wall of my own life. The young guys on stage were laughing, singing, and just loving what they were doing. Hell, at some point in the night, they played one of our current songs and I found myself completely lost and absorbed in the music, just like I used to get. Music speaks for me, it feels for me, and it defines me. And after eight weeks, I had an answer to the first question . . . I do still love music. Now, I just need to figure out if I still love what I do with it.

Chapter NINE

Ava Layne

"GOOD MORNING, SLEEPYHEAD." Emma grins at me as I walk into the kitchen and head for the coffee pot. Both she and Cora are sitting at the table looking very pleased with themselves. They are both itching to say "I told you so," and I turn my back quickly so they can't see me smile. I don't know why I'm smiling—the evening definitely didn't turn out like they think it did—but it still feels good.

"Morning," I mumble.

"Spill it!" Emma yells at me and I jump. Both of them laugh.

"There's nothing to tell." And if there was, I don't know if I would. I pour the coffee and walk over to the French doors off of the kitchen to open them. Only getting to be here for a few days, I need to soak up as much of the mountains as I can;

clean, cold air rushes in, and it feels and smells so good.

"Not good enough, Av. Before you went out to call Mona, you practically bit my head off when I suggested you go over and talk to him, then the next thing I know you're getting a ride home from him. You rode home with him! That is huge! We're shocked and so proud of you! Now spill it. Tell us how you ended up with that piece of mancake and in his truck."

Mancake. The sound of this makes me grin and her comment about his truck has me reliving that feeling of freedom. The night air blowing across my face with the heat on our feet, some of my favorite music ever pumping through the sound system, and the excitement of knowing I was being spontaneous and enjoying the company of a guy. I briefly close my eyes and let out a sigh before turning to face them.

"I hate to burst your bubble, but there's not really much to tell." I pull out a chair and join them at the table. "He went out the back door, scared me, I rammed my knee into his balls, we had a few awkward moments, and then he drove me home. Nothing happened."

"Wait, you crushed his junk?" Cora's eyes widen with amusement and disbelief.

"Yep, he grabbed me to keep me from falling and I over-reacted." A flush burns up my neck and through my cheeks. Both girls burst out laughing, and I bite my lip.

"Av, that is so classic you. You haven't been close to any guy that we know of in years, and your relationship with him immediately starts out with you and his junk." Emma leans back in her chair, smiling from ear to ear.

Years . . . it has been years. Seven to be exact. Maybe that's why in spite of the panic attack, my memory of last night has me smiling and tips toward the memorable side.

Covering my face with my hand, I pinch my eyes shut.

"Oh my God, can we please stop talking about his junk? And I don't have a relationship with him. I don't even know him." In another lifetime though, I think I might like to.

"Did he kiss you goodnight?" I peek through my fingers at Cora.

"Be serious." My mind drifts to an image of his perfect face, those full lips, and I can't help but wonder, what would it be like to kiss him? I was so worried last night that he would in some way be deceitful with ill intentions, that kissing him never even crossed my mind. But now that it has, I'm disappointed. I think I might like to kiss him.

"I am. I got a good look at him last night on the porch without his hat on and you were given the perfect opportunity." She *would* see it as an opportunity. Cora loves kissing guys. She's always said she should have been an actress, because then she could kiss lots of handsome guys with no strings attached. That it would be the perfect job for her.

"It wasn't like that." Not even close. However, there's no forgetting what it felt like to be pressed up against him. My head slid right under his chin, his warmth had immediately surrounded me, and all of our points lined up perfectly. His fingers as they ran across my head and under my hair felt so good. I can only imagine what they would feel like everywhere else.

"Well, at least you'll get your chance today!" Emma chimes in.

"What do you mean?" I squeeze the coffee cup, not wanting to alert them to the fact I just got nervous.

"We invited them back over to barbeque this afternoon," she says so nonchalantly, like having guys over is just an everyday thing.

"You did what?!" Oh no, my heart starts racing. I would be lying if I said I didn't want to see him again, I just never thought that I would. What do I say? He must think I'm a complete nutcase after the way I behaved last night.

"Relax. We're just going to cook some food and hang out down by the lake. I really didn't think it would be a big deal. Besides, it's been a really long time since we've had guys around and you didn't mind being with him last night." I hear what Emma is saying, but now is not last night.

The two of them are watching me and Cora smiles. Oh no, Cora. She thinks he's hot and guys are so easy for her. Nothing happened between him and I, what if he comes here, and he and Cora hit it off? I might be no good for him, but I know for a fact I wouldn't like to see them together.

"Besides, it's Mancake's birthday," she says.

"Why are you calling him 'Mancake,' and how do you know?" It irks me that they seem to know more about him than I do.

"Clay told us." *Clay.* I wish I knew what his friend's name is. I feel awful for asking him for a ride home and then not even asking him his name. "And we call him Mancake because he's delicious and you like cupcakes over candy. Mancake fits him better for you than Mancandy."

"Fits me?"

"Don't be dense. Even if you don't realize yet that you like him, you do. Or you never would've asked him for that ride home. Even Clay said it was out of character for him to offer you the ride. It seems your boy is a little bit of a loner too, and no, he doesn't have a girlfriend. We asked," Emma says smugly.

No girlfriend!

How can he be a loner too? He's so sexy girls must flock

to him, and he must think I'm no different than any other girl throwing herself at him. I'm still shocked at my behavior last night. I mean, who is this guy? In the last seven years, I haven't socialized, ridden in a car with, or been touched by a guy that wasn't someone I hadn't known for a very long time, and all of these things happened on one night. I was so close to him that if he had lowered his arm, we would have been hugging. And although it was just one finger, he may as well have been holding my whole hand.

Oh well, in the end, it doesn't matter if I like him or not. It was one night, one hour from start to finish, and after today, I'll probably never see him again. I live in New York, my professional life is extremely restricting, and I could never be what he'd want me to be . . . assuming that he did want me, that is. I gave up on the idea of being with someone else a long time ago. Dating means affection, affection means touching, and touching is something I just can't do.

It's time to change the subject.

"Speaking of Clay . . ." I draw out. Emma's entire face lights up at the mention of his name, but she deflects.

"No, no, no, we are not talking about me this morning; we are talking about you." She points a finger at me.

"Well, I'm done talking about me. Time to take Tank out." I stand and Tank jumps up at the sound of her name.

"You can run and hide all you want. Doesn't change the fact that he'll be here in a few hours."

Placing my cup in the sink, I shoot them an indifferent look.

"Whatever." If only that were the truth. I'd never tell them, but I am so excited to see him again. Butterflies take off in my stomach just thinking about his blue eyes and handsome face smiling at me. One thing is for sure—this weekend has definitely turned out different than planned.

Walking out the back door, I spot the familiar red of the kayaker from yesterday morning. I don't know what it is about this particular one—there are always people boating on the lake—but the smooth and serene way he glides across the water is beautiful. I've never given much thought to kayaking, but maybe next summer when we're here I'll give it a try.

I hear the truck pull in as it crunches along the driveway and Emma sprints through the house to meet them. While she is excited, I'm so nervous I feel like I'm going to be sick.

A mixture of voices grows louder as they enter the house, and I squeeze my eyes shut knowing that any second now he is going to be in the kitchen. I am so embarrassed about last night. He must think I'm crazy. Not that it should matter to me what he thinks, but for some reason it does.

"Hey," he says from behind me. The sound of his voice awakens the butterflies in my stomach. Act normal, Av. You can do this.

"Hi." I wipe my hands on the apron tied around my waist and turn to face him.

Holy hotness. I thought he was hot last night, but here in the light of day he is just so much more. My eyes wander over the length of him. He's tall and lean wearing a pair of jeans that hug perfectly across his thighs, and he has on a blue and red plaid button-down with the sleeves rolled up, highlighting his muscular forearms, plus a defined chest and broad shoulders. This man is a work of art, and by the time I make it to his face, a smirk showcasing that perfect dimple is winking at me to let me know I'm busted for checking him out.

I lean back against the counter and blow my hair out of my face. Every part of me that had been nervous about his behavior toward me today disappears by this one look from him. His eyes are so blue in contrast to his dark hair that they remind me of the sky on a cloudless spring day. His eyelashes are thick and as he watches me, there's something so familiar about the two of us together that I'm immediately put at ease and those butterfly flurries change their tune to excitement.

"These are for you." I push the plate in his direction. "Happy birthday." My words are rushed; I feel like an idiot.

"You made me cupcakes?" He looks at the plate graciously before he looks back at me.

"Mmm hmm." Apparently, I've forgotten how to talk.

"Thank you. I can't remember the last time someone made me something like this." He swipes the edge of one, covering his finger with icing, and then sucks it off. The move isn't meant to be anything more than him tasting it, but my mouth goes dry. His eyes light up at the taste and he gives me a lopsided smile.

"Well, stick around then, I'll be sure to fatten you up in no time. I love to bake." Oh my God. What did I just say to him? His smile stretches across his face and I suck in a breath. It's really not fair how good-looking this guy is.

"I think I just might," he says thoughtfully. "Hi, I'm Ash, it's nice to finally meet you." He holds his hand out to me and with just a slight hesitation I slide mine into his. His hand engulfs mine, and its warm, comforting. Moments of last night flash through my mind as he had wrapped one hand around my head and held me to him. His thumb runs across the back of my hand, just a little bit rough, calloused—I like it.

He chuckles and it sounds so warm and friendly. "So this is the part in the conversation where you tell me what all your friends call you."

"Ha, sorry. My friends call me Av." We're standing so close to each other and he smells so good.

His eyebrows shoot up. "As in Ava?"

The moment of truth. He hasn't placed who I am yet, and I'm certain that the second he does, things will change. What does it hurt to let him think it's Ava? It's not like I'll ever see him again after this weekend anyway. And I like the idea of being Ava to him. It's like I get to be someone completely different with him, without most of my baggage, or maybe it's that I'm finally getting to be myself.

"Ava sounds good," I shrug my shoulders and his eyes narrow a little. It's like he knows I'm not telling the truth, but he isn't questioning me about it either. Does he already know who I am? Have we met before? No, I definitely would have remembered.

"Why do I feel like I know you?" I ask him.

"I'm not sure, but I have that same feeling. Trust me when I say I'd never forget someone as beautiful as you."

People have been showering me with compliments my entire life, but coming from him, it feels like the first one ever. A blush burns under my skin.

"You do kind of look familiar though," I challenge him.

"So do you." His head tilts just a little as his gaze runs over me from head to toe and back. Oh my God . . . I think my heart just stopped. He smiles again and my heart melts. It's not that I've never noticed good-looking guys before—I have. But none of them have ever made me feel like this. My blood feels like it's vibrating as it flows through my body. I'm attracted to him and this is a foreign feeling. A feeling I'm not sure I like and quickly need to learn how to block. I feel . . . vulnerable and that makes me feel not in control.

People don't understand my need to be in control. I need to say who, I need to say when, and I need to say how. Giving up any of those things makes me feel uncertain and unsure, and with that comes anxiety. Lots of anxiety. Living with constant anxiety is like being a live ticking time bomb. So easy to set off and so mentally, emotionally, and physically destructive when it does. But by being in control, I can slow the burning of the fuse and maintain some semblance of a normal life.

"I get that a lot. The whole blonde hair, blue eyes thing," I mumble.

"No, it's more than that." He runs a hand through his hair, like he's trying to make a decision, and then he reaches out with one finger to hold one of mine.

He wants to hold my hand! I wrap my finger around his.

"Thanks again for driving me home last night. I'm sorry about what happened outside . . . both times." I drop my eyes to the ground. I know I should be feeling incredibly embarrassed by my behavior, instead I just want to laugh remembering my conversation with the girls this morning.

"No worries, I gather you have your reasons, which is your business, and that's all right by me. I'm just glad you're okay." Hearing his kind and genuine words, my eyes immediately lift to his. Most people when they find out I have panic attacks and anxiety, they make me feel uncomfortable and awkward. They probe me with questions and offer unwanted advice. This is the first time I can ever remember someone just accepting me as I am, and he'll never know how much this means to me. I already liked him before, and this just made him so much more becoming.

"Av! Are you two coming or what?" Emma yells from the outside.

"Yeah, she's kind of persistent," I giggle. "We should go join them."

"Or we could leave them and just take off." He tilts his head toward the front door, grinning.

"Nah, we never have guys around. They're super excited." Why did I just say that?

"Really?" He looks at me curiously.

I shake my head, not wanting to answer any more questions. For a brief second, sadness washes over his face and then it's gone. He must realize it's because of me.

"All right then, let's go." He drops my finger and I grab the plate of cupcakes.

"We eat dessert first," I say nonchalantly.

"And now I like you even more." He's flirting with me and I blush.

Stepping out the French doors, both of us blink at the brightness of the sun and he sneezes three times in a row.

"Bless you," I say at the exact same time he says, "Bless me." He runs his hand over his face and then gives me a small one-sided smile. It surprises me how much his face transforms from a rugged expression to a youthful one, and really it's all because of the dimples.

"The sun makes me sneeze." He shrugs his shoulders.

"Every time?"

"Yep," he says flatly.

"That's kind of . . . cute." I smile at him and he cocks a smirk at me.

"Cute? Whatever you say." His smirk stretches into a smile. I really like it when he smiles.

Walking down the steps toward the lake, like a gentleman, Ash lets me go first. I try to argue him on this, but he just looks at me like I'm crazy. What I find interesting is I don't mind it. Yes, I know he's behind me, and I can *feel* him behind me . . . and that's what usually triggers panic. Not this time though. That is until I feel his hand drift across my lower back and I instantly stiffen. He feels the change in me and drops it. I glance back at him and his lips are pressed into a thin line. I hate how my body reacts to being touched. The sad part is I really want him to put his hand there. It's nice.

Suddenly, I don't know how to act normal around him. Not that I am in the first place, but I feel awkward and this is hard. He shrinks the size of the space, sucks up all of the oxygen, and we are outside. I ruined that moment and I'm frustrated. I feel out of control and confused by the way I feel about him. How can I want him to touch me, but not at the same time? And really what does it even matter? In a couple of hours, he'll be gone and this will be over. The last thing I need right now is to have a crush on some guy who I just met. I need to be focusing on my career and the girls.

"There you two are. Get lost?" Emma says as I set down the plate. "You know, last night we didn't formally meet. Hi, I'm Emma." She holds out her hand to him and he takes it. Watching such a simple interaction between the two of them causes my stomach to tighten. I'm jealous of that touch; there's no hesitation, and she so easily accepts it from him.

"Hi, I'm Ash." He nods to Emma and Cora, looks at me, grins, and then back to her. I like that he acknowledged me in this conversation too.

His friend, Clay, chokes on his beer and starts laughing. "Ash! That's what I call you." I don't understand the look on his face or his tone.

"I know. I told her that's what my friends call me." Silence passes over our group as the two guys stare at each other. Ash's expression says "Don't question me on this," and Clay's reads confusion.

Ash nods his head at his friend, and then his blue eyes land on me. Heat floods my cheeks. I probably shouldn't have been watching their exchange, but what I caught on to was the fact that Ash isn't his real name—it's a nickname. So really, I don't know anything more about him than I did last night, except he likes my cupcakes.

"Well, I like the name Ash, it suits you. I'm Cora." His eyes leave mine and skip to her. She holds out her hand and he takes it. They smile at each other, and that pang of uncomfortable jealousy hits me again. This sucks and I hate this feeling. Pulling up the walls around me, I close off any feelings that might have been developing for him and take my seat in between the girls. Nothing good can come of it anyway, so there's no use in thinking about it or him.

Closed off. That's how people have come to describe me and that's how I'm going to stay.

Chapter TEN

WILL ASHTON

I COULDN'T WAIT to get out and stretch my legs. Mornings have always been my favorite time of the day. Most people like sleep, but I've never been one that needs much of it, so while the rest of the world is getting that last little bit of shut-eye, I'm outside running, enjoying the quietness of a new day. Whether I'm back home in Nashville, in some city during the tour, or here in the mountains, I love it.

Every place offers something different.

Whiskey loves mornings too. He loves to run. His only problem is that he likes to play chase. He chases squirrels, pigeons, cars, people—it doesn't matter—so the fewer opportunities he has to come in contact with any of these, the better. The trick with him is to stop running or moving. If you stop, he stops. If you run, he runs, and he'll always catch you, usually by tackling you down. On more than one occasion this has been a problem for us.

Stopping, I turn and stare out at the mist covering the lake. The glow beyond the eastern mountains has grown into morning light. Shoving my hands into my pockets, I can't stop thinking about Ava and how much of a good time Clay and I both had spending the day with her and her friends.

I had hoped to get to know Ava a little more, but as we approached the outdoor living room area where Clay and the girls were sitting, the little brown-haired one—who I learned was Emma—stood up and moved one seat over, leaving the one between her and the blonde, Cora, open. It was an unconscious move too. She was in the middle of introducing herself to me and she just moved. Ava sat down between them and a pang of disappointment hit me. Looking on the bright side, sitting across from her gave me full access to stare at her, and stare at her I did . . . for hours.

Her wild, curly hair was pulled up into a knot on top of her head, she was wearing large hoop earrings, and the only trace of makeup I could see was lip gloss. She had on a long-sleeved, gray t-shirt that slipped off one shoulder when she moved and skinny jeans that were so tight they reminded me just how perfect her legs are. Most of the afternoon, she kept them tucked under her in her chair, but occasionally she would stretch them out in front of her, and damn, if I didn't watch every move and twist she made.

I can't remember the last time Clay and I just sat around a campfire and wasted away the day. Granted I've been hiding out and not doing much, but this was different. It was fun, relaxing, and the conversation flowed so easily. Not once did we talk about our day-to-day lives, and as great as it was to avoid all of that banality, in hindsight, I didn't learn very much about her. She lives in New York City. She works with her friends. She has great taste in music and loves to bake, but that's about it. I had been hoping for an opportunity to come up where she and I could slip away for a bit, but it never happened, and her friends kept her pretty much locked between them.

As the day slipped into the evening, Clay pulled his guitar out of the truck and played for the three of them. I didn't even realize he had brought it, but this was the perfect occasion for it. The music was light and peaceful. Some of the things he played were older popular songs from artists like Johnny Cash and Willie Nelson, and some I had never heard, which meant he's been working on new material over the last three weeks. Several times, his eyes flickered to mine. He knew what he was doing—he knew if he played enough, I would cave, wanting to hear more. And I did.

Right around ten, the girls started yawning. I would have stayed all night, but it was time to go. Walking back up the steps to the house, my gut tightened at the thought of not seeing her again, so it may not have been very original, but I did the only thing I could think of and gave her my cell phone number. At first she looked surprised, but then she smiled so sweetly at me, I had another urge to kiss her, and damn, it sucked that I couldn't. Not yet at least.

I'm going to give her one month. If I don't hear from her by then, I'm going to track her down somehow, by either getting her number from Emma—who I know will be talking to Clay based on their body language yesterday—or Emma's parents. I'm not above getting stalkerish and using public records, such as the purchase records of Emma's parents' house to somehow find a way to get in contact with her. I don't know what it is about her, but I'm interested enough to want to find out. She's different and I like that.

Part of me thinks she's not the type of girl to chase after

guys—which is a welcome relief—but I still want to leave it in her hands. She's shy, quiet, and in a lot of ways, standoffish, so even if the month passes, at least she knows that I want to talk to her and I'm not coming on too strong, too quick.

Even though I know she hasn't called or texted yet, it doesn't stop me from pulling my phone from my pocket and checking . . . nope, but what I do have is a missed call from Juliet.

Juliet.

Needing to face the music, no pun intended, I know it's time to call her. Tapping her name, the phone starts dialing. She answers on the second ring.

"Will, you are so lucky you decided to call me back." She's pissed. I knew she would be, but I had been a little hopeful she'd cut me some slack. I hate making her mad, but she's funny when she's mad and I chuckle at her comment.

She huffs into the phone. "Don't you laugh at me; it's been months!" The faint strain in her voice lets me know she's not just mad, she's worried too. I hate that she worries over me, but it's nice at the same time. Other than Clay, Juliet is the only other person I've allowed close enough for that to happen. In this industry, we meet a lot of people, but I can count on one hand the number of people who really know me.

"Yeah, I know and I'm sorry. I just needed some time to myself." I wonder how many times I'm going to have to give this response over the next couple of weeks. I haven't stayed completely off the grid; I've seen how social media and the tabloids have blown up: *Country singer, Will Ashton, shocks fans after his recent disappearance from the Phoenix concert. What went wrong? And where is he?* There's a multitude of speculations, and unfortunately for them, the answer is really boring.

"Well, are you about done?" she asks, attitude winning out over concern. Attitude that I probably deserve.

"I think so." I frown into the phone, looking out over the lake. The fog has started to lift taking with it the dampness in the air.

I hate the idea of leaving here. It's funny how for so long I wanted nothing to do with being a country boy, and now that's all I long to be. I want to be here where life is slower, roots are put down, and the air is clean. I'm so sick of watching life pass by out the front windshield of the bus, and I absolutely loathe the smell of exhaust. Once Clay and I sit down to talk about what happens next, I'm hoping he'll agree with me that we can spend more time here and less somewhere else.

"Good, because Bryce has been asking for you, and I've had no idea what to tell him."

Thinking about Bryce, my heart squeezes. It's been almost three months since I've seen the little guy and I hate that it's been so long.

"Tell him I'll be home shortly and I'll be over soon." Bryce likes it here in the mountains too. Clay can't argue with that.

"I will, and if you're not, we're coming to you." And she would too. She's never been the type of girl to make a threat and not keep it. "For what it's worth, I understand. I'm surprised it took you this long to throw in the towel. I've never understood how you and Clay can keep the schedule you do. Just following you on the calendar makes me tired." Hearing that she understands in a world where I feel most people won't, warmth floods through me. I've always known being a celebrity comes with a certain amount of responsibility, and for the most part I think I do a pretty good job; I guess I just didn't realize how much I needed her and Clay to understand why this break was so important to me.

"I appreciate that, more than you know, although I'm not so sure the label and our fans feel the same way." Picking up a stick, I throw it out for Whiskey, and he sprints off down the trail as silence lulls our conversation.

"Will . . ." she says hesitantly.

"Jules."

"Am I part of the reason you needed this break?" I knew she'd mention our last conversation, but I guess I never thought she'd think I was hiding because of her. Maybe I should have called her sooner.

"No. Maybe. I don't know. But being here without all the noise, I've thought about it," which is the truth. I don't ever want to lie to her.

"And?" she asks.

"We'll talk about it when I see you next." Which is my roundabout way of saying, "I don't know yet, but I will soon."

"I'd like that," she says softly. "You know, there's nothing wrong with taking some time to yourself. Don't let anyone else tell you differently, okay?" She lets out a big sigh, "And you know I love you, right?"

"I know." Juliet has always been very generous with her affections. I should return them more—it's just not my thing. "I'll call you when I get back to Nashville." I'm ready to end this call.

"You better," she fires at me and I chuckle.

"Later, Jules," and I hang up.

Toward the end of the tour—and even into last week—I was ready to tell Juliet I'm in, but now that I've had a little time to clear my head, I'm starting to second guess that decision. Is it the right one? Or are we just taking the easy way out?

As Whiskey and I loop back to head in, there's another runner a little farther up the trail just past my house and immediately I think, "Oh no." Whiskey sees the runner too, and before I can get him under control, he takes off.

"Whiskey! Here!" He completely ignores me. Damn dog.

"Stop!" I yell at the runner.

Whiskey's running, I'm running, and the runner's still running. The closer I get, I can see it's a woman and there's no way she won't be tackled if she doesn't stop now. The chase has been too great and Whiskey is loving every second of this.

"Hey! Wait up!" Shit, my lungs are going to explode from running this hard.

"You need to stop running!" Either she doesn't hear me or she's ignoring me—either way, she begins to speed up. She has to feel us behind her, and then the next thing I know, Whiskey is airborne. He jumps and his front paws hit her right between the shoulder blades. The entire scene breaks down into slow motion and I cringe. I cringe for the girl, I cringe because Whiskey will have to be scolded, and I cringe for me. This has "lawsuit" written all over it.

The poor girl screams the second Whiskey touches her, and she stumbles forward, reaches out to catch herself, and crashes into the ground. Her hands try to soften the impact, but the momentum is too much, and she slides through the damp dirt. Her head bounces as it makes contact and her earbuds fly out of her ears. That's why she didn't hear me calling her. She whimpers in pain, curls up into the fetal position with her face buried in the ground, and begins to shake. Whiskey is standing over her like he won the biggest prize.

Skidding to a stop, I drop to the ground next to her and

gently grab her shoulder. She jerks away from me, gasping for air. This girl is not okay. I pull off her hat, move her ponytail off her face, and see it's Ava.

No, no, no! This can't be happening. My heart crashes into my chest and aches at the impact.

Her face is red and dirty and she's gasping for air. She's having another panic attack, and I have no idea how to make it stop—and it's my fault. My aching heart breaks for her and anger surges through me. What could have possibly happened to send her repeatedly into this kind of panic? Looking around frantically, there's no one else out here, and I'm desperate for someone to help me . . . help her.

Doing the only thing I can think of, I drop down on the ground next to her, and get as close as possible without touching her.

"Ava, look at me!" Her eyes are pinched shut, tears are leaking out, and she's breathing so hard it's bordering on hyperventilation. A lump forms in my throat as it tightens and my eyes burn. Yesterday she was so composed and happy, and now she's lost in this horrible moment, and it's all because of me. No one should ever have to go through life experiencing this horror. I put my finger under her chin just like I did last time and speak a little louder to her.

"Ava! Open your eyes and look at me!" Her eyes flash open and lock onto mine. I'm met with dark blue waters. There's so much pain and fear in them, my stomach dives. Removing my finger from her chin, with two fingers I motion back and forth from my eyes to hers. I want her to keep her eyes locked on me.

"Breathe with me." I overexaggerate my breathing just a little and watch as tears roll down her face leaving streaks through the dirt. All I want is to gather her in my arms and tell her that nothing bad will ever happen to her again . . . only I can't.

Chapter ELEVEN

Ava Layne

*I*T DOESN'T MATTER how many years go by, how many therapy sessions I've had, or how badly I just don't want to be haunted by this anymore. There are just certain things that trigger the panic and I am instantly transported back to that awful night again.

I love running, and I've found the lake here in Horizons Valley is one of the most peaceful places there is. Every trip up here, I get lost on the trails around the lake and up into the mountains. The dirt is always freshly packed, the air clean and devoid of humidity, and in the mornings, the orange glow of the sun reflects off of the water providing enough light to find my way. Mornings are my favorite time of the day, reminding me that it's a new day, anything is possible, and that makes me feel hopeful.

I'm not sure how long I've been running before I begin to

feel as if someone is behind me, chasing me. I can't hear them over the music, but I can feel them hitting the dirt and total panic sets in. I run harder and faster, my feet trying to match the pounding of my heart, but it doesn't matter, he's going to catch me—he always does. Flashes from that night start slipping into my vision, the cool morning air becomes the mist from that night, and the thumping becomes his shoes on the hardwood floors. I can no longer see where I am or where I'm going. I'm running down a dark hallway and it never seems to end.

The second my back is hit, my heart stops beating. I feel like I've died, but I know I'm still living because he's here, it's him, it's that night all over again. I barely remember hitting the ground, but I do remember his fingers as they grab and yank on my hair, the heat from his breath as it covers my face, and his knee jammed into my back to hold me down. Please . . . just make this quick.

"You know what?" his voice comes up from behind me and slithers under my skin, "I think that sounds like a great idea—let's go to bed." His hands wrap around my arms and he squeezes, pushing me. Tears blur my eyes as the pain and fear take over.

Refusing to go in the house with him, my knees bend and my feet dig into the concrete. "Let go of me, Chris; you're hurting me." I wanted these words to come out strong and assertive, but instead they sound more like I'm pleading.

"It's supposed to hurt," he hisses in my ear.

"Why do you want to hurt me?" He's leaning against me, draped across my back, and my toes push back as hard as they can to keep us from going forward.

"Because it's the only time you'll listen to me, and dammit, you *will* listen." He shoves and the point of my left heel catches on a crack in the driveway. The heel breaks and my ankle twists, throwing us off balance. Flashes of white streak before my eyes as I cry out in pain, crumble underneath him, and reach for my ankle. Chris loses his balance and falls on top of me.

"Shit." He scrambles up and stands hovering over me. The mist surrounding us turns to rain, soaking my hair, skin, and clothes. Time passes and I think he's calmed down. Nope. "Get up!" he demands.

"I can't, Chris, it hurts so bad." Tears are streaking down my cheeks, but I refuse to look at him; he hates it when I cry. Always has. He used to want to slay dragons when I got upset, now he just gets angry and calls me weak and pathetic.

"It can't hurt that bad—all you did was trip. Get up!" He jams his foot into my side, kicking me. The spaghetti strap on my dress breaks, and my bare shoulder scrapes across the driveway giving it road rash. Lying in a ball with one hand on my ankle and the other on my shoulder, I just don't understand how we got to this place. Glimpses of past memories flicker through my eyes: moments when he was gentle, kisses that were tender, and a loving smile that was just for me. My stomach clenches as I prevent the sob that wants to break free.

"Why don't you just leave? Go home, Chris! I want to be left alone!" I keep my face hidden, but I'm loud enough where I know he hears me.

"Go home? Are you joking? After what you said to me in the car there is no way I'm going home. I'm never going anywhere. It's you and me, babe, for life . . . and you need to be reminded why we are so good together."

More tears fall, just like the rain. What do I do? How do I get him to leave? If I can just get inside, I can lock the door and call for help. I'm not sure who to call, but at this point anyone will do.

"Fine," he snaps. "But don't say I didn't give you enough time to get up." With that, my head jerks backward as his hand wraps around my ponytail and he pulls me toward the door.

Screams pierce the air around us and when his other hand comes down and slaps me in the mouth, I realize they are mine.

"Shut up!" Blood floods my mouth as my teeth break the skin behind my lips. He pulls harder as his other hand grabs my arm. I bounce across the ground trying to get up, but it isn't working. My ankle won't support my weight, so my knees and the palms of my hands drag across the ground.

Every part of me hurts. My hair, my face, my mouth, my shoulder, my hands, my knees, my ankle . . . but mostly my heart. He was my best friend and the love of my life. How, after a lifetime together, he could treat me so horribly hurts worse than any physical pain he could ever inflict on me.

I look up into his face, his handsome face that once meant so much to me, and I see someone I don't know looking back at me. I want to help him, and I want to save him from this person that he's becoming. It's not him, I know it's not, but what do I do? And why do I even want to after the way he's treated me?

"Chris! Stop!" He does, and wobbly, I push up off the

ground to face him.

His eyes scan over me from head to toe and then come back to my face. He leans over until we are only inches apart and his eyes lock onto mine. Through the rain, there's no mistaking how dark his eyes have become. Countless hours I have stared into his warm brown eyes, but now all I see is darkness and rage. "Get your keys out and open the damn door," he spits. Blood drains from my face, and with it my body cowers before him.

He shoves my purse in my stomach, knocking the air from my lungs. I must have dropped it on the way to the door. Quickly, I fumble through the pockets and make the mistake of sniffing, alerting him to the tears.

"Are you crying?" he jerks on my arm so I'm facing him again, my skin pinched under his fingers. His eyes narrow and his jaw tics.

"It hurts." I don't want to sound weak—I don't want to *be* weak—but I'm terrified of him and what's to come once we go inside.

"Well, it's your fault. Stop fighting me. Do as you're told. Open the damn door!" He twists his wrist, twisting my arm, and I cry out in pain. Shouldn't it have broken by now? He shoves me forward and my face hits the door. Stars float in front of me and my stomach turns over. Dinner and every drop of bile comes rushing to the top, and I vomit all over the door.

"What the fuck?" Chris jumps backward, and I lean against the house to make everything stop spinning. Rain pours down over me. It washes away any evidence that he and I have on the front porch and chills my stinging skin.

Desperation and panic consume me. I have to get in the house and I have to get away from him.

Pulling the keys, I stick them in the lock and pause. This

is my chance; it's now or never. I turn to face him, and using my hurt leg, I shove my knee so far up into his crotch I hope his balls end up in his stomach. His face contorts as he bends over and cries out in pain. Using all the strength I have in me, I shove him backward so he falls down the steps.

Not wasting one second, I unlock the door, slip inside, and slam it shut. Twisting the lock back in place, I'm frozen as I stare at the only thing separating me from him.

The silence inside the house is a complete contrast to the sounds outside. Instantly gone are the rain and the wind, only to be replaced by the ticking of the grandfather clock and the ringing in my ears.

Taking a step backward, I slip further into the darkness of the hallway. My eyes never leaving the door. My heartbeat is erratic, my chest so tight I can hardly breathe, and I just want this to all be over.

BANG!

The door rattles on its hinges and shrill screams leave my throat.

"Av! Open the door!" His foot kicks the door repeatedly, and I take a few steps further away.

"If you don't open this door right this minute, things will be so much worse for you!"

I can't help but think, how could they possibly be worse? And then there's the silence.

Is he leaving? Is he finding another way in? What's he doing? My eyes dart to the windows, but there's no movement. I also don't hear the engine of his car.

I take a few more steps back and my hip bumps into the hall console table. Grabbing on to it for support, my entire body starts shaking.

Echoing through the darkness, I hear the familiar sound of a key sliding in the lock.

Oh no! I forgot about the hide-a-key!

My head swings to the front door just as the handle turns and the hinges creak upon its opening. There, standing in the darkened hallway, staring at the entryway and into the faint light shining in from the outside, is the blackened silhouette of my worst fears come true.

Fear turns to sheer terror. It blankets me with a weight that is suffocating and I'm frozen to the spot. My skin begins to prickle as awareness sets in. He will most likely catch me, but I can't stand here and do nothing, I have to run.

Turning, as fast as I can, I limp-run down the hallway. Digging through my purse again, my fingers wrap around my cell phone. Yanking it out, I swipe it on to unlock the screen and pull up my favorites list. The pounding of the blood in my ears is so loud, it's completely shut off all the noise surrounding me, leaving only the sense of touch and feel. The sensory for vibration is burning up my legs as I can feel the pounding of his shoes ricocheting across the wood floors—straight to me. Touch is that one sense you can't turn off. I can close my eyes, shut my mouth, cover my ears, and clog my nose, but nothing can separate touch.

One one-thousand. *Oh God, he's going to catch me.*

Two one-thousand. *What's he going to do to me?*

Three one-thousand. *Why doesn't he love me anymore?*

SLAM!

His hands make contact with my back and I know it's over. He's caught me and there's nothing I can do to escape him.

Falling.

Falling.

Down.

My body strikes the ground and I cry out in pain. His knee jams into my back to hold me in place, as one hand wraps around the back of my neck keeping my head shoved into the floor, and his other punches the wood directly in front of my face. Four times. Four times I think it's going to be me, four times I wince from the closeness of the impact, and four times I fear what he is going to hit next.

Leaning over, his nose and then his lips rub against my ear. His breathing is labored, but his words are not.

"I'm so mad, I just might kill you."

His voice lingers in the hallway, taunting me, and I squeeze my eyes shut. Tears roll down the side of my face and I think, "If I don't see what he's about to do to me, then I can't see that memory, and seeing nothing is better than something" My mind closes off and my heart locks down. This can't last forever, right?

Chris is talking to me. His mouth is moving next to my ear and his hot breath is fanning over my face. Desperately I want to move away from him, but I can't. The voice returns, I hear it, but something is off. It's not his. This voice sounds almost panicked, and Chris is never panicked. Yes, he's impulsive, but he almost always stays calm, even in a rage. Focusing on the voice, it gets louder and louder. Slowly, the surrounding noises return and take over the thrumming in my ears. My chest aches, I can't breathe, and I don't know what happened. A finger touches my chin and that's when I hear him.

"Ava! Open your eyes and look at me!" My eyes flash open and stare into the most soothing shade of blue. I know those eyes. Those eyes are kind and at the moment show only complete concern. He waves his fingers back and forth between the two of us, and if I could, I would stare into these eyes forever.

"Breathe with me." Ash is lying in the damp grass and dirt, his face next to mine, but he's not touching me. Obeying, I follow his breathing, and that's when I realize there's no one here but us and a large black and tan dog standing over us, panting. That's what I felt in my ear, not Chris. I haven't been caught, he's not here to hurt me, it's all going to be okay. Relief floods through me, and more tears drip down the side of my face.

"I need you to tell me what hurts," his voice is calm but laced with concern.

My eyebrows pull in because I am not sure why he's asking me this. These tears are out of relief not pain. Chris isn't here and he didn't get me . . . and that's when I feel the shooting pain up my arm. The pain is so fierce, I gasp and immediately know something is broken. Rolling further into the dirt, I want to escape his handsome face. I really don't want him to see me like this.

"Ava, please look at me." His voice is so kind and warm, it vibrates throughout my heart. Along with those blue eyes, I think I could listen to him as well as look at him forever.

"I am so sorry," he says and I peek back over at him.

"What happened? Were you chasing me?" I can't imagine that he would've been, but maybe. With the earbuds in, I never would have heard him call out to me.

"No, but Whiskey loves to play chase, and I yelled for you to stop, but I don't think you heard me." At the sound of his name, the dog leans down and nudges Ash's head, pushing him a little closer to me.

"Whiskey. That's his name?" The dog whines and then lays his head down on Ash's arm, looking at me.

"Yeah. Clay and I found him behind a bar called Whiskey's last year." Silence surrounds us as I roll onto my side to face him. Worry is etched into the lines of his face.

His face.

The uneasiness in my stomach changes and is replaced by nervous flutters. He's so close to me I can feel the warmth of his body as it closes the distance between us. The stubble on his chin is longer than it was yesterday and I like it. His head is covered with a gray beanie leaving only little pieces of his hair sticking out, and there are little freckles under his eyes, making them even bluer than they already are.

"Can you tell me what hurts?" he asks again.

"I think it's my arm, or maybe my hand. I don't know. It all hurts." I shift to my back, clutching my arm to my chest. The pain has started to throb and I know this is not good. He sits up next to me, holds his hand out in front of me so I can see what he's doing, and then slowly pulls my uninjured hand away.

Leaning over, but never moving it, he examines my hand, wrist, and arm. The palm side of my arm is facing up and very tenderly he traces the piano keys I have tattooed across my wrist. "I think it's your wrist. It's already swelling and turning purple."

My wrist. Oh no . . .

Reality slams into me. The panic and fear, the adrenaline

and the pain. The shaking returns and I just give up. I start openly crying in front of this gorgeous guy and there's nothing I can do about it.

"Oh, Ava, I am so sorry. This is my fault." His voice is hoarse and laced with remorse. I glance at him and he looks so distraught. He pulls the hat off his head and runs his hand through his hair.

"Do you want me to call someone? Emma?" His eyes are pleading for me to tell him what to do.

I shake my head no.

"Well, I think you should have this looked at. My house is right there." He points to the house that's up the trail next to us. "Let's go get you a little cleaned up and then I'll take you to a doctor. There's a twenty-four-hour urgent care just on the other side of town. I think that will be quicker than driving you to Asheville to the hospital."

He's right, it needs to be looked at, and it's best that I know what's wrong before I send people into panic mode.

"Okay." He scoots away from me just a little so I can sit up. Showing me his hand again, he slowly moves it to push my hair back off my face. It's not lost on me how considerate he is in the way he handles me. Showing me his hands each time he goes to touch me, allowing me to feel and react first—no one has ever done this.

"I think if it's just sprained, they'll wrap it, and if it's broken, they'll still wrap it and send you to an orthopedic to-morrow."

He's right, I know he is, but I'm devastated this is happening to me. I was so happy last night and this morning, just thinking about him and how he gave me his phone number, and now this happens. Am I ever going to have a normal inter-action with him that doesn't involve me falling apart like a basketcase? My arm hurts, my heart hurts . . . this just sucks.

Ash stands and holds his hand out to me. Placing my good hand in his, he gently pulls me up off the ground and into him. My forehead falls onto his chest, and I moan out in pain, hugging my arm closer to me. Gently, he wraps his arms around me, and now twice this weekend I've found myself tucked up under his chin. Although neither time was for amorous reasons, right now, I wouldn't want it to be anyone else.

"Hey." His hand wraps around the side of my head and he tilts it backward. His beautiful blue eyes roam my face, and very softly with his thumb, he begins to wipe away the dirt and grass.

Everything about this moment is overwhelming me and I begin to shiver. His hand drops to my shoulder as his other pulls on my hip to steady me against him. I take a deep breath and the smell of him fills my mind. I commit it to memory thinking he smells better than anything, ever. As his eyes stay focused on mine, his face changes from one of sympathy to complete seriousness. His gaze is so intense and piercing that I can't look at anything else. His hand moves back to my face and his thumb rubs across my bottom lip as he lets out a deep sigh.

"Come on, darlin', let's go get you checked out." He moves to wrap one arm around my shoulders, keeping me close, and together we walk back toward his house.

Chapter

TWELVE

WILL ASHTON

I FEEL LIKE the biggest asshole.

Oh my God.

Never in my life have I been fascinated by a girl like I am with her . . . and then my crazy dog happens. If I didn't love Whiskey so much, there's a good possibility I would give him to Clay and never look back. Unfortunately, I'm kind of attached to the fur beast.

As we walk back to the house, I'm shocked she lets me wrap my arm around her, but I'm so grateful at the same time. I wonder if she even realizes she's letting me hold her or if she's still lost from the panic and the pain. Replaying that entire scene in my mind, I shake my head in disbelief and pull her a little tighter next to me. Of all the people in all the world, Whiskey has to run her down. I'm wound so tight, the muscles in my neck feel locked up and I could break shit.

First off, I now know that whatever happened to her—to

make her this way—somehow involved a chase. She was running from us, as fast as she could, and she may not have realized it, but she was whimpering from full-on terror. And as Whiskey's paws hit her back, that scream spoke a thousand words. Lying in the dirt with her, watching her cry—those tears represented so much more than just the pain in her arm. I've never felt so helpless.

Step by step, we take the trail leading up the back deck and into my kitchen. My heart is still pounding, so I suck in some of the cold air to try and calm down as quickly as possible. She stops right inside the door and I look around for a towel to help wipe her off. My insides are screaming in complete chaos, but knowing she's watching me, I'm trying my damnedest to appear calm.

"Ash?" The quiet sound of her voice is like an electric shock to my heart. I turn to face her, her expression full of pain and embarrassment. I did this to her and I feel horrible. "Can I please use your bathroom?"

"Of course, it's this way." I turn and she follows as I walk through the living room and to the hallway that leads to the bedrooms. This house is a four-bedroom and each one has its own bathroom. I start to lead her to the room next to mine, but Juliet left a few things behind last time she was here, so I pick the one across the hall.

"I'll be in the living room when you're ready. Don't rush; take your time." I slow my words hoping they calm her some.

Blue eyes blink back at me before she nods her head and closes the door.

Letting out a breath I didn't know I was holding in, my forehead leans against the wall next to her door. I wanted to see her again, but certainly not like this, and now here she is in my house and I have no idea what to do. Running my hand over my face, I glance toward Clay's room. His door is cracked, so I peek in, and see that all of his things are gone.

Last night he mentioned getting on the road early, but I didn't expect it to be quite this early. There's a sheet of paper lying in the middle of the bed, "Call you in a few." Interestingly, the idea of him calling me doesn't stress me out—like it would have last week—it makes me feel more like things are slowly getting back to normal. I'm not real sure what normal is yet, but being a recluse locked up in the mountains doesn't have the same appeal now as it did leaving Phoenix.

Dropping the paper back on the bed, I head for my room to change. I'm covered in dirt too. Slipping on a pair of jeans, a t-shirt, and an athletic pullover, I grab an extra for Ava. She's even dirtier than I am and it's chilly outside.

The house is quiet as I walk back through to the kitchen. Whiskey is sitting by his dishes waiting patiently for breakfast. Tossing him some food and giving him some water, I turn around and find Ava watching me and looking very cautiously at Whiskey.

She's washed her face, and attempted to tidy her hair, but it's the stress lines around her red eyes that let me know she's in a lot of pain.

I grab her a bottle of water out of the refrigerator, open it, and hand her some pain medicine from the cabinet.

"Here, take a few of these. Who knows how long it will be before they can prescribe you something?"

A flash of relief passes over her eyes and she doesn't even hesitate.

"I also grabbed you a clean shirt. Not sure if you want it or not, but it's here." I glance toward the shirt on the counter and her eyes follow. She bites down on her lower lip, looking at the shirt, then at me.

"Will you help me change?" Embarrassment stamps her face and I grin at her. She has no idea how much I'd like to help her change. Part of me wants to be flirty and say, "I thought you'd never ask," but I already know she'd run right out the door. Her eyebrows furrow and little wrinkles form just over her nose. "Why are you smiling at me?"

"Just because. I mean, how hard was it for you to ask me that?" I'm teasing her and her face relaxes a little.

"Really hard," she huffs and my grin stretches into a smile.

Moving closer to her, I keep my eyes locked on hers. For a brief second, there's fear, and I don't know if it's because I'm close to her or if it's because she's worried about her arm.

"Bend over for me." She does and I take the hem of her pullover on her lower back and pull so it comes up and over her head. Once it's over her head, she shrugs her good arm out of it and then carefully removes the other. Her injured wrist looks terrible. On the outside, there's a bump about the size of a lime and it's already turning nasty colors. Looking away from her injury, I take her in from head to toe.

She's wearing some type of workout tank top that hugs her perfectly, almost like second skin, and she looks so tiny. Tiny and hot! Her arms, upper chest, and most of her back is showing. Inwardly, I groan and shift my weight as everything tightens. I could look at her all day, but instead, I drag my eyes back to her face. She's looking at the ground and her shoulders are hunched inward. Shit, now I feel bad for checking her out; waves of pain and vulnerability are pouring off of her. She's so uncomfortable, I quickly grab the clean shirt and help her as she slides her arms into it and then back over her head. Slowly, her eyes travel up and lock onto mine. "Thanks."

In my shirt, she looks amazing, and I'm not ashamed to admit how much I like it.

I give her a small smile and tuck some loose hair behind her ear. "All set?" I ask her.

"I guess so," she frowns, running her hand over the shirt to smooth it down.

Grabbing my keys, we head for the door.

It takes close to forty-five minutes for us to drive around the lake and across the little town to the urgent care clinic. She's quiet the entire way, and I can't say I blame her. At one point I saw her shaking—I wasn't sure if it was the downfall from the adrenaline or because she was cold, but I turned the heat on anyway. Anything to make her more comfortable.

Once we get to the clinic, I'm happy to see it's essentially empty. I've already inconvenienced her with this and feel like a complete ass.

"How can we help you today?" the check-in nurse says. Ava holds up her arm and pulls the sleeve back. The lady winces at the sight of it. "All righty then, I'll need you to fill this out, and we'll call you right back." She pushes a clipboard toward us.

Ava takes a look at it and frowns. It's her right arm that's hurt, her dominant arm, and my heart sinks even more. I take it from the nurse and we make our way over to the waiting room.

"I'll fill this out for you, and I'm paying, so we don't

need insurance information or anything."

She tilts her head to look at me. "I don't mind. It'll just be a co-pay, and I can submit the paperwork later."

Angling my body a little more toward her, I lean over so we are eye to eye. "It doesn't matter; this is my fault." She bites down on her lip, worrying it as her eyes search mine for something.

"Okay," she says, still unsure about it. I give her a lopsided smile and her eyes widen.

Shifting the clipboard between us, line by line I begin to ask her personal questions. I learn her last name is Layne, her birthday, her address, that she had an appendectomy when she was fifteen, and she's allergic to Sulfa antibiotics. It's awesome getting to know these little details about her, and it makes me want to know everything. Right before turning the clipboard back in, I glance at her address and take a mental picture of it.

Sitting back down next to her, her silence continues as we wait. I want to talk to her, but she's propped her head against the wall and closed her eyes.

"Ava Layne." We both look over at the nurse waiting at the door, and we stand together. She looks up at me and the hesitation is written all over her face.

"I'm going with you." My tone let's her know I'm not up for arguing. Irritation flares across her face and then it's gone. I lift my arm to wrap it around her shoulder and she flinches away from me. My heart sinks, so I drop my arm and watch her. I know we haven't known each other for long, and I know she doesn't like to be touched, but throwing an arm around someone doesn't mean anything other than being friendly, and she let me do it earlier.

Leaning up on her toes, I bend down so I can hear her. "This place reminds me of a hospital. I. Hate. Hospitals." She shrugs her shoulders, attempts giving me a small smile, and then walks to the triage nurse. I follow her, but give her distance too. People who hate hospitals have a reason. I wonder what hers is.

It's her wrist, not her arm, and it has a pretty sizable crack in it. It's not broken clean through, so she won't need to have it pinned, but it's going to take some time to heal. I thought the silence was bad on the way to the doctor, but this is worse. I don't know what to say to her, and she's clearly internalizing her thoughts. Just looking at her, I can't tell if it's the pain causing her this stress or something else. She never turns her head to look at me. She just stares out the window, thrumming the fingers on her left hand a mile a minute. There's no consistent rhythm to the movement, and she doesn't even seem aware that she's doing it. I just want to stare at her.

"Do you mind if I use your phone? I need to call my friends." She's been so quiet most of the day, I'm startled when she speaks. I look to her face and those blue eyes pin me to the seat, watching me.

"Sure. What's the number?" I grab my phone out of the center console. "The bluetooth will pick it up."

"Oh . . . okay. It's 646-543-2198." The call connects, ringing echoes through the cab, and is answered on the third ring.

"Hello?" The voice is anxious.

"Hey, Emma, it's me." Ava's voice is nervous, but up-beat. She's faking this call.

"Oh my God, Av, where are you? Cora and I have been worried sick. All your note said was 'Heading out . . . see you later.' Do you know what time it is? We're supposed to leave for the airport in twenty minutes. Why don't you have your phone on you? And where are you calling me from. I don't recognize this number."

I understand why she's worried—Ava's been gone for hours—but the way she's firing these questions, I grit my teeth together. She's had a bad enough day already and being badgered by her friend suddenly rubs me the wrong way.

"Listen, I'm not gonna head back with you guys tonight. I'll catch up with you later in the week." Ava lets out a sigh.

I sneak a peek at her; Ava's fingers are moving a mile a minute on her leg. It's obvious I'm listening to their conversation, but I'm trying to show indifference. Maybe I should have disconnected the bluetooth and let her take this privately.

"What are you talking about? I don't understand. Where are you?" The pitch in Emma's voice rises.

"At the moment, heading back to the house." Ava glances over at me before she looks back out the window. She looks tired.

"Well, hurry up! We'll wait for you." Irritation and impatience leak through in her words and the hairs on the back of my neck stand up.

"No, don't, I need to stay here for a few days," she says firmly.

"Av! You aren't making any sense. Why do you need to stay here? We have stuff to take care of . . ." I look over at Ava as she leans forward and rests her forehead on her good hand. Her eyes are closed and that's when I see the first tear roll down her face. My heart instantly cracks down the middle at her distress.

Shit. I wasn't expecting her to cry during this call. It's stressing her out and I hate this. I want to hang up on Emma. I want to pull over and hug her. I want to make this entire situation go away.

"Hello! Are you still there?" Emma asks. My hands tighten on the steering wheel.

"Yeah, I'm here, sorry. Listen, don't flip out, okay?" Ava sits back and runs her good hand over her face to wipe away the tears. Her eyes are swollen and her nose is red, and I can't help but think she's still so freaking beautiful.

"You're scaring me." In the background, I hear Cora ask what's going on.

"I'm on my way back to the house from the urgent care . . . I fell and broke my wrist." She rushes the words and then dead silence fills the truck as more tears leak down her lovely face. These tears aren't tears of physical pain—this is something else, and my stomach clenches.

"Please tell me you're kidding . . . you're not kidding, are you?" Ava doesn't say anything, she just shakes her head no.

"Av, I'm about to have an all-out panic attack! What happened?" Cora says something again from the background and Emma shushes her.

"I tripped and fell while running."

She just lied to her friends and I don't understand why. I mean, Whiskey chases—it's his thing—I guess I just don't understand why she can't tell them that. Maybe it has more to do with explaining the panic attack, not that it's any of their business. I don't know.

"Holy crap, Av! I'm staying here with you." Speaking of panic, Emma is all but screaming and Ava winces from the volume.

"No, please don't. Please take that meeting for us. I have to follow up with the orthopedic tomorrow and then I'll head back to the city."

This is keeping her from her job. Guilt floods me, and I hope she doesn't get into trouble.

"Oh my God, no! You need to see a specialist in the city, not some country quack!" Ava looks down at her wrapped arm and runs her fingers back and forth across the bandage.

"Maybe you're right," she mumbles.

"Of course I'm right. If it doesn't heal properly . . . oh, I think I'm going to be sick."

I'm confused and my vision tints a little red with anger. I understand worrying about your friend when they get hurt, but why is she acting like this affects her too? Emma didn't break something, Ava did, and she needs to calm down.

"Hey, it's going to be fine. It's just a crack. Look, I know you're upset and I'm really sorry, but I can't deal with this right now, I'm just—"

"Have you called Mona?" Emma cuts her off.

Who's Mona?

"No. I wanted to call you first." Ava's fingers return to tapping on her leg.

"Have you looked at the calendar?"

Ava squeezes her eyes closed. I should be looking at the road and not at her. "No, but I already know."

"How many?" Emma asks.

"Three." The word echoes through the truck cab like cannon fire.

Three what? I'm so confused by their conversation.

"Shit," Emma says under her breath.

"Tell me about it." The fake upbeat tone Ava has been attempting vanishes.

"I don't know what to say right now. I'm shocked, upset for you, and overwhelmed."

"I didn't mean for this to happen," Ava says defensively.

"Oh, Av, I know." Emma lets out a sigh. "And I'm so sorry you're hurt."

Ava sniffs. "Please call Mona for me. I can't deal with her." Ava hugs her arm closer to her chest.

"Okay, Cora and I will take care of everything."

"I really appreciate it. I need a few days to wrap my head around this, and then I'll give her a call."

"I really think I should stay with you," Emma pleads.

"No, don't. I'll be fine."

Will she be fine? I hadn't thought about her needing extra help, and she *is* going to need it.

"Where are you calling me from?" Emma asks.

"Ash's phone." Ava glances over at me and gives me a small smile. God, I love her smile.

"Ash, as in the same Ash we spent yesterday with?" Emma's tone is slightly accusatory and I'm not sure I like it.

"Yep." Ava's smile gets a little bigger and my heart thumps a little harder.

"Why are you with him?" Emma mutters my name to Cora, and Cora animatedly yells, "What?!"

Huh?

"He saw me fall and took me to the doctor." Her smile fades a little. Not being ready to break the connection, I reach over and place my hand over hers. Instead of pulling away from me, her fingers tangle with mine. I know it's such a small thing, but coming from her, I'm elated.

"Be careful," Emma warns.

What the hell is that supposed to mean? My eyebrows furrow in confusion, and Ava pulls on my hand bringing my eyes from the road back to hers. They are soft, letting me know she feels cared for and not afraid. But why would she be afraid of me?

"I will, don't worry about it."

"I am worried about you . . ." she trails off.

"I'll be all right. Listen, I'm gonna go. I'll call you after I talk to the ortho. You're right—I'll see a specialist when I get back to the city."

"Just call me tomorrow. I'll take care of Mona, and Cora will find you the best specialist."

"All right. I really appreciate it."

"Hey, Av, I'm so sorry this is happening to you." I look over and see her swallow. Emotional pain crosses her face again.

"Me too. Later, Emma."

"Bye, hun."

The phone clicks off and silence refills the truck. I have no idea what half of that phone call was about, but I get the feeling a broken wrist means more to them than the average person. Shit, this just makes me feel worse. Ava relaxes back into the seat, lays her head against the window, and closes her eyes.

"Please don't ask me about the call," she mutters on a sigh.

"Wasn't planning on it." And I really wasn't. This girl is locked tight with secrets, and she doesn't volunteer information very easily. Oh well. She'll tell me if she wants to.

"Thank you, Ash."

"Anything I can do for you?" Like give you the moon . . .

"Maybe just drive a little longer so they're gone when we get back."

"I can do that." Slowing the truck, I hit the blinker, and make the turn toward the Blue Ridge Parkway. May as well take the scenic route.

Her injured arm returns to her chest in a protective move and the fingers on her left hand relax under mine. I'm so happy she doesn't pull them away; I'd hold her hand forever.

By the time I turn down Lake Horizons Road, she's asleep against the window and I make the decision for her . . . she's staying with me.

Chapter THIRTEEN

Ava Layne

"AVA, WE'RE HERE," he says quietly so as to not startle me. My eyes flutter open and I turn to meet his. I can't help but wince from the pain and he frowns. It's the same frown he had during my call with Emma.

After we hung up, I closed my eyes to let him know I was done talking. He seems to follow my mood pretty well, and I appreciate him not asking me a thousand questions. Really it isn't any of his business, but I can't blame him if he's curious. That call was kind of cryptic.

I feel bad for lying to Emma. She would never lie to me, but she and Cora don't understand. Over the years, their support and understanding has turned to make me feel more like an annoyance. I know they love me and mean well, but I can't just turn it off, and sometimes it feels like that's what they almost expect. The memories—triggers—are never going to go away, as much as I want them to.

"Listen," the tone of his voice changes. It reminds me of the one in the urgent care when he *told* me he was coming in the back with me. "I think it's best if you just stay with me. How about you let me run in and pack up your things? You can just sit here if you want and I'll be right back."

I would be lying if I said I didn't want to spend more time with him, because I really do. When Emma offered to stay, a huge part of the reason I told her no is because I was hoping he would. I know I'm going to need a little extra help and I jumped on the opportunity blindly, but it felt right. I mean, I wasn't sure how he would feel about it, but I wanted to take the chance. In my mind, he'd come over and hang out—never did I think he'd want to move me in with him. I eye him cautiously. Can I do this? Can I stay in the same house with him? Well, I guess there's only one way to find out.

"Okay," I say timidly, being rewarded with the biggest smile. Even through the pain, butterflies take off at the sight of those dimples.

"It'll be fine. You'll be fine. Trust me." The second the word "trust" leaves his mouth, I flinch. As much as I like him and feel this undeniable connection to him, I don't know him.

"Trust you?" My words are slow, but he needs to hear me. "Trust isn't something that's just given, Ash. It has to be earned."

He regards me for a few minutes and runs his hand across his jaw. "Ah, see, I disagree with you. For me, trust is automatic until you break it." I can appreciate his positive outlook, but mine wasn't just broken, it was shattered. "Look, your friends know where you are and who you're with. You're gonna need some help, and besides, it'll be fun. The apple harvest is this week, so there'll be some town activities we can go to."

Looking into his eyes, I try to match them with distrustful ones I have seen in the past, and there's nothing. They are wide open, letting me in. He wants me to see him. They are clear, light blue, and looking back at me . . . adoringly. Trust. Maybe I can allow him this. After all, in little ways, he's been proving himself since the moment I met him. He respects my physical boundaries, he's been patient and listened to me cry twice, he's never pushed me to answer questions that I don't want to, and in general, he's been very protective of me.

"Okay," I say, sounding a little surer of myself. His smile returns, he leans over, and pats my leg. Heat from his hand quickly spreads and a blush crawls up my neck.

He turns the truck off and opens the door. "Do you want to stay here or come in with me?"

"I'll come in. I just want to make sure everything is locked once we're ready to leave, and I'll need to pack up Tank too." Carefully, I slide out of the truck trying not to jostle my arm, and I hear him sneeze. I know I shouldn't find this adorable, but I do.

"Tank?" he asks, walking over to meet me. His shoes crunch against the gravel and I take in his long legs and broad shoulders. He's still wearing the gray beanie, and it looks so good on him.

"My dog." I grin.

"You have a dog?" He looks at me curiously as we walk up the steps. It dawns on me how bad things were the last time on these steps, and I hope he's not thinking about it too. He holds the door open for me and together we walk in.

"Yep. Right after I got her—"

"Wait, you have a female dog named Tank?" A giggle escapes at the amused look on his face.

"Yep, I wanted the girliest name possible and picked Tinkerbell. Well, within a week it shortened to Tink, and then Cora was over one night and says, 'Tink? Should be Tank because her gas tank never runs out.' Tank just stuck."

"Where was she the other night? I've been here twice and haven't seen her once." As he follows me up the stairs, my chest tightens a little. He's not going to hurt me; it's an irrational reaction, and I hate that I'm having it, but it's not lost on me he'll be the first guy to enter my bedroom in seven years.

"She sleeps in her crate when I'm not home—or travel bag, while we're here—and for whatever reason, she doesn't bark in it. And," we reach my bedroom door, and I pause before opening it. Can he tell that I'm nervous? That he makes me nervous?

Taking a chance, I look up at him. His eyes roam over my face and then drop to my mouth. Oh my. Slowly, he reaches up and pulls my lip out from between my teeth—I didn't even know I was biting it—and he takes a step back. The tightness in my chest evaporates and is replaced by the familiar electricity that runs between us.

"And?" His voice is hoarse, which lets me know he feels it too.

"She doesn't like guys," I whisper. "We kept her inside when you and Clay were here. Otherwise, she would have been a pain the whole time."

His eyes light up and he laughs. "Just like her mom, huh?" He runs his hand over his head, pulling the beanie down and grins at me.

"What makes you think I don't like guys?" I do like guys. I may keep my distance from them, but that doesn't mean I don't like them.

"Darlin', I'm about as tame as it gets and you're even skittish around me." He shoves his hands into his pockets and leans back against the wall opposite me.

Tame—there's a laughable word. Nothing about him is tame. Yes, so far he's shown me nothing but kindness, but he screams sex appeal that would make even the strongest of girls weak.

"Whatever." I open the door and there she is. Her little, sweet face, so happy to see me.

Ash peeks over my shoulder to get a good look at her. "How do you think she'll do with Whiskey?" Just thinking of his giant dog makes me cringe.

"I guess we'll find out. By the way, don't tell her she's a little dog; she thinks she's a big one," I whisper.

"Deal." Right on cue, she growls at him.

"Easy there, killer." He chuckles as he walks over to the fabric bag and picks it up.

"What type of dog is this?" Tank and Ash are having a stare-off.

"Italian Greyhound," I say proudly.

"Cute little thing," he says, winking at me as he passes and heads down the stairs.

Leaving Emma's parents' house, we turn back on the main road, and head further away from town. I know he's staying only a few houses away from us, but I'm surprised at how much the road veers away from the lake, and how long it takes to get to his driveway.

Emma's parents' drive is nothing like this one. Both sides are lined with apple trees and beyond them, fences filled with tall grassy fields. The apple trees are overflowing with apples and my mouth waters at the thought of making cinnamon apple strudel cupcakes. Maybe tomorrow morning Tank and I can wander down here and pick a few; I don't think he'll mind.

As we approach the house and pull to a stop, Whiskey comes running out.

"You have a dog door?" I look up at the house and see it's impressive. How did I not notice this before? Gray stone covers the front, while the rest looks like a huge log cabin. There's a wraparound porch and the landscaping makes it feel welcome and inviting.

"Yep," he says turning off the truck.

"Aren't you worried about other animals trying to get in?" A multitude of animals cross my mind: squirrels, raccoons, fox, bobcats, even bears!

He chuckles. "No, I close it up at night, but if one did, it wouldn't last very long." He looks at Whiskey affectionately.

"How old is he?" The dog, which looks like a cross between a German Shepherd and a Husky, runs over to Ash's side of the truck and barks. His front paws hit the door as he stands on his back legs looking in. Ash smiles at him and then looks back to me.

"We're not sure. Clay and I found him last year, and he's been with us ever since."

"I should have asked you this earlier, but is he nice?" Instinctually, I pull my arm in closer to me. Ash frowns at the move.

"Yes, he's the biggest ninety-pound marshmallow you'll

ever meet. Loyal and extremely obedient, except when he takes off chasing. He loves to chase." His eyes meet mine, filled with remorse.

Silence fills the truck and Ash runs his hand through his hair.

"I'm so sorry about what he did to you, and I'm sorry you're afraid of him—you really don't need to be." His eyes are pleading with me for me to forgive the dog. I find it endearing and think about how he asked me to trust him. I know this is just a small instance, but I'm going to.

"Okay."

A huge smile splits his face and I'm rewarded with those dimples. My heart starts racing at the sight of them. He really is too handsome for his own good.

"Come on, let's get you settled." He climbs out of the truck, sneezes again, and grabs my things along with Tank from the back seat. "Should we let her out?" His eyes find mine over the seats.

"Sure, why not?" Quickly getting out of the truck, I walk around to see Tank and Whiskey circling each other with excitement and curiosity. In an instant, they tear off together and disappear around the side of the house.

"She won't run off, will she?" he asks, glancing back at me as he walks toward the front door.

Following him, I breathe in the air and say, "No, she'll be fine." Part of me wonders if I'm talking about Tank or me.

The first thing I notice once inside are the floor-to-ceiling windows on the back of the house. The view of the lake is spectacular and I gasp at the sight.

"Wow! It's gorgeous!"

"I know, right? I love it." Ash's back is to me as he

moves to the hallway where the bedrooms are to drop my stuff.

Standing alone in the living room, I look around his house, and just like with the outside, I can't believe how unaware I was of everything around me earlier. There's country music playing over the surround sound and I smile to myself because it seems so much like him. A little bit rugged, good ol' country, and in general, calming. To me, country music has always been about telling a story—a story with an ending I'd like.

I'm surprised by how well-decorated it is. He must have hired someone, because it looks beautiful, yet simple, manly, and clean. Cream-colored walls, leather furniture with throw pillows, huge fluffy rugs, photographs instead of paintings for artwork, a large rustic dining table, a fireplace, a giant TV, and a superb state-of-the-art kitchen.

"What do you think?" He holds his arm out and waves it around the room. Over the couch, there are four guitars vertically hanging side by side. Hmm, are they art or does he play them?

"I think it's amazing. Do you always rent this place when you come up here?" It's funny because we've been coming here for years and of all the times I've run around the lake, I've never noticed it.

"Rent? Ah, this is my house." He runs his hand over his face and takes a look around like he's seeing it for the first time. "I bought it a year and a half ago and just finished putting a little facelift on it."

What? This house is not small and looks expensive. Not that I care what kind of house he has, but this one is so much more than Emma's. "Oh, I didn't realize you owned it. What did you say you do again?" I'm curious.

He grins at me. "I didn't actually. I dabble in several

things. Mostly, I've done well with some investments." His answer is evasive, but given that I'm hiding my profession from him, I let it go.

"Do you live here year-round?" If this were my house, I'm not sure that I'd ever leave.

"No, it's just a place to visit when I need some time to re-group and think." He runs his hand through his hair and walks past me over to the large window. With his back to me and the lake in front of him, I'm certain this image will forever be etched in my mind, and there's a good possibility that after these next couple of days are over, I'll never be able to think about this lake without him again.

Moving to stand next to him, I scan the back, looking for the dogs. "So where do you live? I remember Clay mentioning something about leaving yesterday."

He props himself against the glass and faces me. "Nash-ville."

I love Nashville. Mona's conversation flashes back to me and although I'm getting a little ahead of myself, I'm wonder-ing if I'll be able to see him when we're there next month.

"This seems a little far from home." Thoughtful blue eyes blink back at me.

"Yeah, it is, but it's worth it. It takes me about four and a half hours to get here."

"That's not too bad. I love this lake; if we were closer, I'd drive here too. Maybe one day I'll buy a house here and we can be neighbors."

He smiles at me and takes a step closer. He's so close, heat from his body is radiating my way. Slowly, his fingers brush against my cheekbone as he swipes the hair off my face and tucks it behind my ear. Nervous flutters sweep through me, the good kind.

"Listen, you get settled in. I'm going to run back into town, get your prescription filled, and pick up some food. What are you in the mood for?" He drops his hand and reaches into his pocket for his keys.

"I'll eat anything, surprise me," my words mumbling out as his nearness clouds my brain.

"Sounds good." He nods his head, then walks toward the front door.

"Hey, Ash . . ." he stalls and glances back at me. "Thank you." I'm rewarded with a fleeting smile and then he's gone.

Standing by myself, my ears pick up the music, and my body picks up the pain in my arm. Momentarily I had forgotten about it, and I'm suddenly even more thankful he's off to get the medicine.

Part of me wonders if this break might just be a blessing in disguise. I know I should head back to the city to have my wrist looked at by someone more renowned, but I saw the x-ray and it looks pretty small and clean. Laughing to myself, I think staying here a little while longer suddenly sounds like the best form of medicine.

Chapter FOURTEEN

WILL ASHTON

IT DOESN'T TAKE me long to run the errands. I know I'm rushing around like a mad man, but who wouldn't, knowing what's waiting for them back at home? My hands are sweating as I pull the grocery bags from the back seat. Slamming the truck door, Whiskey comes running out to escort me inside.

She's in my house.

My house.

And I'm nervous.

Why am I nervous? I feel stupid for being nervous. It's not like I haven't been alone with a girl before. Maybe it's because I haven't really been alone with this girl before. This girl who after two and half days has somehow managed to embed herself under my skin and in my heart.

Shit.

I don't even know why, I just know that around her everything seems so much brighter, easy, hopeful, and that's such a sharp contrast to when I first got here, eight weeks ago. Yes, she's quiet and mysterious, but there's something about her that feels familiar and it sets off sparks in my soul. I can't quite put my finger on what it is, but I'm determined to find out.

The front door opens, and there she is. My heart skips in my chest. She's showered, changed, and my eyes drink her in from head to toe. Her hair is down and the curls blow across her face from the backdraft of the door. Her eyes are clearer than before, and now she's wearing what look like pajamas—a long-sleeved t-shirt and flannel pants. She looks amazing, and to me, like she belongs here—in this house, with me.

Tank runs out and starts barking, but backs away the closer I get to the door. Dog is cute; it definitely suits her.

"How are you feeling?" I ask as she scoots to the side to let me pass. Strawberries hit my nose and I pause to look down at her. Her eyes widen, she bites her bottom lip, and then sucks in some air like she's forgotten to breathe. Do I make her nervous too? Hell yeah! I hope so, but only nervous in a good way.

"Okay, I guess. I have a headache and my arm hurts; I'm so ready for that pain medicine." My brief moment of joy evaporates. I hate that she's in pain. Guilt assaults me. Maybe I should have brought the medicine back to her before going for groceries.

"I'm sorry I took so long." She follows me into the kitchen and I set the bags on the counter.

"Oh, you didn't. That's not what I meant." She blushes. "Thank you for getting it for me; I appreciate you helping me." She gives me a small reassuring smile as I hand her the bag.

"Anything, you just let me know, and I'll get it for you." And I would. I would drive around the world if she needed me to.

Her smile grows bigger and my heart stutters. Damn, this girl makes me feel funny things.

Blinking, I shake my head and turn back toward the food. "So, I thought I'd make us spaghetti and meatballs for dinner. You know, pasta, comfort food—I'm thinking we can't really go wrong." My eyebrows raise with a hopeful expression.

She giggles and climbs up onto a bar stool next to me. "Sounds perfect."

I grin back at her in relief. "The doctor's office called; they can squeeze you in at eleven tomorrow," I say as I move around the kitchen to pull out the necessary pots and pans.

Her bright smile falls a little. "That's good. I'll go ahead and book my flight for Wednesday then." Her voice is timid, unsure. I'm really hoping it's because she wants to stay longer and not because she dreads getting the cast.

"I'm paying for your flight." There's no way I'm letting her do this. Last minute too; it's not going to be cheap.

She sits up a little straighter, takes a sip of her water, and licks her lips. "You don't have to do that."

My eyes narrow and lock on to hers. "Yes, I do." My tone is a little sharper than it probably should be, but she needs to know this isn't up for discussion.

A moment of silence passes between us as she stares at me with a blank expression. "Okay. Thank you."

"No need to thank me. This is all my fault." I dump the ingredients for the meatballs into a bowl and start smooshing them together.

"Not really," she draws out and her eyes skip over to Whiskey, lying on his bed chewing a toy.

"Well, we'll have to agree to disagree." Mangy beast. He must feel us looking at him, lifting his head to see what we're doing. Ava smiles a little at him. He wags his tail, oblivious to the havoc he's wreaked.

"Can I help you with dinner?" she looks at my hands as they are covered with meatball mixture.

I give her a look that basically asks if she's crazy. "No. But I'd love it if you stayed here and talked to me." I'm giving her an out. If she wants to be alone, she can go and lie down, but I really want her to stay.

"Okay." There's no hesitation on her part, and my heart warms. "So, I suppose this is the part of the day where we sit down and tell our life stories."

I look over at her and see she's dropped her head and is picking at the bandage on her arm. She looks uncomfortable.

"Is that what you want to do?" I ask her. She pauses and there's my answer. Most people love to talk about themselves. Why is it that she wants to remain so secretive? I wonder if it has to do with the panic attacks, or something else. I guess she'll tell me when she's ready. "How about we break the norm and don't. I've kind of liked getting to know you as just you, without all the things that define you day to day."

"So you're saying let's skip the twenty questions. No discussing backgrounds, careers, et cetera." Her energy level perks up at the idea of this.

"Yep." I smile at her and begin to shape the meatballs, tossing them into a large pot.

"I think I like this idea." She smiles at me and takes another sip of her water.

"I think I like you."

She freezes and her eyes dart to mine.

I am an idiot. *Way to go, Ash.* Whatever happened to thinking before you speak?

"But you don't know me," she says softly.

"Sure, I do." I smile and she relaxes a little.

"All right, tell me, what do you know? What do you see?" She shifts on the stool and crosses her legs.

"I see a girl who's thinks exercise is important, as I caught you running—literally—and your body is a testament to that." My eyes fall over the length of her and then back to her face.

She blushes and narrows her eyes at me.

"You love animals as you have your own dog, and I've seen you pet Whiskey more than once already. This also tells me you have a compassionate and forgiving heart. You are fiercely devoted to your friends and them to you, which makes you loyal. You bake, which tells me two things: one, you like to stay in more than go out, and two, you have a sweet tooth and aren't afraid to eat dessert should it come your way."

"Hmm . . . observant, aren't you? Anything else?"

"Well, let's not forget that you love the mountains and have great taste in music." I wink at her.

"Yeah, I do have great taste in music," she says grinning at me. "Okay, maybe you do know me . . . but just a little bit. So if you had to guess, what do you think I do for a living?"

"Well, what if I guess right? Are we breaking the rules?"

She shifts on the seat, thinks about her answer, and then smirks at me. "Nope, I just won't tell you if you're right or not."

"But you're a terrible liar," I say with a straight face.

Her jaw drops open. "Why do you say that?"

"Because your face gives you away every time." I walk to the sink and wash my hands.

"I've been told that before, but go ahead, you'll never figure it out." She shakes her head at me.

I look her over from head to toe, stalling, and her eyes widen slightly. It's then I see that the fingers on her left hand have started tapping on the counter. She's worried that I'll guess the answer. Strange. I'm starting to wonder if she's hiding something.

"Hmm. After tasting the food that the three of you whipped up yesterday, I'm going with caterer. The three of you co-own a catering company with someone named Mona."

She giggles and I love that sound. A smile stretches across her beautiful face.

"Nope, not even close, but what's your favorite food?" she asks. Her fingers stop tapping and she lays them out flat, still.

"Chicken and dumplings." I had thought about making this tonight, but really the chicken needs to slow cook all day, whereas this sauce just needs a few hours.

"Wow, such a Southern dish."

An image of my grandfather smiling and holding a large wooden rolling pin comes to mind, and a pang of grief hits me. He always let me roll out the dough, and never once did he scold me for getting flour on the floor. He would just sweep it up as if it wasn't the messiest kitchen ingredient ever. It's been seventeen years, but that doesn't take away how much he meant to me, or how much I miss him. He was the best.

"My grandfather used to make it for me, it was one of his specialties. He was a big fan of the one-pot dishes and all that—less to wash. Just like with these meatballs." I hold up the pot and then slide it into the oven.

"You're roasting them?" she asks.

"Yeah, I turned on the broiler just to brown them and then I'll put the pot on the stove and add in the sauce. Mix the flavors and all that." I grab a towel from the counter and wipe my

Blue HORIZONS

hands off.

"Sounds tasty." She looks relaxed sitting here . . . and I like it. A lot.

"It is. So, what's yours?" I move across the kitchen to the pantry and grab the peanut butter and bread.

"Barbeque," she states proudly, sitting up a little straighter.

"Really?" Reaching into the refrigerator I grab the jelly.

She nods her head, and I move back to the bar next to her to make the sandwich.

"Well, I happen to know the best hole-in-the-wall barbeque place around here. I'll take you there for lunch tomorrow after the appointment."

"Seriously, you just made my day." Her eyes sparkle at me, so large and blue, and have such a calming effect on me. Warmth spreads through me at the thought of making her happy, but then it's gone. Her day—she wouldn't even be here if it weren't for me. She'd be on her way back to New York.

"What's your favorite dessert?" she asks, angling her body a little closer to me.

"Don't hate me, but it's not cupcakes." She scrunches her nose up with disapproval. "Apple pie." I place the sandwich on a plate, cut it in half, and toss the knife in the sink.

Her face smooths out and her head tilts to the side. "What's your favorite part about it, the pie crust or the apple filling?"

"Apple filling. Warm and gooey, so good." I push the plate in her direction.

"Challenge issued," she looks down at the offered plate and then back at me curiously.

"I didn't challenge you."

129

"Yes, you did, and I accept," she says triumphantly.

Well, this is a new side to her—spunky . . . I like it.

"What's this for?" she looks at the plate and then back at me.

"You need to eat. You have an empty stomach and that painkiller might not sit well."

Her eyebrows pop up. "You're probably right. Thank you."

"Welcome." I stretch my arms in front of me on the counter and lean toward her on my forearms.

She takes a bite of the sandwich and with her mouth full asks, "So, what made you decide to buy a place here?"

"Clay and I are from here, well, a little town just east of here." She pauses midair with the sandwich and looks at me.

"So, you and Clay go way back?" She takes another bite and I can't help but watch the way her lips wrap around it.

"Yep, I've known him since I was thirteen. That's when my grandfather died. His family became my foster family." I don't know what I would have done without Clay and his family. Of all the foster families out there, I was given to them, and every day I am thankful.

She frowns. "I'm sorry, I didn't know."

"Of course you didn't, and it's fine. They were kind to me, loved me in their own way, I was lucky." My lips press together and I give her a smile.

"Well, I think it's beautiful here. I've been coming up with Emma for years now, and this lake is one of my favorite places in the world." Her eyes skip from mine to the window. Can't say I blame her; I try to look at the lake as often as I can.

"Mine too, but it's funny, when we were younger I couldn't wait to get out of here, and now I don't want to leave."

"Then don't," she states so matter-of-fact. If only it were that simple. I already know I'm here on borrowed time. Given my affiliation with the label, they've turned their head for now, but I know at some point business is going to be affected and I can't let that happen.

"When I was a kid, once a summer my grandfather used to bring me here to fish. Those memories are my favorite from my childhood. He loved it too. The last summer we came up here, I was sitting in the middle of the lake looking out at the houses, and I made a promise to myself and to him that one day I would own one of them." Fishing with my grandfather is one of the few things from my childhood that I remember. Sure, images filter in and out, but for some reason, most of it seems blocked.

"That's an interesting perspective, from the inside looking out." She finishes the sandwich and wipes her hand across her thigh. Damn, forgot to give her a napkin.

"I guess. Why do you love it here so much?" I'm curious to know. Of all the places imaginable, this girl from NYC loves it here.

"When I moved to the city, I really wasn't in the best frame of mind. Yeah, I had Emma and classes were going well, but I was nervous and meeting new people was really hard. I mean, you've known me for three days and I've already had two panic attacks and my ridiculous hair trigger sent my knee straight into your groin." She looks away, embarrassed, and takes a deep breath. "I was so much worse then. Anyway, by October I was a complete mess, but I couldn't go home, so Emma brought me here. We stayed for a week and it was just what I needed. After that, we came for Thanksgiving, Christmas break, spring break, and most of the following summer.

Circling the date on the calendar gave me something to look forward to and it made living just a little bit easier."

I want to ask her what happened to make her this way, and why she felt she couldn't go home, but that's intrusive and none of my business. It's too soon.

"Well, I'm glad you love it here." I pick her plate up and drop it in the sink. Looking back at her, the muscles around her eyes are a little droopy. "Tired yet?"

"Now that you mention it, yeah, I am." She looks around the living room and spots the couch.

"Come on, I think that painkiller has finally kicked in." Glancing to the clock, I note the time. In fifteen minutes, I'll pull the meatballs, add the sauce, and let it simmer for a couple of hours on the stove. "We can watch a movie while you lie down."

"Okay." She climbs off the stool, and hugs her arm to her chest.

My lips pinch into a thin line; I hate that she's in pain because of me.

Moving into the living room, she stretches out on the couch, and I throw a blanket over her.

"Thank you," she says quietly.

Squeezing her foot gently, I give her a small smile, and take my place in my leather chair. Grabbing the remote to turn the TV on, my gaze falls to her as she closes her eyes and rolls over onto her side. Tank hops up next her, cuddles down, and both drift off to sleep.

If I had any doubts before, they're gone.

I want this girl.

I want her to be mine.

Now, I just need to figure out how.

Chapter FIFTEEN

Ava Layne

THE SMELL OF coffee lures me out of my bed and I quietly pad toward the kitchen. The house is still and I find it peaceful. I really like it here, and surprisingly—after only a day—I feel at home.

Walking into the kitchen, I find a full pot of fresh coffee, my pain medicine, and a note.

"Good morning. Please make yourself at home. I'll be back by 9, just spending a little time on the lake."

On the lake.

So he's the kayaker that's been out every morning. Of course he is. Even from a distance, I'm drawn to this guy. Slipping out the kitchen door with my warm cup of coffee, I wander to his deck and lean over the edge to see if I can see him. Sure enough, off in the distance, I spot the red kayak.

The picture in front of me is so serene, I'm momentarily

stunned by its exquisiteness. Still mist dances against the water as he slices through it. The grace and precision of his movements are mesmerizing to watch. The sun has slowly begun to rise over the mountain peaks, and its light floods the trees on the western side of the lake, bathing them in warmth and gold. In the distance, I hear the call of the purple finch, and my heart clenches. Everything before me is just picturesque, and even given the circumstances, I am so glad to be here.

Ash has been the perfect gentleman and the perfect host. He's attentive, funny, and kind. Not once yesterday did I have to lift a finger, and this morning, he's already made the coffee.

I've thought several times about our conversation yesterday afternoon in the kitchen. I wanted to ask him more about his grandfather and living with Clay, but that would have broken the rules. Instead, I'm in awe of him and what he's done. I'm not quite sure what that is, but I admire people who have drive and want to make something of themselves. He said he wanted to leave this place, so he did, and in return, by the looks of this house, he's doing very well for himself.

Taking a sip of coffee, cold air brushes across my hand and my face. The wind this morning is slow moving and takes its time as it weaves through the trees, rattling the leaves. A giggle slips through my lips as I shake my head and look down at my arm hanging in a sling. So unintentional and unfortunate, but yet, oddly welcome and surreal at the same time.

I've realized over the years that although life is one long journey, it can better be defined as a series of moments. After all, journeys are usually premeditated. Rarely do people set off without some type of destination in mind, but it's these moments—the good, bad, unexpected—that alter the plan, usually throwing the journey off course.

This is one of those moments.

If someone had told me last week, that I'd find myself here in this one, I would have laughed in their face. I never could have predicted this. Me, here in the mountains, alone with this strange guy and in his house. Never, in seven years, have I allowed myself to be close to a guy in any way, but there's something about him that makes me feel an inner strength I haven't felt in a long time. That strength makes me feel almost ready—ready to break free from the protective bubble I've been living in.

As I watch him paddle further away from me, I think about a quote I once read, *"Life isn't about how many breaths we take, but how many moments take our breath away."* But what if those moments aren't filled with happiness and love, but something dark and haunting? For me, it's those darker moments that've shaped and taken over my life. Yes, most moments are meant to be remembered and cherished . . . if only some could be forgotten.

Clearing my mind, not allowing this moment to be ruined by haunted memories, I think about Ash's face. His dark features make him rugged, sexy. His lips are full, thick, and frame his perfect white teeth beautifully. His jaw isn't too square, but it's well-defined, making it strong. His nose is straight, only dusted with freckles, his cheeks are constantly covered in an even stubble, and his cheekbones are prominent, highlighting the set of his eyes.

His eyes.

Some people when they look at you, you can see the indifference and insincerity shining back. It's as if even though they're talking to you, they're looking straight through you. There's a void, a lack of connection. Sure, other emotions are glaringly evident, but it's not so much what I see, it's what I feel, and I feel nothing.

When Ash looks at me, every nerve in my body stops to take notice. Whether we are talking face to face, or if he's tracking me as I walk across the room, I am fully aware. Those blue eyes aren't looking through me, they're looking in me. They're searching, learning, memorizing, and I feel it from the tip ends of my hair all the way down to my toes. It's like I'm a lightbulb and his eyes are the switch. When they're on me, I light up and burn. When they're off, I feel cool and alone. His eyes take notice, and when they fall into the depth of mine, they command attention, every single time. He makes me feel like I'm the only person in the world.

Letting out a sigh, a whine comes from behind me. I turn around and see Tank and Whiskey sitting there. One's so big and one's so little, I can't help but grin at them. Shouldn't they be off running and playing? I know—they can come with me.

"Come on, you two. If I remember correctly, a challenge was issued. Let's go pick some apples."

I hear Ash's footsteps the minute they hit the stairs on the back deck. A smile springs to my lips and my heart starts racing. I'm excited to see him and I feel optimistic for the first time in a long time.

As the door pushes open, his eyes immediately fall to me and panic streaks across his face.

"Are you okay?" he drops down next to me and starts looking me over. The richness of his voice blankets over me and I'm immediately engulfed in his scent. He smells like sweat, some type of sporty deodorant, and the outdoors.

My heart stops at his nearness . . . in a good way.

"What do you mean?" I ask, looking him over from head to toe. His face is flushed and the stubble is thicker this morning. He has on a gray pullover that's soaked through, white athletic shorts, a dark blue beanie that covers his ears, and his feet are bare.

"You're on the floor and covered in flour." There's tension in his words and around his eyes. He runs his hand over his face and through his hair, pushing the beanie off in the process. His hair is damp from sweat and sticks straight up. He's so good-looking, and with those bright blue eyes, I'm awestruck.

"Making cupcakes," I mumble, trying to ignore the flush that's crept into my cheeks.

"On the floor?" His eyebrows rise in confusion. He then looks around the rest of the kitchen and sees the mess that I've made.

"Yep, needed to use my legs to hold the bowl." His eyes drop to my lap, where I'm sitting cross-legged with the bowl securely in the middle. He lets out a warm chuckle, and it does amazing things to my body: tingles, pounding heart, sweaty palms.

"So, maybe not a caterer." He winks at me, his dimples sink into his cheeks, and my blush deepens.

"Whatever. You said to make myself at home." I bump him with my uninjured arm and he sways, almost losing his balance. "Where are your shoes?" I point to his feet.

"Water shoes, they stay outside," he tilts his head toward the door. "So, what kind of cupcakes?" he peeks into the bowl.

"Apple, of course. Don't you remember the challenge you issued? Here, taste."

I dip the spoon into the batter and hold it out for him. Without thinking, he grabs my wrist and moves the spoon to his mouth. Every muscle freezes, my vision blacks out, and I gasp in fear.

"Ava," his voice drifts in through the haze and slowly the kitchen reappears. I can feel myself trembling, and I look to my hand. His eyes widen at my reaction, they follow my line of sight, and he drops me like I've burned him. "I'm sorry," he says, swallowing. Standing up, he moves one step away from me.

Regret instantly washes over me and I have to look away from him.

"No, I'm the one that's sorry. What you did was completely normal; what I did was not."

I'm so embarrassed. He didn't do anything wrong, and I've just made him uncomfortable.

He regards me for a moment and silence builds between us. I drop the spoon back to the bowl and watch as he shifts his weight back and forth on his feet. I hate that I ruined this moment. I mean, do all of our interactions have to include me having some type of mental breakdown?

"Ava, it's okay to have boundaries. I'm sorry I crossed them. Won't happen again." He tucks his hands in his pockets and gives me a small sympathetic smile that feels a lot like pity.

"That's not it." A lump forms in the back of my throat.

Letting out a deep breath, my eyes burn with unshed tears. I'm so frustrated with myself. All morning, I've felt like maybe, just maybe, he could be something more. I'm not afraid to admit that for the first time in a long time, I feel something other than fear, I feel something for him, but what good does it do either of us if every time he touches me I black out? And why would he want to deal with me when there are plenty of normal girls he could be with?

"Then what is it? I don't ever want you to be afraid of me." He props his hip against the counter, leaning away from me.

"I'm not afraid of you. If I were, I wouldn't be here. It's just sometimes my brain gets triggered, it disconnects, and then it takes it a little bit to catch up. I'm trying to be better." This sucks. I lower my eyes and shake my head to myself.

"You don't need to try to be anything for me. Just be yourself and we'll learn as we go. Okay?" His eyebrows lift in question.

His understanding makes my chest tight, and I nod my head instead of speaking. If I do, tears may just fall, and I don't want to cry in front of him again.

"Hey," he says to get my attention and I look back up at him. He smiles one of his million dollar smiles and the dimples come out. After a slight hesitation, he slowly leans down, wraps one hand around my head, and presses his lips against my temple. "By the way, that batter tastes delicious. If cooked they taste anything like this, you crushed the challenge, and apple cupcakes will definitely be my new favorite dessert." Releasing me, he stands back up and grins at me.

Oh my.

My heart drops to my stomach and then soars. All I can do is stare at bright blue and dimples.

He taps me on the shoulder and walks out of the kitchen.

"I'm gonna take a shower while you plop those in the oven," he throws over his shoulder from the hallway. "I'll help you clean up when I get out, and once they're done, we'll set off for your appointment."

My mind sticks on the word "shower" and immediately I wonder what he looks like naked. Squeezing my eyes shut, heat spreads up my neck and into my cheeks. I shouldn't be thinking of him like this, but I can't help it, and I can't help but wonder . . . what if?

Chapter

SIXTEEN

WILL ASHTON

GETTING THE CAST takes longer than we expect, and by the time we get to the barbeque restaurant, we're starving. I don't think I've ever seen anyone eat as fast as she is. I'll never tell her that, but I love it. In my industry, girls are fickle and vain; eating is an issue. I understand wanting to be thin, but guys like girls who eat, and right now I am overjoyed.

"You were right, the food at this place is amazing," she says as we climb back into the truck. "I can't wait to bring Emma next time we're down here."

"At least you got the sauce to take back. She'll be able to try it."

As we were leaving, she spotted a bookshelf full of mason jars of sauce for purchase, and asked me if I'd buy her one. She was so cute, I bought her two: traditional and spicy.

"Heck no, this is for me." She hugs the bag to her lap and gives me a look like I'm crazy.

I can't help but grin at her. "What? You won't share it with her?"

"Well, maybe, but it's gonna cost her."

I bust out laughing and she laughs with me. Damn, I love that sound. It's good to see her relaxed. After the little incident on the floor this morning, she's been a little closed off. I have no idea what she's thinking, but I sure wish I did. I'm trying not to take it personally, but something tells me she's like this with all guys, the first clue being the way my manhood became one with her knee outside Smokey's.

Turning back onto the Blue Ridge Parkway, she rolls down the window, and just like the other night, her hair whips out as the wind blows across her face. My ears ring at the memory of her singing along with our songs, and all of a sudden, I have to know: how much does she know about our band?

"So, I take it you were a Blue Horizon's groupie; tell me more."

She looks back over at me with bright eyes and she giggles. "Trust me when I say that I was not a groupie. I couldn't tell you one thing about those guys except that they changed their name after the lead singer, and personally, I think in the process lost their originality."

Holy shit.

Nothing like hearing the brutal honest truth. Then again, she isn't really telling me something I don't already know.

"The music used to be so good, and now, well, it's more mainstream, I guess, than soulful. I only saw them play three times, but of all the concerts or shows I've ever been to, those were my favorite. Maybe it's because the venue was small or maybe it was the sound of his voice, but something about those songs were magical and stuck with me, not the band. Different music speaks to different people, and the lyrics in their songs spoke to me. That's all." She shrugs her shoulders and loosens the seat belt. It must be pressing too tightly on her arm, which she keeps close to her body.

Well, I'm speechless. I've never heard anyone talk about how my music is magical and speaks to them, and my eyes begin to burn. People love music for all different reasons, but ultimately it's a form of self-expression. Especially to those of us who are songwriters. Everyone loves a catchy chorus they can sing along with, or a fun beat that they can dance to, but rarely do people actually stop and think about the meaning of the words and where they might have come from. The songs I wrote during our days of Blue Horizons weren't necessarily for the fans—yeah, I mean, I wanted them to love the songs—but they were for me. They're about what I was feeling and my life. And I completely understand what she's saying, because over the last couple of years, the songs have drifted more toward the general population and how they can be relatable to the fans.

Needing a moment to myself, I turn on one of the original albums and she smiles at me.

"Do you hear it? Do you feel it?" she quietly asks me.

"Yeah, I do," but right now it's her I hear and feel. My hands grip the wheel and out of the corner of my eye, I see her put her head back to the window, her eyes slip shut, and she begins to sing along.

I'm officially lost in this girl.

Rolling my window down, I turn up the music, and in the comfortable silence, I soak up her company. They say everything happens for a reason, and just maybe she is mine. My reason, and for the first time in a long time, I feel inspired, and

I'm ready to pick up my guitar.

With Clay, I realized I still do love the music, and with Ava, I've realized I still love what I do. I love writing music, I love letting it speak to me, and I've always loved when other people appreciated what we played. Clay and I may have fallen off track a little, but the tunes he was playing the other night let me know he's well on his way to finding his voice again too.

A flare of excitement ignites under my skin. It's been snuffed out for so long, and damn, if she isn't the inspiration that lights the match. I'd forgotten what it feels like to have the urge to write, and once she leaves tomorrow, I know I'm headed back to Nashville to get started.

Once she leaves.

Shoving the wave of sadness aside that she'll be gone, I turn down the music, and smile affectionately at her. She returns my smile with one of her own, and it's so beautiful.

"So, other than Blue Horizons, what type of music do you like?" I want to learn as much as possible about this girl as I can.

"I like all kinds of music. In fact, can't think of one I don't like." This statement is such a turn on to me. Knowing she appreciates the variations between music genres, I seriously haven't found anything about this girl that I don't like.

Remembering the piano keys, I'm now curious if she plays. "The tattoo on your wrist, tell me about it."

She looks down at the cast and stretches her fingers underneath it as she thinks about her answer.

"I love the piano, it's kind of my thing, and on my wrist it can be easily covered if I want it to. Do you have any?" she looks back at me.

She sings like an angel and plays the piano, so freaking

sexy.

"Nope. Although I like the idea of them, they're not for me.. All right, new guess . . . you're a music teacher?" My eyes skip from the road to her. She busts out laughing and my heart soars.

"Nope, but I do have perfect pitch," she says proudly.

"What?" My hand grips the wheel. I'm stunned.

"Do you know what that is?" she asks, her head tilting to the side.

"I do, and I've never met someone who has it before. I'm thoroughly impressed and dying to know what you do now."

"No, no, no," she shakes her head smugly. "We made a deal."

"Yeah, but you can't drop something like that and leave me hanging. That's a huge piece of information." She must be in the music industry. She *has* to. Then again, just because she loves it doesn't mean she has to make a career out of it.

She grins at me, close-lipped, and I groan out in frustration.

"Fine then, don't tell me. So, back in town, they're having live music every night this week for the Apple Harvest festival, and I thought it might be fun to go and listen. That's why I asked you what type of music you like. Alison Krauss and Union Station are playing tonight."

"Blue grass! Count me in," she squeals, sitting up a little straighter.

I can't remember the last time I met a girl who genuinely likes blue grass. Most agree with me, just to agree, and Juliet hates it. She's always complained about how it's too twangy and she'd rather listen to pop instead. I love it. I grew up listening to my grandfather and his friends playing together. It's mountain music; it's in my roots.

"All right then. I threw some stuff in the back of the truck before we left, so we're all set." I smile at her.

"Thank you, Ash." She reaches her hand over and places it on my thigh. She's proactively touching me, and now I want to grab her, throw her across my lap, and squeeze her. Instead, I cover her hand with mine, and thread my fingers between hers.

"For what?" I rub my thumb over the back of her hand.

"All of this, everything." She shrugs her shoulders, looking at me shyly.

I would give her everything if she let me.

It's on the tip of my tongue to ask her to stay. Hell, I'm pretty sure I want to ask her to stay forever, but it's not the right time. Instead, I smile and turn the music back up.

Hours pass.

We got here early and the crowd was still small, which played to our advantage. I grabbed a baseball hat out of the backseat to try and stay hidden, and we found a great spot near a tree. I swear this is the best afternoon I can remember in such a long time. The music is exceptional, the weather is perfect, and she's talked and laughed more than she has over the last three days. There is nowhere else I'd rather be than here with her.

I feel carefree and young. Not that I'm old, but stress makes me feel like I am.

Today, on this blanket, I don't feel like I have to be the person that the world sees and knows. Being a full-time public figure, it's draining. Here, no one is watching us—not that I've noticed—no one is taking pictures trying to skew them into something they're not, and no one is asking for an autograph. I get to be a regular guy, doing a regular thing, and I get to do it with her.

"Do you think the dogs are okay?" she asks. Shadows from the tree have moved away from us, and her skin is bathed in golden light from the setting sun. My muscles tighten just at the sight of her; damn, what she does to me.

"Of course. I left the dog door open, so they're good." I sit up and shift a little closer to her.

"That's right, I forgot about the door. Oh, look at that cloud over there." Ava is lying on her back staring up at the sky.

I glance at the cloud she's pointing to and then turn my attention back to her. God, she's stunning. Being this close to her on the blanket, I'm dying to touch her.

"Don't you think it looks like a pirate ship?" she looks up at me, her eyebrows raised in question.

"Mmm hmm." I don't want to look at clouds; I want to stare at her.

Right after we got here, my phone buzzed with a text, and it was her friend Emma wanting to know what's going on. Instead of calling her, Ava had me text back that she's headed home tomorrow. I logged on to my Delta account and booked her a flight. She doesn't know it's first class; hopefully that will be a nice surprise for her tomorrow.

Tomorrow.

I feel like I'm running out of time, when I just want more.

147

"So, what are your plans for the holidays?" I grab a piece of grass and roll it between my fingers. I'm suddenly nervous, and I don't know why.

She looks back at me and her eyes find mine. "I'm not sure yet. I might have to work Thanksgiving weekend, and usually for Christmas, Emma and I head to her parents' house."

"Any possibility you might head this way?" My heart starts beating a little harder. I desperately want her to say yes.

"Ah, Ash, do you want to see me again?" She's being playful, but I'm dead serious.

"Yes. I want to see you a lot actually." My tone is firm, and honestly, if she had been wondering at all about what I thought of her, the way I'm looking at her now should leave no room for question.

I want to kiss her. I want to kiss her so badly.

The smile drops from her lips and my eyes drop to her mouth. I hear the intake of breath as her chest expands and my eyes travel back up her face to her eyes. She's watching me and pink stains her perfect cheeks.

I know I should be concerned about being outside in the wide open for anyone to see, but I just don't care. From the first second our eyes connected, there's been chemistry between us, and after four days, that spark has just gotten stronger. I feel it and I know she feels it too.

Without touching her, I lean in, place my hand next to her head, and hover over her mouth, separating us by just mere inches. My eyes are so focused on their intended target, everything around me drifts away: the mountains, the people, and even the music. The only thing—the most important thing—I see and feel is her.

"Ash . . ." Her voice cracks with nerves, and the heat from

her breath fans across my face.

Dragging my eyes away from the part of her I want most, I glance up and our eyes collide. Blue to blue, time stalls. For months, I have felt lost, but lying here staring down at the most beautiful face I have ever seen, I feel found. I'm struck by an overwhelming sense of devotion to this girl that feels a lot like love. Call it wisdom, call it maturity, call it whatever the hell you want, but I know once this kiss is sealed, I'll only ever again have eyes for her. Eyes that are spellbound by hers; hers that are reflecting back at me with hesitation, curiosity, and mostly desire.

"If you don't want me to kiss you, tell me now." My voice is gravelly and laced with longing. If it's that apparent to me, it has to be to her.

Her eyes widen slightly, her lips part, and that's when I feel her fingers slide across my rib cage and fist into the back of my shirt.

The pull I have to her is so great, I'm not sure I could stop this kiss even if I tried. Licking my lips, my willpower is completely shattered. Not wasting one more second, my mouth lands on hers and my eyes slip shut.

Lip to lip, neither one of us moves. Blood rushes through my ears, roaring by, and pools at the place of contact. My lips feel like they are burning up on hers. Does she feel it? Can she feel what she's doing to me?

Easing the pressure I've applied, she lets out a sigh that parts her lips against mine.

Holy shit.

With my heart racing, I'm overcome with a fervor I don't understand, and my arms have begun to shake as I hold myself up. I have to force myself to remember to be gentle, when gentle is the last thing I want to be. I want to devour this girl and drink her in until we become one.

Licking her bottom lip, a groan escapes me at the fullness and flavor of her. Needing more, I sink my tongue into the deep recesses of her mouth and savor what has to be the best damn thing I have ever tasted in my entire life.

I knew kissing her would be something else, but I never imagined this. Damn, it's perfect. *She's* perfect.

Chapter
SEVENTEEN

Ava Layne

M̲Y MIND, MY body, and my heart are all at war with each other as I feel the magnetic pull between us. My mind is saying, "If you do this, he's going to touch you. Are you ready for the reaction this might cause?" My body is saying, "If you don't do this, I will hate you forever," as it's vibrating for him. And my heart is saying, "If you do this, there's no going back. He will mark you indefinitely." But as he stares down into my eyes and the battle plays out, the voices quiet, and I feel the body winning.

I had wondered if he would kiss me before I left for home. A girl would have to be blind not to see some of the glances that he's given me, not that they were suggestive in any way, but the attraction was evident. Had I been someone else—say, someone like Cora—I might have even initiated it, but there's no way I could have. It's just not in me, even though I've thought about it endlessly.

Ash's eyes are penetrating mine, and as he leans in closer to me, an invisible weight pushes me flatter onto the blanket. I swear I'm not trying to move away from him, I'm certain I want this just as much as he does, but it's been so long. Doubt creeps in and mixes with the butterflies. The muscles around his eyes tighten, and his eyes move away from mine and search my face. What does he see when he looks at me? Can he see the apprehension? Does he think it's just nerves? What if I'm not any good at kissing and he's disappointed? My heart is racing, and I will it to calm. I don't want to ruin this moment.

Time suspends between the two of us as he thinks this through. Looking up into his handsome face, I memorize every detail from the curve of his jawline to the length of his eyelashes—which are so long and dark they brush the top of his cheeks when he blinks. I want to remember everything, and I see in his eyes the moment he makes the decision. It's like there were greyish blue clouds lingering and instantly they've cleared, leaving them as blue as the afternoon sky. His eyes flicker from mine to my mouth, he licks his lips, and that's it.

No more time wasted.

My hand, which is tangled in the back of his shirt, pulls as he moves. I'm not even sure which hits me first, the heat from his breath or the heat from his lips. Not that it matters, I welcome them both, and flames race throughout my entire body as his lips press to mine.

Oh my God.

His lips . . .

On mine.

I've died and gone to heaven. Every bit of nerves evaporates and in their wake, a sense of rightness settles in that I haven't felt in a long time. A sigh escapes me and my bottom lip falls between his.

His lips . . .

Feel like everything.

They are warm, full, and right this second . . . mine.

He runs his tongue over my bottom lip, tasting me, and coaxing my lips further apart. I groan into his mouth at the sensation and his breath mixes with mine. I want him to deepen this kiss. I want to lose myself in him and drown in a passion that's so absolute it makes my insides tighten and leaves me sweltering for more. I want this with him—no, I need this with him—because it has to *be* him. These feelings are *only* for him, and I've never wanted it more.

Sliding my hand around his back, I pull him tighter against me, and his chest brushes against mine. He pauses for just a second to catch his breath and the sound of his breathing combined with the beat of my heart hits my ears. The cadence of the two together creates the perfect harmony. It's sexy and intimate, causing the heat from the flames to radiate off my skin. It's a sound I never want to forget, and knowing what's coming next, my eyes squeeze tighter in anticipation . . . then he gives us what we both so desperately want. He claims me completely.

Shock charges surge through my heart as his tongue caresses mine. In and around, he takes what he wants, giving me something so beautiful in return tears burn in the back of my eyes. He's gentle, but commanding, and there's a hunger lingering just beneath the surface that's just begging to be let free. I desperately want him to set it free, but I know he won't. Instead, his lips, his tongue, and his breath all tangle with mine and in the most delicious way.

He tastes like apple from the cider we were drinking earlier, and fall. Why he tastes like fall, I don't know. Maybe it's because I now associate this time of year with him, or maybe it's that his mouth is warm while cool air hits my skin. Either way he tastes like fall, which has instantly become my favorite season, and it tastes so good.

Surrendering myself over to him, he explores my mouth with such devotion, he's stealing a piece of my heart and he doesn't even know it. This kiss is beyond amazing and clarity sinks in as I realize I have *never* been kissed before. Yes, I know that Chris is the only person I've kissed so my experience is limited, but it never occurred to me how completely different it can be from one person to the next.

Kisses like this can't be normal, right? Then again, movies, books, songs, and poems have all been written about longing for and experiencing the perfect kiss, and I know without a doubt I'm having mine. This kiss is going to devastate me and revive me all at the same time.

Pulling back, he rests his forehead against mine and takes in a few breaths, each one falling across my face as he exhales.

"Wow," he murmurs, his eyes still closed.

Breezes from the tree blow over us, and I hear laughter in the distance. My heart slows as we both lie here, neither moving, just breathing each other in.

"It's been so long since I've been kissed," I whisper into his mouth.

His ocean blue eyes open and find mine. Silence stretches between us as he searches for answers. He knows asking questions will break the rules, and I hope he does break them. I think I'm ready to tell him more. He shifts his weight so he's lying on his side, and he props his head up on his hand.

"How long?" His other hand moves to cup my face and

his thumb runs over my cheekbone. The move is tender, affectionate, and my skin burns from his touch.

"Seven years," I mutter, a blush warming my cheeks.

His eyes widen in shock. "How is that possible? You're the most beautiful girl I have ever seen." He shakes his head in confusion.

My blush deepens at his compliment as his thumb moves to run over my bottom lip. It feels swollen, but in the best possible way.

"I don't think it's really hard to figure out. You've met me, right?" I give him a small sympathetic smile. Sympathetic for myself, because I know I've missed out on some great life experiences.

"Ava," he breathes out with sadness.

Sudden guilt engulfs me and the blush vanishes.

He's been so good to me and I haven't even told him my real name. Soon. I'll tell him soon. If I tell him now, it might ruin the moment, and I'm *really* enjoying this moment.

I shrug my shoulders and look at his lips. They're so pink and flawless.

"Well, if you feel the need to make up for some lost time, I'm your guy." He gives me a lopsided grin and one dimple peeks at me.

A giggle escapes and my eyes reconnect with his. There's an amused glint in them, but they look thoughtful and kind too.

"I just might take you up on that." My heart rate picks up at the possibility of him kissing me more.

His grin grows to a full smile, and his eyes flicker back to my lips.

"Good," and just like that he closes the distance between us.

This kiss doesn't have the desperate edge to it that the first one did, and he explores my mouth with fascination and skill. His movements are slower, deeper, and this time he's touching me.

He's touching me! And I'm not freaking out! Not once have I felt even a glimmer of panic or fear. If anything, what I feel is normal. He makes me feel normal. How did I get so lucky to be here, with him, under this tree, on this gorgeous day? I want to bottle this moment up and carry it with me always.

His hand moves from my face, to the back of my head, and down to my neck. I feel like he's marking me and I want more. More of him . . . and that's what I get. I'm not sure how long we actually lie here kissing. No one stops us or complains, the songs change one after another, and the dusk sky easily slips to night. This is the best date I have ever been on, and yes, I'm calling it a date.

"Do you want to stay a little longer?" he murmurs against my neck, sending goosebumps fluttering down my arm.

"Do you mind?" This night has been so magical for me, I want it to last as long as possible.

He pulls back and smiles at me. He's so gorgeous. I'm not sure how I keep forgetting, but I do, and each time, it's like looking at him for the first time all over again.

"Nope," he blinks at me. "I'm having the best time." His thumb strokes my cheek and I want to melt into his touch.

"Me too. The company's okay, but the music is so good." I shrug, giving him a playful look.

He busts out laughing. "Let me guess . . . you're a comedian?"

"Only part time." I grin at him.

"Right," he drawls out. "I like you like this." His face

switches to a sincere one.

"What do you mean?"

"I don't know, it's like you're more open, having a good time—being yourself."

He's right. I have been more open with him. He makes it easy, and he makes me want to. His fingers move to tuck some loose hair behind my ear. I love it when he does this.

"How about if I go and get us another drink?" he asks.

"I'd like that." I run my hand over his side and down to his hip, memorizing the bumps of his ribcage.

"Okay, I'll be right back." He leans over and brushes his lips against mine one more time, hops up, and graces me with the most content, pleased, and devilishly handsome smile.

Be still my heart.

Watching him walk away, he adjusts the hat and pulls it down lower. It's then I notice that the crowd has definitely filled in since we arrived, and my cheeks warm at the thought of someone watching us kiss. But then I realize I don't care.

I now understand the true story of *Sleeping Beauty*. For seven years, I have been in a dark slumber, and one kiss from Ash has brought me back to life. I feel invigorated and new. Colors are brighter, smells are stronger, and things sound sharper. The bubble has popped. I feel awake, and I feel set free.

The blanket vibrates and I look over to see Ash's phone lying near the edge. He either left it, or it fell out of his pocket, and the name Juliet flashes across the screen, disappears, and leaves his phone illuminated to the home screen. There, right in the middle, is a brown-haired boy grinning back from ear to ear at whoever took the picture.

My stomach drops and reality crashes over me.

Oh my God.

Does he have a son? And who is Juliet?

For the first time in four days, I really wonder what his story is. Frantically, I flip through our conversations and remember him talking about his grandfather, but not once did he mention a sibling, so this can't be his nephew, right? Not that I have a problem with him having a son, everyone has a past, but this is a huge piece of information to not disclose.

My heart starts pounding, and not in a good way. I reach up and push on my chest. Quickly, anxiety and confusion trickle in under my skin, and my back breaks out in a cold sweat.

How *is* it possible that a nice, handsome guy like him is unattached? My mind drifts back to him sitting at the bar, the first night I saw him, and the conversation I had with Emma. I hate to think the worst of him after he's been so nice, but what normal guy just sits at the bar while his friend is out meeting girls, having fun? I said it then and now I'm worried . . . maybe he does have a girlfriend . . . or a wife.

The phone turns off, fading to black, and I stare at it as if it holds all the secrets of the world.

I'm so confused.

Dropping my head to my hands, I fight back the blur of tears trying to form, and I suck in as much cold air as I can. I don't want to jump to any conclusions, but the little boy did have brown hair and olive skin just like him. Granted his eyes were brown and not blue . . . oh, I don't know.

He wouldn't lie to me, would he? Then again, I haven't been completely honest, but it was his idea to leave out our personal details. Mistrust swirls through my mind, and I hate that, because as far as I know, he hasn't done anything to break it. He's only earned it, just like I said.

I hate how five minutes ago, visions of happily ever after were skipping across my heart, and now I'm beginning to think all of this is more likely to be one moment in time.

What happens at the lake, stays at the lake, right?

Disappointment consumes me.

Chapter
EIGHTEEN

WILL ASHTON

SHE LEAVES TODAY.

Waking up this morning, instead of an instant grin hitting my face at the thought of seeing her, I'm stuck on the fact that this will be the last time I see her until who knows when. I don't like this, at all, and I need to figure out how I can spend more time with her.

I'm bewitched by her, and that kiss . . . it was better than all the kisses I've ever had combined. I could get lost for days in that little dip in the middle of her bottom lip, and just thinking about how it felt when her tongue danced with mine and the way she tasted, I'm addicted. I don't think it will ever be enough.

When I got back from getting our drinks, she was sitting in her chair. Yeah, I was disappointed, I wanted to lie on the blanket with her some more, but the high of that kiss overrode any negative thoughts I had. I could feel her trying to put some distance between us, but given she just told me it'd been seven years, I gave her the space I assumed she needed to process.

How am I going to do this? How am I going to let her go? Maybe I should just lay all my cards on the table and see what she says. I hate the ambiguity that's developed between us. I want to know her, and I want her to know me. No more secrets . . . but if she's not ready yet, or I push too hard, things might not go in my favor.

Shit, this sucks.

Climbing out of bed, the reflection of the lake flickering on the wall calls to me. I don't want to be tense or locked into myself today; I need to burn some of this off so I can enjoy our last few hours together. Throwing on some clothes, I wander out to the kitchen to find her leaning against the counter, staring out the window, already drinking a cup of coffee.

"Morning," I say to her. She turns to look at me and smiles. She looks so good here in my house that my insides squeeze. I grab a cup and pour myself some coffee as both of the dogs tear by and out the door. She giggles and my heart soars at the sound.

"Sleep okay?" I ask.

She shrugs her shoulders.

"How's your wrist feel?" She's got the sling off and has the cast lying on top of the counter.

"All right. I took some more medicine. As long as I don't move it too much it's fine." She looks away from me and back out the window.

She's still distant and I hate this. How do I get us back to where we were? I want her smiling, laughing, and talking to me.

"I have an idea—how about you come out on the lake

with me this morning?" She brings the cup to her lips and takes a sip of her coffee.

"But my arm?" She looks over the cup at me.

"We can wrap it up, but you'll be fine. I have a canoe out back that I use for fishing, so unless you stand up and move around, there's no reason for you to go over or get wet." I prop my hip against the counter and try to look as relaxed as possible. If I'm relaxed, maybe she'll relax.

She lowers the cup. "So, you'll paddle me around, *Notebook* style?" Her eyes spark and she smiles at me. I think it's working—this smile is a little more friendly and open. I like this smile.

"*Notebook* style?" I'm confused.

"Yeah, like the movie," she says very matter-of-fact with her big blue eyes blinking at me.

"I haven't seen that movie in over ten years!" And even then, once was enough.

"Well, are there swans?" she smirks. Spunky Ava is back, so freaking sexy, and I can't help but laugh.

"No swans, but there *is* something I'd like to show you. You'll need to add a few layers; it's gonna be chilly." I look her over from head to toe. She's wearing a long-sleeved t-shirt, stretchy pink pants, and striped socks. Her hair is down and all over the place. She looks amazing.

"Okay." She smiles at me, and my heart rate picks up.

"I'm gonna go pull the canoe. Meet you down by the lake?" I ask, just to make sure she's really coming.

"Okay," she says again. Her eyes follow me as I move past her to put my cup in the sink. I like her eyes on me. I like it a lot.

Whiskey follows me out as I head down the back steps and under the house. The house is built on the side of the mountain, so underneath the deck, I left it open and it acts more as covered storage.

Grabbing the canoe, I drag it down to the water's edge. I've only used this canoe twice. Once to fish, and once to take Bryce out on the lake. Thinking of Bryce causes my heart to hurt. I'm way past due to see him, and if I'm feeling like this, I can only imagine how I've made him feel. Guilt consumes me.

"Whatcha looking at?" Ava asks. I didn't know she had made her way down here, and I wonder how long I've been standing here.

Turning to face her, I find her watching me. My skin heats at the sight of her. She's fully bundled now in warmer clothes and I have to ignore the way they hug her body. Her hair is pulled back into a ponytail and there's no makeup on her face. *Shit*. She's just so beautiful.

"Nothing really, just thinking." I pull the beanie off my head, run my hand through my hair, and let out a deep sigh.

"About what?" she tilts her head to the side—studying me—and puts her good hand on her hip.

"Stuff I have to take care of when I get back to town." That's really the best answer I can give her without divulging my whole life.

"When's that going to be?"

"Probably tomorrow morning," I let out another deep sigh and look across the lake. Damn, I'm going to miss it here.

"Have you been here for a while?" she crosses her good arm over the hurt one, closing herself off.

"Longer than I should have. Come on, I'll help you in." The ground next to the lake's edge is muddy, and I don't want her feet to stick and throw her off balance. I walk toward her and hold out my hand. She takes it, and as she steps into the canoe, my hand slides up her arm and my fingers wrap around her elbow to steady her.

She turns to smile at me in thanks, but I still catch the distance in her eyes.

Shit. Insecurity sweeps over me, and I'm never insecure about anything. Maybe she has regrets about last night, maybe she's wishing she knew a little more about who I am, or maybe she's just worried about being on the lake, who knows? I just wish I could get a better read on what she's thinking, or better yet, I wish we were in a place where I could ask her.

Stupid rules. Why did I offer that as an option?

"You're sure you want to go with me, right?" I ask, wanting her to be open with me.

"I'm sure." She smiles up at me again as she settles onto her seat and Tank jumps in. She giggles and pets the dog. Can't say I've ever had a dog on the lake before.

"All right then, hold on." Carefully, I push the canoe into the water. Stepping in, it wobbles a little and she grips the edge. Using my paddle, I push us out away from the shore.

The lake is quiet this morning. There are a few birds up singing, but mostly everything is still. Quiet.

Taking my time, I slice the calm waters with the paddle and push us further onto the lake. The colors of the leaves have turned even more over the last couple of days and its vividness is extraordinary.

By the time we reach the middle of the lake, all of the stiffness Ava has been carrying is gone. I lay the paddle across my lap, and the boat comes to a stop.

"I completely understand what you were saying now about looking from the inside out. At the house, we enjoy the beauty of the lake, but here it's like we are the lake," she whispers.

She's right. In the middle, there's a three-sixty view of the mountains surrounding us. Homes are littered across the mountain side, mostly camouflaged by the trees, but from here it's like nothing else exists. Just the lake and the mountains, and it's magnificent.

"My grandfather used to joke that we were fishing in a fish bowl, but I never saw it that way. Even though I grew up in the mountains, there's just something about this place that felt more magical, more mine, and I always knew I'd have a place here."

"You talk about him a lot." She frowns at me.

"I guess." I shrug my shoulders. "It's been a long time, but I do miss him. Anyway, I just wanted to show you this part of me. Why I love it here in Horizons Valley so much."

"This is a good spot." Her eyes and head turn as she fully takes in the view.

"Do you see the ski clearing over there?" she points toward the northeastern side of the lake.

"Yeah."

"That's where I learned to ski." She smiles proudly at me.

"I've never been skiing."

"What?! How's that possible?" she sits up a little straighter, her eyes widening.

"I just haven't. As a kid, my grandfather wasn't a fan of it, then I moved in with Clay's family, and by the time I was a teenager, it was easier to say no, than explain I didn't know how."

She giggles at my answer.

"Maybe I should teach you," she offers up.

"If it means more time with you, count me in."

Her cheeks shade pink, but the smile she gives me looks

almost hopeful.

"So, what about you?" I ask.

"What do you mean?" she bends over and pets Tank.

"It's called sharing." I grin at her. "I tell you something and then you tell me. Come on . . . who are you? Tell me something I don't know." I feel like I'm starving for any tidbit she'll throw my way.

She glances over my shoulder at something behind me and her face relaxes as she thinks about her answer. Why is it so hard for her to tell me who she is? That feeling that she might be hiding something comes crawling back to the edges of my thoughts.

"I'm just a girl who's trying to be." Her eyes are thoughtful and her good hand starts rubbing the cast over her wrist.

Be? What kind of answer is that?

"Be what?" I'm confused.

"Be everything. I want to be brave. Be fearless. Be kind. Be strong. Be beautiful. Be badass." A chuckle escapes me and she laughs softly. "And at the end of the day, I just want to be me." Her eyes are clear. She's happy with this explanation, even though I really don't understand it.

"Why do I feel like after four days, I still know nothing about you?" Time is running out and I'm disappointed. This shouldn't be so hard.

"I seem to remember the other night you being very detailed about who I am and what you see." She smirks at me, trying to lighten up the moment.

"I guess so."

Her eyes match the sky, the tiny diamond stud in her nose keeps reflecting the sun, and her lips are glossy. She's breathtaking and I want to reach over and pull her onto my lap.

"I just want to know everything about you," I tell her,

placing the paddle back into the water, breaking eye contact. "One more thing to show you and then we'll head in."

"Thank you for bringing me out here, it's beautiful." She grips the edge of the canoe as we turn toward the southeastern end.

"You're beautiful." My eyes connect with hers and hold. She blushes and then looks out across the water as a comfortable silence falls between us.

Pulling around the last curve of the lake, I paddle to the edge so we don't get pushed back by the runoff.

"Look, do you see it?" I point off to the right.

"I do."

Tucked in and barely noticeable to the average passing person is a small rocky river, and about a quarter of a mile down, there is a waterfall. The water from the river feeds into the lake, so between the current and the rocks, it's a little more challenging than flatwater paddling.

"Do you ever go down there?" she asks.

I look down the river and notice the fog has lifted in a way that canopies over the top of the trees. Memories of Clay and I flash before my eyes.

Right after we were hired to be the summer band at Smokey's, we found a small house for rent just outside the edge of town. We were young, naïve in so many ways, and so excited to be following our dreams. We kayaked the lake, found this river, and spent hours talking about how life was going to be once we made it big. It's on those rocks down by the falls, five years later, we agreed to change the name of our band and move to Nashville.

"Yeah, in the summer, Clay and I kayak down and go swimming." To my knowledge, he's never brought anyone, and Ava's a first for me. It's one of those places you just don't share with everyone.

"It's so pretty. I wish I had a camera. Are there any trails leading down to it?" She leans to the side of the canoe, hoping for a better view, and I counterbalance her weight.

"Not that we've seen, so unless you travel up the river, you aren't getting any closer. It's pretty secluded."

"Maybe next summer we can go." She looks back to me.

My eyes dart to hers. It's the first time she's really mentioned anything about us and the future. My heart swells with hope.

"I'd love to take you down there. It's a great place to swim if you can handle the cold water." Thoughts of skinny dipping with her come to mind, but I keep that to myself.

"I'll manage," she smiles.

"Good. It's a date," I declare.

"Pretty sure of yourself, huh?" Her eyes light up.

I smile back. "When it comes to you, I'm very sure. You may be leaving today, but this," my finger moves back and forth between the two of us, "isn't over. It's just beginning."

Chapter
NINETEEN

Ava Layne

RIVING TO THE airport, both of us sit in complete silence. With each mile that passes, I feel the distance between us growing even more, and I hate it.

I don't want to say goodbye to him, but what would be the point in saying otherwise? I know he wants to see me again, but I fear if I do, I'll lose myself to him completely, and I'm not sure if I'm ready for the repercussions if it were to end badly, because that's what it would be for me . . . bad.

Sensing the tension growing between us, he reaches over and lays his hand on top of mine. My fingers were tapping on my leg and I didn't even know it. Flipping my hand over, he laces his fingers through mine and brings it up to his lips for a kiss.

I watch as his kiss sears and brands the back of my hand.

Ash completely surprised me this morning by offering to take me on the lake. He didn't have to do that—he could have gone off on his own, but he didn't. He wanted me to see why he loves it here so much, and in return, it made me fall for him even more.

Most summers, the girls and I rent a boat and go tubing on the lake. We pack a lunch, speed around, and laugh at each other as we fly off the tube. But I can honestly say, not once have I truly taken in the view around me. Maybe because it was morning and it was calm, or maybe because it's fall and the colors are so vibrant, or maybe it's because I was with him, but I felt like I was seeing the lake, the valley, and the mountains for the first time. And I loved it.

I'd be lying if I said Ash and the lake didn't steal a piece of my heart today, because they did; and when he asked me who I was, I really did want to answer him, and I hope one day he'll understand why I didn't. Despite my broken wrist and his mysterious call last night, this was the best weekend I've had in a really long time. I know it's selfish, but I wasn't ready to give that up by having to explain all the details of my life. It would have changed things, without a doubt.

"Ava," his voice pulls me from the lake and back to the truck. As if reading my mind he says, "Thank you for the best birthday weekend I've ever had."

I sigh contentedly and squeeze his fingers between mine. "I'm not sure what I did, other than cause you trouble, but you're welcome."

"You'd be surprised actually. You were exactly what I needed." He looks away from me and out the front windshield of the truck, his thumb rubbing the back of my hand.

I want to ask him what he means, but there's that gray area again where we really don't talk about life and reality.

"Well, I'm glad I was able to do something for you, other than eat all your food and spend your money." I try to lighten the mood, but his eyes are troubled when he looks back at me.

"I truly am sorry about your wrist. Never in a million years would I ever wish pain upon you, but . . . I wouldn't trade these last couple of days for anything. I meant it when I said I don't want this to be over. I want to see you again soon. And any time you want to come to Horizons Valley, the house is open for you. Just shoot me a text, let me know, and leave some of those apple strudel cupcakes on the counter." He gives me a small smile.

"I appreciate that, thank you." I think back to my reaction last night to that call, and suddenly I feel stupid. He has a life. He's surrounded by people, just like I am. It was wrong of me to just assume the worst. After all, he wouldn't knowingly open his home up to me if he was with someone else, would he?

He brings my hand back to his mouth, kisses it again, and then places it on his leg. I wish there wasn't a console in between us; I'd unbuckle and slide over just to be close to him again.

Pulling into the airport, Ash parks the truck at the Delta curb, and neither one of us moves. There's an electrical current running between us, and with each second it seems to be getting stronger. It isn't a sexual one, granted after his kiss from last night I'm thinking I wouldn't be opposed to it, but it's more like an electrical connection where we're drawn to each other in an inexplicable way.

Letting out a sigh, he opens his door, and sneezes as the sun hits his skin.

"Bless you," I say smiling at him. As rugged and manly

as he is, it really is adorable every single time.

"Thanks," he says, flashing me one of those dimples, opening the door to the back seat. He grabs my suitcase and Tank, then slams it shut. As he walks around the back of the truck, I watch as he takes in a big breath of air before he lifts his head to face me.

Neither one of us says anything, but both of us are searching for answers to the questions we agreed not to ask. And even though he says he wants to see me again, my eyes burn with the knowledge that I might not—he may change his mind—and I have to fight to hold back the tears.

Setting Tank's travel bag down, Ash steps closer, tucks a few pieces of hair behind my ear, and runs his thumb down my cheek to my jaw.

"Don't do that," he says.

"Do what?" I bite on my bottom lip to try and stop the tears, and he reaches over and pulls it out. My lip burns at his touch.

"Look so sad. I can't take it. Keep it up and there's a good possibility I get on that plane with you." My hand finds his hip and holds on tight.

"Would you, if I asked you to?" I study his face to see if his eyes stay clear with the truth.

"Yes." He lets out a sigh, and they do. This makes my heart leap with hope. "Give me a couple of weeks to take care of some work things. I'm behind and people aren't happy with me. Once the dust settles, I'd like to see you again, maybe over the holidays?" His eyebrows lift in question.

Over the holidays!

He just made the hope I've been holding on to tangible, and I'll take it.

"I think I'd like that." I'm so happy I could burst.

"I think I like you. I think I more than like you." His cheeks tinge pink and I find it charming that this man just got nervous.

My breath catches as he leans down and just barely brushes his lips against mine. Standing on the curb, neither one of us is moving, just our breaths as warmth mixes with the cold air slipping between us.

Willing him to move closer, just one last time, my hand moves up from his hip and my fingers graze the shirt covering his stomach. He feels the faint touch and his muscles contract underneath.

He groans against my lips, moving one of his hands around to my lower back, pulling me to him; and he moves his other into my hair, holding my head.

Heat from his body surrounds me, along with the fresh scent of sandalwood, clean laundry, and musk. It's a smell that is so distinctly him, it's comforting and intoxicating at the same time.

His fingertips tilt my head backwards, and my lips fall open and invite him in.

Ash doesn't kiss me like he did at the concert, instead, he holds more restraint and kisses me tenderly. His lips savor mine, his tongue gently caressing mine, and I find myself getting lost in the moment.

Yes, we are standing in plain sight for anyone to see, and I just don't care.

I take what this man is offering and give back just what he wants.

Changing the angle of my head, his hand slides down to the back of my neck and tightens. One by one, his fingers imprint me and my world goes black. No longer is he intimately holding me, he's clamped on to me . . . no, he's squeezing me . . . no, he's pinching me . . . no, he's digging his fingers in, bruising me. How did he find me? Fear consumes me, and I start shaking all over.

"Ava," I hear in the background.

It's such a calming voice, behind closed eyes I search past the pounding of my heart to hear it again.

"Ava, open your eyes," says the voice and I do.

Blinking through the tears, Ash is down at eye level looking at me.

"Focus on me." He waves two fingers between us, and I see he's not touching me. "And breathe with me."

He's placed my hand on his chest, just like he did before, and his heart is beating against it in a soothing rhythm.

Keeping my eyes on his, shame and embarrassment wash over me.

"I'm sorry," I whisper to him, and his eyebrows furrow.

"Hey, I told you before, you don't have to apologize for anything. Just tell me what I did." There are worry lines around his eyes.

Swallowing, I push down the lump that's formed in the back of my throat. "Neck."

He runs his hand over his face and lets out a breath. "Okay, now I know," he says slowly, smiling at me, understanding.

"Ash." My chin quivers and eyes again fill with tears. I'm terrified this is going to ruin us. Ruin what we've started.

One hand reaches up for mine, takes it off his chest, and he links our fingers together. "Ava, it's okay. I told you, we'll figure it out as we go." His other hand comes up and his thumb wipes away my tears.

Pulling me closer, my hips lean against him and I arch my

back to look up at him. "You need to get moving," he says, while leaning down and brushing his lips against mine one more time.

"Okay," I murmur once he releases me, and I let out a deep sigh.

"I'll text you soon." He gives me one of his signature smiles, dimples and all.

"Can't wait," I say, smiling.

His eyes hold mine as he takes another step back and toward the truck. My hand drops, but I don't move. I can't move. I'm about to watch the one person I've allowed myself to feel anything for in seven years drive away.

I hate how final this feels, but I'm going to have faith in him that it's not.

Chapter

TWENTY

WILL ASHTON

PULLING AWAY FROM the curb and leaving her here at the airport is by far one of the hardest things I've ever had to do. My hands grip the steering wheel and I squeeze with as much force as possible. If I don't, there's a good possibility that I'll pull over and go right back to her.

I hate those flashbacks. They cause me physical pain to see her so easily sucked right in. I also hate that I'm not given any warning signals to back off. I mean, what the hell? I have no idea when, where, or what happened to her to make her this way, but I swear, if I ever meet this guy, I will end him.

Glancing in the rearview mirror, she's still standing there, and my heart swells at the thought she isn't ready to say goodbye to me either.

It feels so strange to have a girl be interested in me, because of *me*, and not who I am out in the world. As far as I can tell, she has no idea that I'm Will Ashton, country superstar, and that makes me feel so good. I don't really feel like I'm deceiving her—after all, I'm being me when I'm with her, so hopefully once she finds out, she won't be angry with me.

Rounding the corner as I pull out of departures, she disappears. My heart crashes into my chest and panic settles in on it. I really hope she meant it when she said she would see me over the holidays. I'm not past going to her place in NYC to make that happen if I have to.

I'm in love with this girl.

One weekend—that's all it took. Hell, one look was enough. I'm surprised, shocked, and elated all at the same time. In thirty years, I have never felt about a girl the way I feel about her. Damn, it was so hard not to lay every bit of it out there, but I have so many other things that need to come first.

Reaching into my console, I grab my phone and pull up her name.

Me: Is it too soon to text you yet?

I know I'm breaking some unspoken guy code by not waiting, but I just can't.

Ava: Nope. Your timing is perfect.

Her response makes me smile and the pressure on my chest eases.

Me: Good. I forgot to tell you to have a nice flight.
Ava: Thank you, and it looks like I will. I just got my boarding pass and am looking at a very low seat number.

So low, it says 2A.

    Me: Nothing but the best for you.

And I mean that; I want to give her the world.

    Ava: Ah, how sweet...

I can just see her face and hear her sarcastic tone. A smile stretches across my face. Damn, this girl makes me happy.

    Me: Funny girl is back, and just so you know, I like her too.
    Ava: I'm glad. Thanks again for the ticket.
    Me: Anytime.
    Ava: By the way, what's your last name?

Oh no. I understand why she might want to know, and I do know hers, but if I tell her and she just by chance googles Ashton, there's a good possibility photos of me will come up and I'm not ready for that yet.

    Me: Nice try there, detective, but I'm not telling.
    Ava: That's not fair, you know mine.
    Me: I do, and I promise I'll tell you everything next time I see you.
    Ava: Everything? Do you have a criminal record?

A loud laugh escapes me and echoes throughout the truck.

    Me: Let me guess . . . Are you a reporter?
    Ava: Nope. Actually despise them.

I wonder why?

Me: Me too.

She's going to hate them even more once they catch wind of her. Anxiety washes through as it occurs to me that I might need to hire her a bodyguard. Some of these people from the media can get handsy. Just the thought makes me see red.

My phone chimes.

Ava: Aren't you driving?
Me: Yes.
Ava: Then you can't talk to me! Should you crash and die, I'll be left hanging and never find out who you really are!

I laugh at her reasoning, but I'm certain if she really wanted to know, she'd figure it out. After all, Clay and Emma probably exchanged information.

Me: LOL. Fair point. Text me when you land?

I need to know when I'm going to talk to her again, and I need her to know that I want to.

Ava: Yes. :)
Me: Looking forward to it.

Walking into the house, I head straight for the living room and pull my grandfather's guitar off the wall. I don't know why I'm nervous to play it, but I am. It's only been two months; it's not like it's been three years.

Sitting on the couch, Whiskey curls up and places his head on one foot. His eyes are droopy and he looks depressed, and I can't help but think I know exactly how he feels.

The house seems bigger, emptier, and definitely quieter. That little dog of hers had nails that clicked on the floor everywhere she went.

Pulling the pick out from between the strings, I strum a G chord, a D chord, an E minor chord, and a C chord. My fingers are a little stiff, but getting back at it is just like riding a bike—you really never forget.

The harmonies of the chords echo through the room, and the familiarity it brings calms me. Why I let the weeks pass, I'll never know. Playing the guitar was never something I just wanted to do; it was something I *needed* to do. It's always connected me to myself and given me a release that I've not been able to find anywhere else.

Playing the chords again, I think about a Willie Nelson quote—"Three chords and the truth, that's what a country song is."

That's what my songs used to be . . . true.

Ava's right—we've lost our originality, and it's time to get that back. Shifting my fingers, I play the intro to "Why Can't the Future Be Now," and lose myself in remembering what her voice sounded like singing my words.

Her voice.

I wonder if she's ever considered singing professionally. She said she plays the piano and has perfect pitch—maybe she's a songwriter too.

Thinking of her and some of the things she's said, I pull my favorite composition book and a pencil out of the drawer of the coffee table and jot down some potential song lyrics. I should have known she'd be a muse as well. The thoughts and feelings I've had around her over the last four days, I could write a dozen songs about.

My phones buzzes next to me, and I see that it's Juliet calling. I contemplate not picking up, but she did call me last night too and I never called her back. Dropping the pencil, I answer my phone.

"Hey, Jules."

"Hi," a little voice says back to me. It's so good to hear his voice, instantly I smile.

"Hey, Bryce, how's my little man?" I set the guitar down and walk over to the large windows along the back wall.

"Good. When are you coming home?" he asks.

I glance toward the sky and see some clouds moving in. Rain means the leaves will drop, and along with them, the temperature too. The fall season is officially winding down and snow is just around the corner.

"Tomorrow." I had thought about tonight, but I'll wait out the weather.

"Promise?"

"I promise." Just the thought of seeing him so soon has me excited. I can't wait to hug him.

"Okay." I can hear the smile in his voice.

"Has Uncle Clay come by?" I sure hope he's checked in on them.

"Yes, but mama wants to see you. We miss you." I run my hand over my jaw and close my eyes.

"I miss you too, buddy. Tell your mom I'll be there for dinner."

"Okay," he says softly. Gotta love little kids on the phone.

"I love you, Bryce."

"Love you too." My heart gets bigger every time I hear this from him.

"Later, cowboy."

He giggles at my nickname for him. "Later," and he hangs up.

Placing the guitar on the couch, I walk back to the room Ava slept in. Opening the door, strawberries float my way and I breathe in the smell of her. She's made the bed, and her towels are lying on the end of it. Looking around the room, she's left nothing behind, and a pang of sadness hits me; I don't even have a picture.

Lying down in the middle of her bed, I glance at the clock. Two more hours until she lands. Two more hours until she texts me. Twenty-four more hours for me to figure out how to implement what happens next in my life.

Chapter
TWENTY-ONE

Ava Layne

*I*T'S BEEN A little over four weeks since I've seen Ash, and not a day goes by that we don't talk.

I still don't know what his last name is, and honestly, I don't care. I asked him that one time, and never again. I don't think he's hiding anything crazy—he seems pretty genuine, and he's always told me he'd tell me the next time he saw me.

Part of me wonders if it has to do with money. He's only thirty and his house at the lake must have cost a fortune. People with money tend to not want other people to know just how much. If I knew his last name, I'd be able to search for him on the internet, and that might give it away.

The girls asked me about him right when I got back from North Carolina, but I left my answers pretty vague, and in return, they left me alone. Once, we talked about this gig tonight and the possibility of us trying to meet up with Ash and Clay, but Emma hesitated, so I dropped the subject.

Every day he sends me a text good morning, every afternoon he sends me a photo of whatever he's looking at, and every evening we talk before going to bed.

It's the day after Thanksgiving, and the girls and I are in Nashville. Word of our arrival for the benefit tonight has created a bit of a buzz, and sure enough, in front of the hotel, paparazzi have staked out.

Closing the door to the limo, people start tapping on the window, trying to get our attention.

"Seriously! Who says, 'When I grow up, I want stand around and take bad photos of good people'?" Emma growls.

It's the one part of this job that I hate the most.

"It's not that bad, just ignore them," says Scott, the intern tagging along with Mona. Emma, Cora, Mona, and myself all turn to glare at him.

"Who said he could speak?" Cora asks, pinning Mona with a get-rid-of-this-guy look.

"What?" he says, completely unaware of the irritation floating between all of us.

Smoothing out the skirt to my gown, the clutch on my lap vibrates. I unsnap the clasp and pull out my phone.

Ash: When can I see you again?

A smile instantly lightens my face.

Me: Who says I want to see you?
Ash: Ouch, you wound me.
Me: I highly doubt that.
Ash: I'm serious. Tell me when and where and I'll be

there.

    Me: Tomorrow too soon?

    Ash: Where are you?

    Me: Wouldn't you like to know?

    Ash: I would, very much so.

    Me: Well, it just so happens I'm in Nashville.

    Ash: Really? Why didn't you tell me you were coming? If I didn't have to work tonight, I'd come find you. Btw—why are you here?

    Me: You're working on a holiday weekend?

    Ash: So now you're curious . . . wouldn't you like to know?

    Me: I would.

    Ash: All right, let's talk about all this tomorrow.

    Me: Text me when you wake up.

    Ash: You know I wake up early.

    Me: I do.

    Ash: Hope you have a great night.

    Me: You too.

    Glancing up, I realize the car has gone silent and everyone is watching me.

    "What?" I can't help but ask with a grin on my face.

    "Who are you texting?" Emma eyes me suspiciously.

    My grin turns into a full megawatt smile.

    Emma gasps, "I knew it! Oh my God, this is huge! You're going to see him tomorrow, aren't you?" She claps her hands together and then leans over to squeeze my leg.

    "Yep."

    She squeals and bounces up and down in her seat.

    "Who? Who is she going to see tomorrow?" Mona's looking at me a little panicked.

"Ash," Cora chimes in, excitedly.

Mona's eyes narrow as she locks in on me. The wheels are turning in her head, and it's all business related. I've always been the perfect client to her. Never has she had to deal with my publicist, or clean up any messes that usually come with being in the entertainment industry. I don't go out, I don't drink very much, I don't use recreational or prescribed drugs, and I don't date.

"Have you talked to Clay?" I ask Emma.

She shakes her head. "No. I mean, I have, but no, I didn't tell him we were in town." She looks away from me and out the window. I thought she liked him . . . hmm.

"Who's Clay?" Mona's eyes dart back and forth between the two of us. Poor Mona.

"Oh, Clay's his best friend," Cora volunteers, grinning.

"Girls, I don't like surprises. Av, I'm surprised at this little tidbit, but excited for you. Please keep me in the loop." She gives me the mom voice.

My phones buzzes and I look down.

Ash: I'm really excited to see you tomorrow.
Me: Me too. :)

The limo finally comes to a stop at a red welcome carpet for incoming guests. More photographers have lined the steps and street looking to see who will be at tonight's event.

"Wow, they went all out," says Emma as she climbs out of the limo.

"Yeah, I think it's nice." I stare up at the six large columns that grace the entrance. Flashes erupt against the night sky, momentarily blinding me, and I drop my head.

Together, the three of us walk up the front steps of the Schermerhorn Symphony Center, home to the Nashville Symphony. It feels very surreal to me. Emma and I once came to a performance here years ago, right after we started at Julliard, but neither of us has been back since. Not even when we were on tour. It's a shame too, it's known for its acoustics, stunning architecture, and recognized as one of the best concert halls in America.

Right and left, people are calling our names. I hate it. Why they think that's actually going to work in gaining someone's attention, I'll never know. But each of us plays our part, ignoring what we can.

"Don't forget to smile," Mona sings out from behind us.

At the top of the steps, we are ushered over to a photographer standing in front of a NO MORE backdrop. The three of us pose and then head inside.

The main lobby is just as grand as I remember it. My eyes soak in the massive white marble columns and the chandeliers. Blue accents have been placed throughout the space, to represent the NO MORE logo, and everyone is dressed elegantly for the black-tie affair.

"Ladies," a voice comes from our right. Mr. Lang, the lead organizer for tonight's event, is walking our way. "I'm so happy to see you again. You'll never know what it means to have each of you here tonight to perform for us." His hands land on my upper arms and he leans in to kiss my cheek. I freeze, suck in a deep breath, and he pulls back. The greeting is over. I hate how this makes me feel. Allowing someone into your personal space should be asked first, not assumed.

He cheek kisses Emma, Cora, Mona, and shakes Scott's hand. My eyes roll at Scott's apparent haughtiness, when he shouldn't even be here.

"We're happy to support this cause. Thank you for invit-ing us," I say, taking a step back away from him.

"If you don't mind, I'd like to personally introduce you to a few of our top supporters this evening. It shouldn't take too long."

"Of course, we'd love to meet them," Emma says with her usual grace.

"Fantastic." He claps his hands together, and leads us through the lobby and into the concert hall. The theater-style seating has been removed and in its place is a gorgeous hard-wood floor. Round tables have been set up in the back half of the room, and along the walls. They've left the front near the stage open for dancing.

"Ah, here we go. Mr. Hale, I'd like to introduce you to Ms. Layne and her friends. They've kindly agreed to perform for us this evening." Mr. Lang smiles at all of us.

"Hey, I'm Beau, it's nice to meet you." He reaches out to shake my hand, Emma's, and Cora's.

I'd recognize Beau Hale just about anywhere, Mr. Heart-throb Tennis Champion himself.

"This is my friend, Jude Jamison." He tilts his head to the guy standing next to him.

Cora steps in a little closer to me and reaches out to shake his hand. Jude's eyes widen and run over the length of her, clearly liking what he sees. Pinching my lips together, I hold in a laugh. She may be from the Upper East Side, but she has a thing for athletes over the suits of Wall Street, and she just might have found her next challenge.

Pulling the attention off of them, I face Beau. "So, why NO MORE?" I ask him.

"Why not?" he beams. It's easy to see why he's frequently found on the cover of magazines. Tucking his hands in his pockets, he smiles genuinely at me. "I have a vested interest in raising awareness for those who suffer from abuse, no matter what kind. People should be made to feel they have a way out that's positive and not a dead end, if you catch my drift."

He winks at me; I like this guy. The stories about him being sincerely nice seem pretty accurate.

"I do." We smile at each other and share a knowing look.

"Thank you, Mr. Hale." Mr. Lang reaches out to shake his hand again, alerting all of us that it's time to move on.

"Of course." He smiles at Mr. Lang and then winks at me again.

News of our arrival spreads pretty quickly. As we move around the room, people are now full-on staring, leaving me uncomfortable. Giving Mona a look that she recognizes, she nods her head understanding that it's time for us to go.

"I just have one more person, and then I'll let you be on your way. Last I heard, he was down front enjoying the music." Mr. Lang waves his hand in the direction of the stage. A small ensemble of the Nashville Symphony is currently on the stage playing jazz.

Approaching a high top table set off to the side, the man's back is to us, but his black cowboy hat immediately has the hairs standing up on my arms. With the heels of our shoes clicking on the floor, he feels us approach, turns, and my world stops.

"Ash." His name slips from my lips just barely a whisper. The only person to hear me is Mona, and her head whips from looking at me to him.

He is even more attractive than I remember, and my eyes drift down the length of him. His face is smooth, stubble free, and he's wearing a classic black tuxedo. He's holding a high-ball glass with an amber liquid, and his other hand is tucked into his pants pocket. Add in the hat, and one word comes to mind: sexy. He's so handsome, it should be a sin.

Blue eyes appraise me, and my body flushes under his perusal. I'm at a loss as to whether I should say something or not, but then again, I'm not even sure I could. Just being in his presence, he fills all of my senses. My mind is scattered, and as he pinches his lips together, I'm consumed with the few moments we've had together and what those lips feel like on me.

Mr. Lang leans over and places his hand on Ash's shoulder.

"Will, I'd like to introduce you to Ms. Avery Layne. She and her friends have graciously agreed to perform for us this evening and we couldn't be more thrilled to have her here with us. Ms. Layne, this is Mr. Will Ashton. You may already know of him, but what most don't know is that he is one of our largest supporters, and this evening we consider him to be a guest of honor."

Wait!

What?

Did he just say Will Ashton?

Cora gasps next to me.

My eyes flip back to his and his face is expressionless. Seeing him now, here with the cowboy hat, how—just how—did I not recognize him? Apparently, Cora didn't either.

My mind starts racing and several things hit me all at once.

I spent the weekend with the great Will Ashton—a legend in country music.

Will Ashton, as in lead singer of the Blue Horizons.

No wonder he didn't tell me who he was.
Suddenly, I feel faint.

Chapter

TWENTY-TWO

WILL ASHTON

I NEVER IN a million years expected to see Ava tonight. The Ava that I know is quiet, reserved, not a large crowd type of person. She has crazy, white blonde, curly hair, her nose is pierced, her beautiful skin is covered in freckles, her eyes are blue, and she wears rock band t-shirts. But looking at her standing in front of me now, I'm starting to think that I don't know her at all.

I'll be damned.

This woman before me looks like an angel, and seeing her like this, I was right when I thought there was something familiar about her. I've seen her numerous times on television, at different awards ceremonies, and in various venues over the last couple of years. I thought maybe I was recognizing her on a deeper level, like a down-in-my-soul level, but now I don't know.

For a split second my mind begins to doubt Mr. Lang and

that this couldn't possibly be her, but as my eyes lock onto hers, I see a mutually shocked expression in them. I know this look; I've seen it before. That look reaches right into my stomach and squeezes.

Her hair is straight and so long it falls almost to the arch in her lower back. The nose piercing is removed, her makeup is done so her skin looks flawless, and her eyes are green. *Green.* She's wearing a strapless, pale pink, sparkly gown that is fitted to her waist and flows in layer after layer to the ground. The skin across her shoulders and upper chest look polished and has some type of shimmery sheen on it. Her makeup is soft, her lips are glossy, she has in earrings that dangle diamonds, and she looks more exquisite and elegant than anything I have ever seen. She takes my breath away, even in this nearly unrecognizable state.

"It's nice to meet you." Ava reaches out her hand for me to shake and instinctively I pull my hand from my pocket and my fingers slide in between hers. She's shaking. She's nervous. I hate that. Unable to not have her closer, I pull her forward to brush a greeting kiss against her cheek. The familiar scent of strawberries wafts by and calms me with the comfort that the girl I met is in there buried under all this. As my lips connect with her cheek, she tilts her head slightly into me, laying her face against mine. My eyes close at the contact and I let out a breath. Mr. Lang's voice breaks the moment as he continues talking, not realizing that neither one of us is paying him a whit of attention.

"Ms. Layne," says Mr. Lang.

Ava pulls back and blinks but she never breaks eye contact with me.

"Mona here told me that wandering through eager fans

isn't something you usually do, so thank you for taking the time to come out here and for allowing me to introduce you to our supporters, especially this one. This venue isn't overly large, so if you feel up to mingling after your performance, everyone here will be kind to you, I assure you."

He's so proud of himself and this event, as he should be, but there is no way she's going to walk through this room, and if I get my way, she will be leaving with me.

Neither of us acknowledges him and from the corner of my eye, I see Mr. Lang's head bounce back and forth between the two of us. I can't take my eyes off of her and can't get my mouth open to say anything. The woman standing next to Ava shifts her weight—this must be Mona, and she has to be the same Mona she called from my car. She must be Ava's manager.

Someone steps up next to me to join our little circle and I feel an arm wrap around mine. *Juliet.* Ava's eyes glance over to her and then flick down at the same time Juliet slides her hand down my arm and lightly grasps my hand. Ava looks back at me one more time, her face paling. The expression in her eyes has never been clearer—she is angry and hurt, and the walls that had gradually come down over the last couple of weeks are slammed back in place.

Shit!

I should have been honest with her about Juliet. The problem is I wasn't being honest with myself. How do I explain my relationship with Juliet to her? She never would've understood, and if I'd said something sooner, she never would've let me get to know her the way that I have. She feels betrayed and I did this to her. I feel like a complete and utter ass.

She returns her gaze back to Mr. Lang and squares off her perfect shoulders. "Thank you so much again for allowing us to perform this evening. Believe me when I say, I'm glad I came this evening for more reasons than one. After the show, we have plans to head back to New York and wish we could stay to mingle; what you have put together here tonight is truly marvelous." Her eyes skip back to Juliet before they land on me. "Mr. Ashton, it was a pleasure to meet you." The tiniest bit of sarcasm is interlaced between her words, and it's definitely meant for me. Her cheeks are flushed, and with one last look, she dismisses me and turns towards her manager.

"Mona, we're ready to go get started." Mona's eyes widen as she takes in Ava's flushed and stiff appearance.

"Of course. If you'll please excuse us . . ." She and Ava both turn to smile at Mr. Lang one more time before the group turns to walk away.

"Avery, wait." Desperation in my voice hangs in the air over all of us, and wow, did it feel weird to call her by a different name.

Everyone stops, and as she faces me, her eyes are glassy as they regard me. Disappointed hope shines back at me and my teeth clench together. There is no way I'm letting her walk away like this. Without taking my eyes off of her, I lean over and whisper in Juliet's ear. Juliet tenses, looks up at me questioningly, but then takes a step back releasing me.

"Before you go, dance with me." I put my glass on the table, hold my hand out to her, and she looks down at it. More people around us have stopped to watch our exchange and I don't care. Her eyes slide up my arm, over my chest, and settle on mine. She has to see the pleading in them, because I am— I'm desperately pleading that she not leave me, not yet.

Slowly she lifts and places her hand in mine.

Heat races up my arm as I tighten my fingers around hers.

Pulling her away from our little crowd, I hear a gasp come from behind us as I walk her to the dance floor. There are quite a few people surrounding us, but as recognition takes over, the space widens. Whatever, let them watch; let the whole world watch. I want them all to see us together.

"Ash, what are you doing?" Her breath floats across the skin on my neck as I pull her in close. Her free hand slides underneath my jacket and around to my back. My hand settles on her hip and my eyes drift shut as I lean my head down to rest next to hers.

"I saw your face, Ava. I couldn't let you walk away without saying something," I whisper in her ear.

"Nothing needs to be said; I understand." There's sadness and resolve in her words.

I pull our joined hands between us, and see that the cast is gone. In its place is a neutral-colored brace. I carefully kiss her fingers, and rest them against my chest. "No, I don't think you do." The air crackles around us as I breathe her in: her hair, her skin, her presence.

I flatten her hand over my heart, like I have several times before, only this time I hope that she feels how hard my heart is pounding. She's doing this to me.

"Do you feel that?" I push her hand harder against me. "It's for you, all of it, it's all yours." Every word and every moment we've shared, it has to have amounted to something. I have to erase the doubt that so easily slipped in.

"Avery," a female voice comes from beside us. Pulling apart, I glare at her manager for interrupting us. The expression on her face is a mixture of astonishment and suspicion. Dismissing me, she directly faces Avery with a thousand questions flying out of her eyes. "We really do need to get going now."

"Okay." She glances back to me and gives me a polite "Hollywood" smile. I hate that smile. It's the kind that looks perfect, but only touches the surface; there's no connection to it. That just won't do. My fingers squeeze hers—I won't release her like this—and the warmth returns to her eyes.

"Nice hat, by the way," she says softly.

Taking a step away from me, her hand drops and an emptiness rushes up my arm and settles into my chest. I feel the separation instantly, and I'm frozen to this spot, watching as she heads toward a door leading them to a private hallway, not glancing back once. Mona leans over and says something to the guy following them around, and he sprints off to the back.

"Most of the time, these tabloids airbrush so much one can never be sure as to what someone really looks like, but she's just as beautiful in person as she is in the magazines, don't you think?" Juliet has stepped up next to me.

There are more questions than just this one lingering in her voice, but I'm not ready to answer them and my hands sink into my pockets seeking the warmth they had found with Ava—I mean, Avery.

"Hmm, yes, she's very beautiful." How did I not put two and two together? All that time I kept thinking she looked familiar, and this is why. Stupidly, I had thought it was more than an exterior recognition, but I was wrong. Everyone knows Avery Layne—it's a household name—and I feel like an idiot.

"I'm so excited to see her perform this evening. Word on the street is she canceled some of her recent shows and hasn't performed in weeks."

"She did cancel them. She broke her wrist," I volunteer without thinking.

Juliet stiffens and turns to face me. I don't want to look at her and see the confusion in her eyes, so I remain focused on the door that Avery walked through.

"How do you know that? Do you know her?" There's a wariness in her voice. She's not going to like the answer, or maybe she will. I'm probably blowing this out of proportion for nothing.

Clay walks over with three glasses of champagne and his gaze bounces back and forth between the two of us. He feels the tension and his eyebrows furrow. Looking at my best friend, he raises an eyebrow at me, but all I can do is shake my head no. Having this conversation with him or Juliet right now just isn't going to happen. Without saying a word, I take one of the glasses, walk out of the hall into the lobby, and climb the stairs that will lead me to the balcony level. No one tries to stop me, maybe it's the look on my face, but I'm grateful.

Looking around, there are only a few people up here, and I'm relieved. Wandering over to a cocktail table next to the railing, I peer down towards the stage and see Clay and Juliet deep in discussion. My heart aches; I should have told her on Thanksgiving.

I hate that I feel lied to somehow, even though we agreed to keep our regular lives out of it. She did exactly what I did, and I should understand why better than anyone. "Pull yourself together, Ash. Process quick and lock it down," I mutter to myself.

The side door to the stage opens, Emma and Cora walk in, and wow, they too look just as amazing tonight. I had been so focused on Avery, I never even really saw them standing right next to her. Three seconds after, Avery follows behind. The random guy tries to usher them along, and none of them spares him a glance. As he reaches Avery, he grabs her arm to push her along, and she jerks backward out of his grasp. I see red and heat floods my face. No one touches her. Emma, who's standing closest to her, sees this interaction and storms toward them. Leaning into his personal space, she fires something at him and I realize I'm white-knuckling the railing. I would've loved to hear what she said.

Why is that guy even with them? He's too small to be a bodyguard, he's not talking to the press so he isn't a publicist, and he's not their agent—that woman Mona is. It makes no sense to me. And why did he put his hands on her? Is he stupid enough not to realize she doesn't like it? He has to have been warned.

Emma takes Avery's elbow and the three girls walk to the middle of the stage. Avery takes a seat at the piano, fluffs out her skirt, and my heart starts pounding in my chest. Emma picks up a violin, and Cora takes up a cello. I am certain by now Clay is filling Juliet in on our summer.

Avery, Emma, and Cora are even more well-known than I am. The three of them can create any genre imaginable and are sought after by everyone. From opera to pop music, they are incredible. Their signature sound is classical pop, think Taylor Swift mashed with Mozart. Most recently, I saw them in a commercial performing a flashmob for the #ShareaCoke campaign in Times Square. Little girls love them and so does every red-blooded male out there—including me.

"Good evening, ladies and gentleman." She's leaning forward into the microphone and out toward the audience. "I'm Avery Layne and these are my two very dear friends, Emma White and Cora Rhodes. We'd like to thank you for coming out tonight on behalf of NO MORE. NO MORE is a symbol. It is a symbol that is used to increase visibility of the reality of domestic violence and sexual assault. Every dollar raised is directed to one of hundreds of partner organizations in hopes to create more awareness and provide resources that will touch the lives of individuals affected. I personally hold this symbol very dear to my heart. I have a friend who could have benefited from what these amazing people do every day, and I wonder if just maybe her life would have turned out differently had she seen the symbol or felt the strength behind what it stands for."

She looks over at Emma and the two share a knowing look. My heart aches because although she's never told me any specifics, I know she's talking about herself.

"To learn more about NO MORE, please visit their website or make sure you stop by and speak to any of the many volunteers who are here tonight. They'd love to hear from you."

Racing her fingers across the keys, she looks back out over the audience and smiles. "We hope you enjoy the music tonight . . . most of it you will recognize, but we've thrown in a few new songs too. Thank you."

With her hands on the keys, she glances over to the girls, and the three of them begin to play. Her hands move so swiftly, and the music is beguiling. As she closes her eyes and begins to sing, I'm spellbound. I knew I was falling for her before, but it's in this moment I know I am completely in love with this girl. She owns every part of me and I'm hit with the realization that I know exactly what to do next. My life has always been about the music, but listening to her beautiful voice, it's as if all the unknown pieces have found their way together, becoming complete.

Time passes. I'm not sure how long I've been standing up here, or how many songs she's played, but I feel someone come up next to me. Glancing over, Clay leans against the edge, his eyes are focused on the stage. His arms are crossed over his chest; he's closing himself off and I'm not sure why, but it's easy to see he's just as mesmerized as I am.

"I don't even know what to say right now." He runs a hand through his hair and lets out a sigh.

"Yeah, that makes two of us." Silence falls between us as Emma takes two steps forward and solos on her violin. The sound of the strings is piercing and alluring.

"Did you know?" he asks, his eyes drinking her in.

"No, did you?"

He shakes his head. "No, she never said anything. I mean, I can understand why she didn't, but seeing them like this . . ."

"Did Juliet ask you about her?" I look around the dance floor to see if I can spot her.

"She did. I gave her an abbreviated version of our time with them. She asked if you had feelings for her, and I hope it wasn't too presumptuous of me, but I told her that although you haven't said anything, I thought you did. She decided to call it a night and catch a cab to head home early."

I let out a deep sigh and rub my hand over my face. "I guess it's better she knows." I do love her, I'm just not in love with her. I hate that she's going to get hurt in the end.

"She'll be fine. You know she wants what's best for you." He pats me on the shoulder and a look of understanding passes between us. "Come on, let's go down there and wait for them to get finished."

We take the large staircase down and walk along the wall toward the front of the stage. I figure this is as good a spot as any to try and catch up with her as she leaves. She must have questions and I'm ready to answer them.

"All right, ladies and gentleman, we hope that you all

have had a wonderful evening. This will be our last song of the night, and even though I can't take credit for writing this song, I have always loved what it has meant to me. Life can change when you least expect it, and the person who inspired me to sing this one tonight has changed mine for the better. It's called 'That Place in Time.'"

She leans back and the strings cut into the silence with the opening bars. Avery's eyes close as her fingers play the chords on the piano that I usually play on the guitar. She leans into the mic, begins to sing, and another piece of my heart breaks off and is now forever hers.

"Ash . . ." His voice trails off as we watch the girls. "This entire night is definitely going down in the books."

I can't take my eyes off her.

"That Place in Time" is off of the first Blue Horizons album. It's over ten years old and is one of the first songs we ever sang as one of our own. She'll never know what this moment means to me. Not to be too full of myself, but surely she knows of the singer Will Ashton—it feels like everyone does—but very few remember Blue Horizons. We were just a local mountain band that was discovered and reinvented. She has to have put two and two together . . . right?

My eyes prick with unshed tears as her voice and the melody bounce off of the concert hall walls and land straight in my very essence. I'm speechless. All I can do is stare. This amazing girl is on stage right now singing a song to me that I wrote, and in her own creative way. The combination of the piano, the strings, and her beautiful voice causes me to tremble. I am so moved. Never has anyone ever done something so personal and thoughtful to me, for me, or about me. The ache in my chest is so strong, all I can do is reach up and rub directly over my heart.

Watching her on stage, I don't really know how to describe it, but she's got that *thing*. That thing that's so unique and so rare that I can't put my finger on it, let alone describe it. It's in the way she moves, walks, talks, sings, and presents herself. It's that thing that is so special, I'm not even sure if I've ever really even seen it before. Passion is pouring out of her hands and through her words, and it's contagious. Watching her eyes light up doing something she loves causes that fire to light inside of me. I was already well on my way back to that place I once used to be, that place where the music just means more, but this reignites the desire and ambition I had lost.

She finishes the song and stands up to face the audience. The room erupts in applause and cheers, and I find myself clapping along with them. She is the complete package with qualities that make her so much more beautiful than I ever thought. Emma and Cora both go and stand on either side of her. All three of them are beaming and laughing. They hug each other, wave goodbye to the room full of people, and turn to leave the stage.

As if it were my show, post-performance adrenaline races through me, and suddenly my excitement turns to nervousness. My hands begin to sweat, and my heart begins to pound.

Is she going to want to see me, or will she walk right by?

Chapter
TWENTY-THREE

Ava Layne

*T*HE CROWD IS cheering and applauding, and I honestly feel better than I have in a long time. Half way through the performance, my wrist began to ache, but there was no way I was stopping. I just told myself, "One more hour and I'll wrap it up tighter."

Emma and Cora come over and engulf me in a huge hug. Both knew I had been nervous about tonight—between my personal feelings about the event and the cause and how my arm would hold up—and I'm so glad everything went as smoothly as we had hoped.

Walking toward the edge for one final wave, I look up and see Ash and Clay standing by the wall near the stairs that lead up to the stage from the dance floor. Ash's hand is over his heart on his chest, and his eyes look glassy. His lips are pressed together and there's just the faintest hint of a smile. He looks proud of me and that makes my heart swell. I had been worried about his reaction to my career, but maybe it turns out I don't need to be. After all, if there's anyone out there who understands the pressures of being high-profile, it's him.

I don't see the girl anywhere, and feel nothing but relief. I don't know who she is, but he can tell me later. The anger and hurt I first felt at seeing him with her has pretty much dissipated, and the more I think back over the last month, there is no way he could've been with her because he was with me, wasn't he? Too many texts, too many kind words, and so much time he's given me throughout each day. The minute Mr. Lang said his name, I instantly knew who he was, and vice versa. I feel kind of stupid for not recognizing him sooner, but sometimes when a person is removed from their setting, it's hard to place how you know them. Although I feel a little lied to, reality is, I lied to him too. But did I? I am who I am, and that's a girl who likes to be with her friends, feel carefree, bake cupcakes, vacation in the mountains, listen to and write great music, and sing. Most of these things he already knows. A name is just a name—it shouldn't define me, and so shouldn't it be the same for him?

A crowd begins to gather at the bottom of the stairs and anxiety ripples through me. We are supposed to walk down to a roped off area in front of the stage and for fifteen minutes stand and pose for pictures. Some of the guests this evening paid—or contributed to the organization—to have a photo with us. This isn't anything out of the ordinary. I usually just stand between the girls and they keep people away. It's understood through the industry that I have a "germ phobia," so no touching or hugging. I lock eyes with Ash. His brows furrow as he sees something in my expression. He moves away from the wall and begins to walk toward me. Emma is in front of me, Cora behind, and Mona and Mr. Lang are at the bottom of the stairs . . . and so are all the people.

My chest tightens and I start counting. One, two, three, four, five . . . I know by the time I get to fifty I will be behind the ropes and away from all of these people. I can feel my fingers as they tap out onto my hip, and I focus on the feeling. Playing my part, I just smile. People are talking to me, but the noise in my ears is a buzz and it's getting louder and louder.

Eleven, twelve, thirteen, fourteen, fifteen, sixteen . . . I'm so thankful Ash is so tall. Emma gently grabs my hand and keeps me steadily walking toward him—she must have seen them too—and I keep my eyes locked on his. There's a carpet at the bottom of the stairs that leads to our designated place behind the ropes. He's positioned himself next to the carpet, and with each step, I'm getting closer to him. He smiles and the pressure on my chest begins to open. Thirty, thirty-one, thirty-two, thirty-three, thirty-four . . .

Suddenly, without warning, someone slams into the back of me. Heat erupts along my spine, long fingers tightly wrap around both my upper arms, and they begin to push. Fear streaks through me, everything flashes white before it blacks out. I squeeze my eyes shut; I don't want to see.

It's happening.

Again.

There's no more music, just the deep rumble of thunder and the pelting of rain from the storm outside. Losing my balance, I trip over the fabric of my dress and my weight drops. The warmth that shines down from the stage lights is immediately gone and is replaced by the coldness of the wood floor as my knees hit and I'm shoved face-first down on it. There's no more Ash, no more benefit concert, no help, only darkness.

Hands. I feel them all over me, and as tears find their escape from my eyes and roll off my face, all I can think is . . . please make it fast.

In the movies, bad scenes always happen at night and during a thunderstorm. Loud, rolling booms and flashes of lightning light up the screen to intensify the terror of the moment. Glimpses of the victim and the attacker are shown to heighten the anxiety, and as we wait for the striking moment, our knuckles strain white as we squeeze the person next to us. Only for me, this isn't a movie—it's my reality.

My reality, minus the flashes of light. Yes, there is rain, and yes, there is thunder, but no light other than the muted faint glow coming from the windows in the living room. The hallway is dark. I can't see him and I have no idea what's going to happen next as he squeezes the back of my neck in a pincer grip. There's no one here but him.

"I'm so mad, I just might kill you." Spit from his words lands on my face and the heat from his breath burns the side of my cheek.

Fear.

There's a difference between simply being afraid of something, or someone, and being consumed with fear. Fear has roots. Roots that rapidly stretch, wind, and grow, choking out everything in their path. They embed themselves into the smallest of places and anchor into the largest. They wrap around all that is good and crush the life right out of it, leaving strength and courage in crumbles.

Fear is paralyzing.

It's in this moment, I truly fear for my life. I never thought Chris would hurt me, yet here we are, and now I'm faced with the possibility of death.

The roots suck out the warmth, and cold barbs sweep down my body. My heart races with acute understanding. It too fears that it might soon stop.

Unwanted tears silently escape my eyes, slip across my skin, and land on the floor.

"You know that you and I are fated to be together." He shifts his weight and an unwanted groan of pain escapes me as my raw shoulder and knees press into the floor. "Is this how you want to spend your life? Running from me, making me angry? Why? Why do you do things like this?" he yells.

Grabbing me by the hair, he yanks backward and a blood curdling scream ricochets off the hallway walls. Slamming my head back to the floor, a crack from my face resonates through my ears. Blinding pain and tiny fuzzy flashes dance behind my closed eyes. I try to blink them away as my stomach rolls from dizziness.

The familiar, tangy, metallic taste of blood pools at the side of my mouth. My heavy tongue runs across my lips and teeth trying to find its exit point.

"Do. Not. Move. Do. Not. Make. One. Sound," each word staccato and snarled. His fingers reclamp onto the back of my neck, the tips of his fingers mashing my windpipe.

Closing my mouth, I grit my teeth and suck in air through my nose. Bubbles of snot catch in my throat and I cough, desperate for another breath. Doesn't he realize he's choking me?

Roughly, while still pushing my head down on the floor

with one hand, his fingers from the other grab the zipper to my dress, and yank on it to pull it down. The fabric on the front side of me doesn't give and cuts into my skin.

Feeling the cold air hit my skin, more tears leak from my eyes. I know what his intentions are, and if I could just relax and allow him to get this over with, things will be so much easier. But I just can't. How do I willingly accept this? How do I get out of this? What can I do?

Pain in my shoulder pulls me back to the moment—he's bitten me, hard.

"Chris," I cry out. "Please stop." Sobs break free; I can't stop them even if I try. What did I ever do to deserve this?

He grunts at my request and bites me again. "I always did love the way you taste."

In an instant, I'm flipped over, and he pins both of my arms over my head with one hand.

Opening my eyes, I stare at the blackened image of Chris above me. My ears start to ring, replacing all the sounds around me, and things begin to move in slow motion as my mental awareness shuts off the ripping of my clothes and the bite of the cold air on my skin. I know he's moving and doing things, but I don't know what. What I see is his hair as it falls over his forehead and sways as he moves. I see the outline of his shoulders, shoulders that I've hung onto countless times while dancing, riding on his back, playing chicken in the pool, and even while he kisses me. Random memories flash, and I focus of those in hopes of not making new ones. In many ways, I'm having an out of body experience as he forcefully shatters my soul and devastates me in every way.

Light floods the hallway, blinding me, and again, I close my eyes. I don't want to see him. I don't want to remember him. I don't want to remember any more of this than I already will. But someone's here, I know it! Someone's turned the lights on. Keeping them closed, I wait.

And wait.

And wait.

Floating.

That's what I feel like. His weight is no longer on top of me, and somewhere in the back of my head I hear men's voices. The floor thumps with what feels like dancing, or scuffling, either way it's the same as when Chris charged in after me.

Fear. It chokes me.

Not again!

Please don't let him touch me again.

Screams.

Piercing.

Desperate.

Mine.

Hands land on my arms, and I jerk away.

"I'm so sorry. I'm so sorry," I hear through the thickness. It's a woman. It's my mother.

Crying.

Wailing.

Not mine.

Sirens.

Tired.

It's like my body suddenly knows help has arrived and instantly my heart rate slows. The pounding of the beats dulls, and I drift in and out of consciousness. Everything hurts so much that nothing hurts at all.

Numbness.

Darkness.

Chapter
TWENTY-FOUR

WILL ASHTON

AVERY IS WALKING toward me, her eyes so focused on mine that my heart rate speeds up. People are calling her name and taking her picture, but she isn't focused on any of them—just me. Without thinking my feet start moving in her direction. She has this pull on me that I've never experienced before, and it's like we are two parts of a magnet that are constantly searching for each other. There is no way I can't not go to her. Emma's head peeks around Avery to see where she's headed, spots me pushing through the crowd, and her eyes slide past me to Clay. She lights up. A huge smile breaks out on her face, and just as quick as there was joy, her expression switches to one of something else: curiosity, regret . . . who knows?

I'd worried that Avery would be angry, but she doesn't look like she is. She looks determined to get to me, and I'm so thankful for that. Once I explain everything to her, I know she'll understand. She has to . . . her life is the same as mine, and rarely do people like us find real, genuine love. That's what I have for her: love, in its purest form.

Keeping my eyes focused on hers, the closer we get, I can see the tension all over her face and my hands tighten into fists. She doesn't like being this close to all of these people, and it's sending up every protective flag I have, but she's doing okay.

"Hang in there, baby, just another minute or so, I'm almost there," I whisper to myself, moving over to a spot on the carpet between the stairs and the roped off area. Once she's done and makes it to the back hallway, I'm taking her away from all of these people and this place. I need to be alone with her, just the two of us.

Somewhere in that minute, there's a blur off to the side. The guy who's been following them around comes up from behind her, grabs her arms, and starts pushing her. Immediately her face blanches, the panic sets in, and she closes her eyes tightly. With the force of him pushing her, she stumbles, releasing Emma's hand, and lands on her knees. Instead of hitting the floor completely, he's now wrapped his arms around her, crushed her back to him, and is attempting to pick her up and carry her out of the room.

Sweat breaks out across my forehead, under my hat, and every fight cell I have in me stands to attention just asking to be released.

A crowd instantly forms, the commotion around them intensifying, and people rush in front of me to see what's happening.

In the back of my mind, I know this entire scene is happening very quickly. And unless you know her, no one has any idea what she's experiencing right now, and all I see is red.

What does this guy think he's doing? I don't know him, but I know I'm going to kill him.

"Move!" The tenor in my voice is loud, and that along with who I am has people scattering. Clay is right behind me, and I pray to God that he's prepared to restrain me, because I'm not stopping until my hands are around that asshole's neck!

As we approach the side door of the hall, the guy shoves Avery through and the girls quickly follow. Security stops Clay and I, and although they can see how angry I am, they won't let me through. She needs me, I need to be there for her, and these guys won't move.

"Sir, you need to back away from the door!" The two guys puff their chests as if this is going to intimidate me.

"Are you crazy? Get the hell out of my way before I remove you," I snarl at them.

"Sir . . ." one yells, but is cut off because Emma pushes between the two of them and grabs my hand. I'm so worked up and about to lose my shit, I can't even hear what she's saying. Blood is roaring through my veins and ears.

As we push through into the hallway, my eyes zero in on Avery as she is frozen in fear and having a complete panic attack. She can't breathe, she's crying, and shaking all over.

"Let go of her right now!" I storm toward the guy. He still has his arms wrapped all the way around her from behind. Why isn't he letting go?

"Who the hell are you? And no way! Something is wrong with her," he snaps at me.

I look at Clay and he knows. He grabs Avery's arm, yanks her forward, and the creepy guy let's her go, not expecting the move to come from him. Immediately I slam my fist into his face, and he falls backward to the ground. I hear a few gasps, but I have no idea what direction they're coming from; they seem to be coming from everywhere.

"I told you to let go of her! You don't touch her, ever! Do you understand?" I point at him.

Leaving him on the floor, I turn around and see Emma trying to calm Avery down while Clay is still holding her. They don't understand; she won't calm down because she is being touched.

I glance at Emma and say, "I'm sorry" and then I shove her out of the way. More gasps come from around the room.

"Ash! What are you doing?" Emma grabs on to my arm and tries to pull me out of the way.

"Give her to me, Clay," I say calmly, shaking Emma off.

"Ash, you need to leave her alone." Emma sounds desperate, but I don't even acknowledge her, my focus solely on the beautiful pained face of the girl standing in front of me. Clay gently hands her over and moves to stand next to Emma. Pulling on Avery's elbow, I move her closer to the wall and away from prying eyes. Using my body as a shield, I block everyone out so she won't see them when this is all over.

Placing her hand on my chest, I put one finger under her chin, and say, "Ava." Remembering the name she gave me, and just me, her eyes fly open, and it's green to blue. She's still trembling from head to toe. I absolutely hate this haunted look in her eyes and I want to kill whoever put it there in the first place. I also now hate the color green.

"Ava," I say again and wave two fingers back and forth between our eyes. I can see the recognition in her face and she understands what I'm doing. "Breathe with me."

Tears drip down her cheeks leaving tracks in her makeup and as much as I want to kiss them away, I know right now I can't touch her, at least not yet.

This breaks my heart. This panic attack is the worst one that I've seen yet.

As the seconds painstakingly tick by, the rise and fall of her chest slows, her face relaxes, the panic leaving, but the heartache of the situation remaining. Her fingers on my chest tighten around the lapel of my jacket as she leans into me and buries her face in my neck. Loosely, I wrap my arms around her, bringing her closer, and tuck my face into her hair. I don't want her to feel trapped, but I so desperately need to hold her. She pulls her other arm in between us and snuggles in closer.

The trembling changes to shaking as more tears begin to fall. I can't even imagine what it feels like to experience this, and for it to happen in front of a room full of people—this wrecks me. I want to hold her and protect her forever.

Moving my lips next to her ear, so only she can hear me, I whisper, "Listen, I'm gonna take my jacket off, wrap it around you, and then we're leaving. I'm taking you home. Okay?"

She nods her head, sniffs, and then responds, "Okay." Her voice is hoarse and it grates across my heart. Leaning back from her, I tilt her head up so I can look into those eyes of hers and smile. This terrible moment is passing and I already know she's uncomfortable with the situation, but she is mine and I am hers. She needs to know this. Her hands move to wipe away the tears, while I pull my jacket off and wrap it around her shoulders.

"My girl," I say, wrapping my hands around her head and tangling my fingers in her hair. She blinks three times, sniffs again, and then gives me a small one-sided smile. I return her smile with one of my own and lean down to kiss her forehead.

Together we turn around, but I keep her facing me so she

doesn't have to see all of the people in the hallway. I know how she feels about these moments and the less she remembers about it and who saw her like this . . . the better. Her eyes stay focused on mine.

There are at least fifteen to twenty people standing in the hall in complete silence, just staring at the two of us. Emma takes a step toward us and I instinctively tighten my grip on Avery and shake my head. Avery feels the nonverbal action and steps closer to me. Emma stops, and gives me a small reassuring smile. She understands. I don't want anyone coming near her. I just want to get us out of this mess.

I look over at Mona, to the creepy guy standing next to her rubbing his jaw, and then back to Mona. My glare sharpens in on her and I say the only thing I can think about at this time.

"He's fired. Immediately."

Mona sucks in a huge gasp of air. Both of them begin to squirm and his face turns beet red.

"You can't fire me. One, you don't work for the label. Two, I don't have any idea who you even are. Three, I didn't do anything wrong!"

Emma turns around, stalks toward him, and slaps him directly across his face. Clay moves to stand behind her as this guy clutches his face in shock, and looks at her angrily.

"Let me tell you something, Scott! One, I told you on the stage that if you put your hands on her again you would have to deal with me. Two, you signed a contract and it explicitly states that under no circumstances are you to touch Avery Layne, ever! And three," she looks back over at me and smiles, "If Will Ashton says you're fired, then you're fired!"

He pales as recognition sweeps in. "You're Will Ashton?"

I raise my eyebrow at him.

Mona turns to face him and squares her shoulders. "I

hired you as a favor to your mother, which I am regretting more by the second. You broke the contract, which is a physical assault on Ms. Layne, and as clearly you aren't aware, Mr. Ashton here is a partner at the label, meaning you work for him, or should I say 'did'?"

His eyes widen in disbelief as he looks at me, and mine narrow at him. Taking one more glance around the hall, I look down at Avery—it's time to go.

"We'll see you later," I say to no one in particular, but to all of them as a whole.

On that note, I turn us around, take her hand, and begin walking toward the emergency exit. I pull my cell phone from the outside pocket and call my driver to come and get us at the northwest exit.

The air is cold tonight, but the sky is crystal clear. Even though we're in the city, stars are shining through. Draping my arm over her shoulders to keep her close and warm, one of her arms wraps around my back and one settles on my stomach. I love it when she touches me.

Five minutes pass and the car pulls up in front of us. I open the door for her, she climbs in, and I slide in next to her, placing my hat on one knee. Neither of us has said a word yet, and as the car pulls away from the curb, I tell the driver to take us to my high-rise. She looks over at me and I watch her eyes as she scans my entire face. It feels like she is tracing me with her fingers. It feels intimate and I reach out to her again. She scoots up next to me as I tuck her in and she moves to hold my hand.

Looking down at our interlocked fingers, my thumb rubs over the back of her hand. I loved her hands before, but now I love them even more. What they are capable of doing, the music that they can create . . . I'm spellbound.

Needing to break the tension and the silence, I ask, "So, how about some pizza?"

She looks up at me like I've lost my mind, and I smile at her.

Damn, she's beautiful.

Chapter
TWENTY-FIVE

Ava Layne

HAT WAS BY far one of the worst panic attacks I've had in years. I am so embarrassed and humiliated that I don't even know where to begin or what to say. My heart is still pounding and even though the car is warm, and I'm wearing Ash's jacket, I'm still shaking.

I don't know what I would have done if Ash hadn't been there. I can't even remember what I used to do before him. Granted, I haven't had this many in years—it's like something has reopened inside me and I can't shake the constant fear. Maybe I should go back into therapy. Clearly whatever I've been doing isn't working anymore.

I can't believe that guy grabbed me the way he did. Any given day, I can handle people touching my hands, arms, shoulders, whatnot—but he came up from behind when I wasn't expecting it, and I just couldn't escape the darkness from taking over.

When Ash's voice breaks the silence suggesting pizza, I can't help but to look up at his expression. Only Ash would think about something so completely off base to distract me from what's currently running through my mind.

"I mean, I didn't really eat much tonight and after watching you perform, I'm certain you must have worked yourself up an appetite. So, I was just thinking that we could throw on some comfortable clothes, eat some pizza, and watch a movie." I really don't know what to say to him. Not only is he the kindest person I have ever met, he knows how to handle me perfectly.

"I think that sounds great, but I'll need to borrow some clothes." I smooth the dress down with my free hand. It really is such a pretty dress.

He smirks at me—one dimple making an appearance—his eyes giving away his train of thought. Heat creeps up my neck and over my cheeks.

"There's no borrowing; you can have whatever you want. And for the record, you look absolutely beautiful tonight. Different," he trails off, appraising me. "But . . . wow. The hair, the makeup, the dress, I was speechless when I saw you. Although, I don't like the eyes."

A blush creeps into my cheeks and I reach across for one suspender, pulling it so it snaps back. "You don't clean up so bad yourself, and the eyes, well, it's all part of it. Curly hair and blue eyes is me. And I've discovered that on any regular day they make me look 'like that famous girl,' but not really. Not enough to stop people."

He doesn't say anything back. Nothing needs to be said. He understands.

Lifting my hand to his mouth, he gently brushes a kiss

across the brace where my wrist was broken. The tenderness makes my eyes burn and my heart swell.

As the car continues to drive, we fall into a comfortable silence, and it makes me appreciate him even more. His fingers play with the brace directly over my tattoo. Pulling the Velcro, he loosens it, slides it off, and stares down at my wrist. Streetlights flicker in and out of the backseat as the car moves down the road, giving him enough light to see it clearly.

Lifting my arm, he runs his finger across the second key and the fifth. The "B" and the "E."

His eyes find mine, and I know he remembers our conversation on the lake.

"Be." His voice is a whisper, but the word lingers between us, and a magnetic charge fills the air.

His eyes drop to my mouth and tiny flutters sweep through my stomach. Gently pulling on my arm, he closes the distance between us, and his warm lips find mine. This kiss isn't urgent or consuming, it's compassionate and healing. It could be seconds or minutes that pass, I'm not sure, but once the fingers of his other hand wrap around my head and into my hair, I surrender.

Deepening the kiss, he thoroughly explores my mouth, breaking free every so often to place random kisses across my face. I feel cherished and loved, and I know when it comes to him, I never need to be afraid.

"Sir, we're here," a deep voice comes from the front seat.

"Thank you, Ryan," Ash says, pulling away from me.

Taking my hand, we climb out of the town car and walk into a large, high-rise condo building.

"Is this where you live?" I ask him looking around at the posh interior.

"Yep. Clay and I were still living in North Carolina when the label first offered us a deal. We had driven into town to sign the paperwork, they handed each of us a signing bonus, and when we walked out the front door, the first thing we saw was this building. Headquarters to the label is a few blocks that way." He points behind us. "Some of it was still under construction, so they were selling the units at a preconstruction discount. We were going to need a place to live and saw this as a good way to kill two birds with one stone. Invest the money and get a home. Clay's condo is next door to mine, so we both have the same view. I can't tell you how many times we've talked about cutting a doorway between the two units, making it one large condo."

"Evening, sir." The security guard greets Ash as we walk by and head to the elevators.

"John," he nods his head and smiles in return.

"Don't you worry about people coming in? Staking out and waiting for you?"

He pushes the call button for the elevator and we wait.

"No, Clay and I pay for the security. We increased the monitoring of the lobby level, the stairwell, and our floor. And once we became more well-known, the builders were very accommodating in changing out the elevator to one that required an access key. Us living in one of their buildings being great publicity for them and all."

The elevator door dings and we climb in. I watch as he pulls out the key, inserts it, and hits the button for his floor.

"We have a doorman at ours in New York." My voice trails off as I take in a deep breath and look at the ground.

"Hey," he says softly, squeezing my hand, regaining my attention. "Just relax, okay? Everything is fine."

"I know. All in all, it was a really great night, I think I'm just tired—on an emotional level."

"I get it." He cups my face with his free hand and runs his thumb back and forth across my cheek. It's so comforting, I want to roll into him like he's a security blanket.

The elevator dings and he pulls me out. The hall isn't very large and there's only one other door. As we walk toward the one on the right, I assume the one on the left is Clay's.

"Just two units here?"

"Yep, about two and a half years ago, Clay and I did a little remodeling. We bought out the other units, had design plans drawn, and while we were out on tour had the construction done." He pulls his keys, and unlocks and opens the door. Black and tan fur comes barreling at us, and a laugh escapes me.

"Oh, hi, Whiskey," I coo at him. He rams his head into my leg and almost knocks me over. "Geez, buddy, I'm happy to see you too!" He circles around us, Ash pets his head and guides us into the foyer.

My eyes sweep up from Whiskey and pass over the condo before me. I'm shocked by the detail and overall ambiance of his home. This condo looks like it could be featured in *Architectural Digest.* Where his lake house is all rustic, this space looks more like a contemporary loft, but still accents his country roots, making it his. From the columns, crown molding, marble flooring, soaring ceilings, lighter coloring, and clean lines to the soothing shades of blues and browns, draped windows, plush throw rugs, and oversized furniture, it looks like him, and immediately I feel at home.

Stepping down into the sunken living room, my eyes fall to a far wall that holds all of the music awards he's won and framed images of his albums and concert tours. There are pictures of him and Clay that span their years together, and most noticeably to me, their days as the Blue Horizons.

Ash comes to stand next to me as I look at all of his successes across the wall.

"You know, I kind of feel bad for what I said to you about the music now." My thoughts turn to how I basically told him his new music wasn't any good.

Turning to face him, I watch as he runs his hand across his jaw, taking his time before he answers. "Don't. You didn't tell me something I didn't already know. I think the music, how I felt about what we were singing, it became my biggest problem." He looks away from me and back to the wall.

"I suppose we have some things we need to talk about, huh?" I lean into his side.

"Yeah, we do. I have so much to tell you, but most can wait until tomorrow. I have to say though, I wouldn't change a thing. You not knowing about all of this meant you got to know me for me, and not what I can offer you. Although, knowing you now, I don't think it would have mattered, or maybe it would have been different in some other way, but what did matter to me was no one's ever taken the time before. I have to imagine you probably feel the same way."

Taking my hand, he begins walking toward the hallway.

"Then again, had I known who you are, I definitely would have done things differently." He flashes me one of his gorgeous smiles. "So, I'm glad I didn't know. Don't get me wrong, the emotions I felt today when Mr. Lang introduced you were all over the place. I was completely floored by your beauty, starstruck, and embarrassed to think that I probably should have figured this out sooner, but I didn't."

"I agree with you. If I had known you were 'The Will Ashton,' I never would have let myself get to know you. Part of your allure was that I got to feel like a nobody with another nobody. Not that you're a nobody . . ." I blush. "But you know what I mean. So is that your real name?"

He laughs at my question and walks us into what I assume is his bedroom. It's decorated in dark grays and white with dark wood furniture and thick carpet. He has a fireplace, more windows that have treatments, and a huge built-in entertainment center. "Yes, it's William Ashton, no middle name. Everyone calls me Will. You and Clay are the only two who call me Ash. What's yours?"

"Avery Emerson Layne, but my friends all call me Av. It's nice to meet you, William Ashton." I smile up at him. I love the sound of his name.

Letting go of my hand, he helps me out of his jacket and tosses it onto a nearby chair. Being bolder than I have in a really long time, I reach up and gently stroke his cheek with my thumb. He tilts his head into my hand and his eyes close. Just knowing that my touch is affecting him this way makes my heart beat faster. His eyes open, lock onto mine, and I can't help but bite my bottom lip. His eyes drop to my lips, but he doesn't move.

Being close to him makes me so nervous, and not in the way that I've become accustomed to, more along the lines of good nervous butterflies, but at the same time I'm not nervous with him at all. I haven't been this comfortable with a guy since Chris—well, before things turned bad—but with Ash, it feels effortless.

Desperate to get this dress off and into some of his comfortable clothes, I slowly turn around and look at him over my shoulder.

"Do you mind helping me with the zipper?" I ask confidently.

"Ah, Ms. Layne, is that your way of asking me to take your clothes off?" he smirks at me and winks.

My eyes narrow and his smile grows wider, forcing those dimples to make an appearance. It's not lost on me that this is the same flirty Ash from the night we met. Only this time, his off-handed comment doesn't leave me blacking out and running for the street.

"Do you trust me?" he tilts his head as his eyes assess me.

"You know I do," I say quietly.

Silence fills the room and heat assaults my back as he steps closer to me. My heart starts racing and my breathing picks up in anticipation of him touching me.

Gently, his hands come down on my bare shoulders and he rubs them up and down. I gasp at the sensation and squeeze my eyes shut. Every muscle tightens, and his hold on me stills as I start to tremble. I'm trying to fight the ghosts, I really am, it's just so hard.

"Avery, who's behind you right now?" he asks, sliding his hands over my back to gather up my hair. Pushing all of it over one shoulder and to the front, his hands flatten against my skin and run over my shoulder blades to the top of the dress.

"You are." My voice is rough and strained.

"How does this make you feel?" He unfastens the eye hook, grabs a hold of the zipper, and slowly starts to pull it down.

"I don't know." I'm feeling so many things, it's hard to pinpoint one specific emotion.

He stops moving his hands. "Tell me."

I know what he's doing. He's trying to keep me in the present, here with him, by talking.

"Nervous." My hands are shaking, and I will them to stop.

"In a good way or bad?" The warmth of his breath brushes across my ear.

"Bad," I whisper.

He pauses.

"Well, that just won't do." He pulls the zipper to the bottom and cold air finds its way between us. Clutching the dress to my front, one of his fingers starts at the base of my neck and runs over the bumps of my spinal cord. My body likes this and goosebumps chase after him. He hums with approval.

Nuzzling his face, which is slightly rough, against my neck, he kisses me under my ear.

Oh my God. His mouth is on me.

Instantly, the ghosts disappear. It's not lost on me that all it took from him to release me from the roots of fear is just one kiss. One kiss to make them wither up and die.

Sinking into him, he molds himself to my back and runs his hands down my arms.

Time slows, and I memorize every detail. The feel of the fabric of his shirt, the press of the buttons into my skin, the softness of his hair against my cheek, the size of his warm hands as they run across my skin affectionately, and his smell. He smells so good.

Eventually, he pulls back. The warmth is immediately gone and my back chills. His hands drift under the fabric of my dress, and around to my stomach. I release my hold on it, and it slips off my body and pools at our feet. Wrapping both arms around me, he pulls me back against him so my head falls to his shoulder, and he hugs me tightly.

"Avery, relax." There's a gentle command in his words. I didn't realize I was still so tense, and I let out a sigh to release it.

One of his hands can stretch almost the entire width of my stomach and as he begins to move them, I decide his hands are one of my most favorite things about him. They move across my stomach, up over my breasts, back and forth across my collarbone, down my sides, over my hips, and up the insides of my thighs.

Time stops.

Over and over, he repeats the pattern.

He's loving me with his hands; he knows this is what I need. He's replacing old memories with new ones. New ones with him.

Turning around, my breath catches at how incredibly sexy he looks. His dark hair is sticking up, the blue in his eyes has darkened, his cheeks are flushed, and his lips are wet. Needing to see more of him, I start to undress him by unclasping his suspenders, pulling the dress shirt from his pants, and unbuttoning it.

He doesn't move. He just watches me.

Pushing the shirt onto the floor, my eyes catch his as I pull the white undershirt up and off too.

Ash is so handsome. The muscles, the lines, the dips, his skin, his coloring . . . he's flawless.

Reaching up, my hand falls to the middle of his chest. His skin feels like it's burning, and I love it. Deliberately, I drag my hand down the front of him and he trembles just before catching it with one of his. He moves my hand back up and wraps it around his neck, using his other to pull me in closer.

No words are said. But as his eyes lock onto my mouth, and he licks his lips, I feel as if that one move speaks volumes.

Leaning forward, he captures my mouth with his, and I've died and gone to heaven.

When Ash kisses me, I feel like I'm the only girl in the

whole world he's ever kissed. He's shown me a tender side, and he's also shown me desire. But right here, right now, he's on fire. There's a hunger to this kiss that leaves no question for how he feels about me.

His arm has completely banded around my waist, keeping us so close. His heart is pounding through his chest and into mine, and his other hand has wrapped around my head and into my hair, giving him the ability to position me any way he wants to . . . and he is. He's taking what he wants, and what he wants is me.

Moving my head back, he exposes my throat, and drags his mouth across my skin, tasting me as he goes. Both of us are breathing hard, and both of us are completely caught up in the moment.

"God, I could do that all night with you, but pizza's here," he gasps into my skin.

"What?" I freeze. "When did you order that?" And how does he know?

"I didn't. I texted John downstairs when we came in, and he ordered it for us. Makes getting food deliveries easier." He steps back from me, leaving his hands on my hips.

No! Stay close.

The doorbell rings; I must have missed it the first time.

"Help yourself to the closet. You should be able to find some clothes in there." His eyes drop and run over the length of me. "Or don't," he says grinning at me.

Leaning forward he kisses me on the forehead and then turns for the front door.

My eyes trail him as he goes, and my heart trips in my chest. The muscles in his back move gracefully as his arms swing by his side, and the dips that fall below his waist peek out as his pants have dropped to sit low on his hips. He's not just hot, or handsome, or gorgeous, he's something all on his own. To me . . . he's beyond word.

Chapter

TWENTY-SIX

WILL ASHTON

DIDN'T MEAN to get so carried away with her tonight in my room, but having her nearly naked and being allowed to freely run my hands all over her gorgeous body, there was no stopping it. And had the doorbell not rung, I'm certain that tonight would have ended very differently. In hindsight though, I'm glad we were interrupted.

After we ate the pizza, we curled up on the couch and turned the TV on. The emotions of the evening finally caught up to her, all the adrenaline wore off—from the incident and me—and she crashed. Within minutes, her head was on my lap and she was asleep with me running my fingers through her hair.

The straight hair throws me off, but just a little bit. Now the eyes, that's different, and relief settled in when she came out of my room and I saw they were blue again. She'd chucked the contacts, thank God.

At midnight, I scoop her up into my arms and move her to my bed. Needing a little more time to unwind, I wander back to the living room. At twelve fifteen, there's a knock on the door. Only two people come to my door, John from downstairs and Clay.

Sure enough, as I open the door, there's Clay, together with Emma, both still dressed in evening attire.

"Hey, guys. Come in." I push the door wider and Clay leads her in by the hand. They walk into the living room and sit on the couch in the exact spot Avery and I had just occupied. Whiskey climbs up next to Clay, and he chuckles as he pushes him back down to the floor. "Want anything to drink?" I ask.

"Nah, we're good," Clay says, wrapping his arm around Emma's shoulders. Emma's looking around, just like Avery did. I suppose it can be a little overwhelming to someone who hasn't been here. With the addition, the space is right around five thousand square feet.

I move to sit across from them in a big chair, and Emma looks at me.

"How is she?" she picks up a piece of her skirt and starts worrying it between her fingers.

"I think she's okay. She ate pizza, laughed a few times, and then went to bed." My bed, where I plan on going very shortly.

She lets out a deep sigh and relaxes into Clay's side. "Oh, thank God. I was so upset, and I've been on pins and needles to get out of that place and over here."

"What took so long?" I look back and forth between the two of them.

"Cora and I still had to take the pictures with the patrons who paid, we were stopped by a few journalist, you know . . .

it's never as easy as you want it to be."

"Yeah, I guess I do." Being delayed at functions is pretty much guaranteed.

"Will, I want you to know she's been different over the last month, and I know it's because of you. She hasn't talked about you, but it's you. It's like she's happier, looser, and maybe even brighter. People like her have a tendency to have this sort of black cloud that follows them around. I don't know, but I think the cloud is shrinking. So, thank you." She blinks at me a few times and then smiles.

Silence fills the room as I let her words sink in. I know I should take the compliment, but instead I feel slightly agitated. The two of them watch me as I bend over and pet Whiskey's head.

"What do you mean, 'people like her'?" I pin Emma with a slightly hostile look. Clay uncrosses his legs and then crosses them on the other side. He sees my mood shift.

Emma's eyes widen a little. "Just people who've experienced what she has. Has she told you about it?"

"No, but I've never asked." Never really felt like I could. Maybe it's time.

"How did you know what to do with her tonight?" Her brows furrow as she tilts her head to look at me.

"That's not the first panic attack I've seen her have," I say leaning back in the chair. Whiskey readjusts himself and curls up at my feet.

"Really? I haven't seen her have one in a really long time." Her hands stop moving, she's surprised.

I give her a small smile and decide not to divulge. If Avery didn't tell her, then it's none of her business, but on the flip side, it's not going to prevent me from asking questions.

"How long has she been this way?" I ask her.

"As long as I've known her. So, seven years now." She starts messing with her dress again, and Clay's fingers begin to move over her shoulder. She settles.

"The person who did this, did she know him?" I've thought a lot about what she might have gone through, granted I don't know the details yet, but I've been stuck on wondering if this was personal or not. Seems to me that would somehow change the victimization of all this.

"Yeah, he was her boyfriend." She looks away from me and frowns as some memory comes to mind.

Personal.

Shit.

"You're kidding." My hands clench into fists and I feel Clay watching me. I understand there are some people out there who want what they can't have, and tragic inexcusable things happen. But her boyfriend? The person who is supposed to love her? That makes this domestic violence. I will never understand how anyone could physically hurt her—she's so perfect.

"Nope, and they were together for a long time too. What happened to her wasn't a one-time thing; it was a long-time thing."

My jaw tenses and I swallow to try and push down the fury I feel at this moment. "Tell me."

"You have to understand, Avery's always been beautiful. For as long as I've known her, whenever she walks into a room, guys literally stop what they are doing and just stare at her. They don't just stare at her because she's beautiful, no, there's always a look in their eyes that says, 'more.' She's viewed as a beautiful object, a trophy, something to own and show off, instead of the kind, loyal, amazing person she is. In the end, that's what the asshole thought of her and he tried his hardest to make her. He wanted to possess her, and each time she didn't do, dress, or say exactly what he wanted, he got a little angrier."

Angry doesn't even begin to cover what I'm feeling. Sweat breaks out across my back.

"When they were in public, he would stand behind her, and squeeze her arms or the back of her neck, bruising her, and then later on he would laugh at the marks and tell her it's her own fault."

"Jesus." Her reaction to my hand on her neck at the airport flashes through my mind. Dread and pain slip in under my skin.

"Yeah, I know." Emma pinches her lips together. "But what makes all of this so much worse is that she loved and trusted him."

No wonder her take on trust is earned, not given.

She told me tonight she trusts me, and knowing what I do now, this trust means so much more. I need them to leave soon so I can climb into bed with her, and wrap her up in my arms.

"I know what you're thinking—why did she stay with him?" She's studying me.

"Actually, I was thinking how I could find this guy and end him," I grit out through my teeth and glance at Clay. He's tense like I am.

"He wasn't always mean to her, but the last time was just . . ." She frowns.

"What happened the last time?" Anxiety washes over me.

"She can tell you that." She gives me a small smile. It's an apology for leaving me wondering, but I understand—this is the part of the story that's Avery's to tell.

"What happened to him?" I ask as my fingers dig into the armrests of the chair.

"Nothing." She shrugs her shoulders.

What?

"How does someone like that just get to go free? Do you know if there were any others he treated this way?" My knuckles strain and turn white.

"One other, that I know of. A few years ago Avery's father called and told her he had gone to jail for doing something similar to someone else. I think he thought it might make her feel better to know he was behind bars and not out running free, but it did the opposite. She cried for him."

"Why?" Why would she cry for that asshole? More like good riddance!

"She loved him. She never wished bad things upon him."

"She should have pressed charges."

"Maybe, but her parents didn't want to do that. It would have damaged the reputations of both families. Small towns are funny about stuff like that, and in the end, she got out."

"So, the boyfriend and her parents betrayed her." Not one person, but three. The three most important people in her life. My heart hurts for her and I drop my eyes to Whiskey.

"You're catching on quickly," she says.

"Hmm." I don't know what to say. I'm so furious at those people who call themselves her family. No wonder she never wants to see any of them. It's not just the bad memories of going home; it's so much more.

"Talk to her. She'll tell you what you want to know." Emma's voice is calm and assertive.

Slowly, I suck in a big breath and bring my eyes back to hers. "I suppose it's time. I just didn't want to push her."

"Push. She's ready." Emma nods her head and smiles at

me.

"And, on that note, so am I." Clay breaks the silence and stands up, pulling Emma with him. She giggles and I smile at my friend. He nods his head to say good night and the two of them leave hand in hand.

Chapter
TWENTY-SEVEN

Ava Layne

CLICKING. THAT'S THE first thing that I hear.

No, typing.

Gradually opening my eyes so they can adjust to the light, I look across the room and see Ash sitting at his desk, working on a laptop.

I'm in his room.

I'm in his bed.

My eyes shift to the empty side of the bed, and yep, it's rumpled. He slept next to me. My faces flushes at the thought, and then I realize I'm disappointed I don't remember it.

The clicking stops, and I glance back at him. He's watching me.

"Good morning, or should I say afternoon?" He smiles a lazy smile, sits back in the chair, and runs a hand through his hair. It sticks straight up and I stop breathing at the sight of him. Red pajama pants, a white t-shirt, bare feet, and that just-climbed-out-of-bed look—where do I sign up to get this every morning for the rest of my life?

"Hi." I sit up and look around the room. There on the table is one of my travel bags. "What time is it?"

He glances at the clock on his phone, which is sitting next to the laptop. "A little after noon. Are you hungry?"

What?! I haven't slept this late in years.

I run my hand over my stomach, nothing. "No, not yet, maybe in a little bit."

"Cora came by this morning and brought you that." He tilts his head toward the bag.

"She did?" I look at him curiously.

"Mmm hmm. And Emma came by last night to check on you." He crosses his arms over his chest and a dark look passes over his face. This throws me, and suddenly I'm worried about what they talked about.

"Wow, I must have passed out hard." I remember being tired, but not that tired. Then again, I think his bed is the most comfortable bed I've ever slept in.

"You could say that." He smiles at me, tracking me with his eyes as I get up to go inspect the bag. She packed half of the things I brought to Nashville. Maybe she's as hopeful as I am that I get to stay the rest of the weekend.

His computer dings, and he leans forward to read what just popped up. I know what he's doing—he's checking for backlash.

"How bad is it?" I walk over and place my hand on his shoulder.

He immediately grabs it and brings it to his mouth for a kiss. "How bad is what?" he glances up at me.

239

"Social media."

He chuckles. "Well, it's not what you think. There are very few mentions of what happened in the hallway. The blow up has more to do with you and me dancing."

"Really?" Relief floods through me. People know I'm standoffish, but no one needs to know why. I've worked so hard over the years to try and prevent anything like this from ever leaking to the media. I had just assumed this would be front page news.

He goes to Google, types our names into the search bar, and tons of links pop up, along with quite a few images of us together last night. The pictures look very intimate, certainly not like that was our first time dancing together.

"Yeah, it seems people like the idea of you and I being together." He looks back up at me and grins.

I return his smile—I like the idea of us being together too.

"What are they saying?" I ask, walking back to my side of the bed.

He follows me, leans against the headboard and stretches out his legs. "Well, they aren't too far off from the truth. There's a lot of speculation about my disappearing act after Phoenix and your cancelled shows. What was it I read? Oh yeah, we were off on a secret romantic rendezvous."

I giggle and boldly move my head to lie on his lap, just like last night, and his fingers immediately start playing with my hair.

"I did hear about you walking out after Phoenix; I think the whole world did. What did they call it, 'Where's Waldo . . . No . . . Where's Will?'"

He snorts.

"Why did you do it?" I roll a little so I can see his face.

"I had to." He looks down at me and smooths the hair off

my forehead. "No one understands. Well, maybe Clay." He shakes his head and frowns.

"I'll understand. Tell me." I run my hand down his arm; his skin is warm.

"It all used to be a dream. At twenty, I knew what I wanted to do, and what I wanted to accomplish over the next ten years of my life. But somewhere along the way, as we started making those things happen, visions for the future became less clear. Now I'm thirty, and when I think about life ten years from now, it feels like it can happen in the blink of an eye. I panicked. Spring turned into summer, summer turned into fall, and every weekend as I stood on stage, my hand would go numb on the mic. The lights felt like they were pressing down on me, I've hated the direction our songs have gone, and by Phoenix, I was pretty sure my heart had stopped beating. I just couldn't do it anymore. I felt suffocated."

I'm grateful that he's talking to me, but it's upsetting him. Taking his hand, I place it on my chest over my heart and let him feel it beating. It's what he does to me, and he looks down, meeting my eyes.

"That day in the truck, you were right about the music, and I'm glad you said it. I needed to hear it from someone other than me."

"I thought about that last night and I felt bad."

His fingers stop moving through my hair. "Don't." He shakes his head.

"Why did the music change?"

He takes in a deep breath, his chest expanding, and resumes playing with my hair. "I think it's probably a combination of us wanting to make the label happy, thinking they knew what was best, and lack of time. We used to have all the time in the world to write great songs, but once the tours started, free time vanished. It was easier to pick a pre-written song than to sit down and create a number one hit from scratch."

I do understand. Completely. The girls and I have experienced some of this ourselves.

"So, what happens now?"

"Back at the lake when I told you I needed to take care of some work things, that people weren't happy, this is it. Clay and I have had several meetings with the label about our direction going forward. He's in agreement with me—we're not ready to give it up, but things need to change."

"Did I hear Mona say you are part owner of my label?"

He grins at me. "I did tell you I've made some great investments over the years, and Three Little Birds Records is one of them."

"That kind of makes you my boss." I scrunch up my nose with apparent distaste.

He throws his head back and laughs. I love that sound.

"So what did Emma say?" My heart rate picks up; it's my turn to do the talking.

"Not much. She did fill me in a little about why the panic attacks happen, but I'd like to hear it from you. All of it, if you can." His eyes scan my face.

I know I need to tell him, but it's so hard.

Hesitating, I take a deep breath, and he smiles at me to give me support. "Chris and I were born to be together." He shifts his weight under me, not liking how I've started the conversation. "He's two months older than I am, and for eighteen years, we were together just about every single day. Our parents were best friends, and they loved the idea that he and I would one day end up together, uniting our families once and for all."

242

"Sounds medieval," he mumbles, frowning.

"It wasn't, and honestly, up until he changed, I had the best life ever." I shrug my shoulders and know my expression shows my sadness. Staring up at the ceiling, I'm sure it's easy for Ash to see that I really did love him.

"What caused the change?" He looks at me with a genuine question in his eyes.

"Steroids." I hate this word.

Complete loathing drips across his face and he swallows to stamp it down. "Did you know he was taking them?" His hand runs down my arm and picks up my hand, lacing our fingers together.

"No. Not until after it was all over, but it makes sense. He wanted to be bigger, better, faster, and well, he was. Right around the same time, he'd started having these random episodes where he would flush red and completely overreact to the littlest things. He would get aggressive and have spurts of crazy violent behavior. Punching the walls, breaking things, throwing things, and every muscle would strain from his neck to his fists."

Ash looks out across the room, his jaw locked tight and his chest moving up and down with the effort of staying calm.

"He hurt you." His blue eyes flicker down to mine.

"He did," I whisper.

Shaking his head, he sits up a little straighter and pulls his hands off of me. "I'm so mad right now, but I'm afraid to be mad near you because I don't want to scare you." He looks away from me and his hands fist next to his hips.

"Ash, I'm not afraid of you. You don't scare me." I roll so I'm off my back and facing him.

"He didn't either, until it was too late," he grits out between his teeth.

"Look at me." His eyes find mine and what I see in them isn't scary. Yes, he's mad, but it's a protective anger. "I've read a lot of articles about 'roid rage,' and there's a consistent theme across the board. Most experts believe that people who develop it already had a tendency to get angry, and he did. I've never seen you angry, but even if you were, that's a normal emotion and reaction to things. His was just more, and it was like one day I woke up and he had undergone a complete personality change."

"Emma mentioned something about the last night. What happened the last night?" The blue in his eyes is darker, troubled. I hate that he feels this way, but love it at the same time. He cares. About me.

"I'm not that girl, Ash, so please don't think that I am. After a while, once I realized things were only going to get worse and not better, I began to make plans. I deserved better." Tears fill my eyes, and his expression changes, softens. "That was the night I told him we were over."

Beep.

Beep.

Beep.

The beeping doesn't stop as awareness sinks in.

Every movie and every story has it right—the beeping always registers first.

Light slowly filters in through the thinness of my eyelids,

creating a muted darkness versus an empty blackness.

I wiggle my toes and pain shoots up my leg.

Pain. Dull, but present everywhere, mostly in my heart.

I know where I am.

One by one, words and images are conjured up to the forefront of my mind, reminding me of the things he did and said. My already broken heart dissolves into liquid and its tears escape from my eyes. How could he do this to me? What happens now? Keeping my eyes closed, I lie here praying for a fast death just to avoid my impending reality.

I don't want to be here.

I don't want to do this anymore.

"Mr. Layne, we're sorry to bother you during this sensitive time, but since we can't ask Avery, we need to know if you have any suspicions of who you think might have done this to her?" a deep masculine voice asks my father.

"I'm sorry, officer, her mother and I have no idea."

What? He sounds distressed and convincing.

"In Kensington County, we take rape very seriously. The sooner we can catch and prosecute who did this, the better. Please give us a call when she wakes up."

Rape.

My ears start ringing and chills crawl across my skin.

"We will," my father assures them. "Thank you for stopping by." There's a shuffling of movement and the sound of footsteps as they leave the room.

I tighten the muscles between my legs and feel the leftover soreness. This isn't a new soreness—tender intimacy flew out the window between us quite some time ago. Chris takes. He's been taking from me for a while now, but hearing someone define it in such a harsh way has my chest closing in on me. I feel ashamed and completely degraded.

No. I can't think of it as such, and will not acknowledge it as that. I don't even care what that says about me or the false sense of reality I've allowed myself to believe. The joining of two people is supposed to be beautiful, and they're just trying to make it ugly. I don't want it to be ugly. And if I admit to it, then I'm admitting to the monster that he's become. For so long, I'd been hanging on to hope. Hope for us.

Us.

There will never be an "us." Never again.

An extreme sense of helplessness consumes me. I feel more vulnerable and out of control than I ever have in my whole life. Any last vestiges of strength drain from my body and I've officially lost all trust in everyone and everything. An unwanted sob escapes me and the machine starts to beep faster.

"Avery." It's my mother's voice. It's weak and pathetic. A creak from the door being pushed open bounces around the room. "Oh, sweetheart, you're awake." Instead of maternal concern, I hear pity. I don't want her pity. I just want to be loved.

Moving to wipe the tears off my face, my fingers hit a bandage where I expect my face to be. Wincing from the slightest touch, I can tell there's a lot of swelling.

"What is this?" My voice is almost nonexistent, shredded to a raw whisper by his chokehold. Swallowing, more pain slides down my throat. I attempt to open my eyes, but only one cracks open. I decide it's best if I don't see what's around me anyway and let my eyelid fall shut.

"Your cheekbone was shattered, and they had to put a plate in. But don't worry, they went in through the gums above your back teeth, so there'll be no scarring."

A gasp escapes me and my lip pulls. My lips feel huge. Running my tongue across the inside of it, there are the rough and foreign bumps of stitches. Moving my tongue to my back teeth, I feel the stitches there too.

Only my mother would be worried about physical scarring. Why doesn't she see the emotional scars are the ones destroying me?

More tears leak from my eyes.

"What else?" I ask, not really wanting to hear the answer.

"There's a lot of bruising and a hair line fracture in your ankle," she says softly.

Bruising. I'm certain there's more than that. Between the driveway, teeth, and fingers, I'm certain that I'm covered in bruises, road rash, scrapes, and who knows what all.

Tears.

Lots of them.

Other than the beeping, silence fills the room.

My fingers twist in the sheets as an overwhelming sense of worthlessness presses down on my chest. How is this my life? How could Chris think so little of me after all this time? Does he know what he did to me? Does he even care? I never want to see him again, and the worst part is, I warned them.

Attempting to turn my head toward her, it won't move; it's been braced. I feel trapped and my heart gallops in my chest.

"I told you and you didn't do anything." My voice is hoarse but accusatory. My throat aches even more from the strain of the emotions running through me.

"And *you* aren't going to do anything either," my father chimes in with his domineering, don't-question-me-on-this, lawyer voice.

"What?" They can't possibly think that I'm going to return to him as if nothing happened.

"The families have settled this," he says.

Of course they have. It's all about protecting the family names, protecting him . . . why aren't they protecting *me*?

Lies. Betrayal. Abandonment.

It suddenly dawns on me that my perception of hospitals is all wrong. Hospitals are cold, sterile, and filled with sickness and death. Hospitals are supposed to be healing, but instead I'm lying here and feeling infected by the deceit and manipulation around me. Hospitals are cruel and unforgiving. Hospitals are where hope goes to die.

"Get out." The machine starts beeping even faster and my breathing mirrors the sound.

"What?" My mother is confused.

"You heard me. Get out!" Piercing pain shoots across my forehead and a moan slips out. My hand moves to cover my face; I don't want them to look at me. I don't want anyone to see me.

Oh, God, can't you just make it all go away?

"Come on, let's let her sleep," my father says.

The legs of a chair scrape across the floor as my mother stands up. Through my heavy breathing and with my face hidden, I listen and track their movement across my room. There's a soft click as the door closes. I'm left alone, and in more ways than one. Along with my misperception of hospitals, I've come to see who my parents really are. They're selfish and vain, and I want nothing to do with any part of them. I'm done being their pawn. I'm done with them all.

Alone.

Strangely, I find comfort in this, and I get a glimpse of what my life is going to be like after all this is over. I've planned my future and it's finally time to move on from what this will become—my past. No guilt, no questions, no more.

Two months. That's what I have left of this life.

Two months left to endure, two months for the physical wounds to heal.

Two months till New York and if I have my way . . . I'm never looking back.

White horror blankets Ash's face, before it turns red with fury. Sliding out from under me, he gets out of bed and starts pacing the room. He runs his hand through his hair repeatedly and squeezes his eyes shut. Stopping to stand at the foot of the bed, he puts his hands on his hips, and stares at me.

"He almost killed you?" His voice is deep with distress.

I sit up and watch him. "Yes," I whisper and he doesn't move.

"Who found you?" he asks.

"Our parents. I tried to get away from him. I had pulled my phone out and somehow dialed my father before he hit me from behind and I dropped it. He heard what was happening, located me through a GPS tracker, and my parents raced home. His and mine, they all found us."

Mumbling expletives to himself, he starts pacing the room again.

"You should have pressed charges." He glances at me, breathing heavily.

"Maybe, but I didn't. I never wanted to make his life worse. I just didn't want to be a part of it anymore. If anything, I've always felt a bit guilty."

"What? Why?" He stops walking and pins me with a shocked look.

"Because when the going got tough, I walked away. If you love someone, you stand by them, you fight for them."

"No, not when they are using their fists to fight you," he argues, running his hand over his face and then through his hair.

He's upset with me. Tears fill my eyes and drop, leaving wet trails down my cheeks.

Ash will never understand. There's really no point in trying to sway him otherwise. In the end, Chris's dad used their influence, money, and relationship with my parents to get everyone to keep this quiet. Chris was hauled off to a back room and paramedics were told an intruder attacked me. That money allowed me to cut ties with my family, move to New York, and it paid for Julliard. It's ironic really—because of him I was trapped and because of him I was set free.

"I don't want to fight with you. It was a long time ago, and now you know." I pull the blankets tighter around me.

He looks back at me, sees the tears, and instantly his demeanor changes.

"I'm sorry." He lets out a sigh and moves back to the bed. Climbing in next to me, he pulls me onto his lap and crushes me to his chest.

Silence wraps around us as my ear is pressed to his heart. It's racing, and it's racing for me.

"Emma asked me once why I couldn't just get over it—after all, it was only one night. But what she and everyone else don't realize is that it wasn't. Yes, that final night was traumatic and ultimately the end point, but the emotional pain of his behavior started months before. All wounds heal, and all wounds leave scars. Inside or out, they're still there."

"So what happens now? How do we make this better for you?" His voice vibrates against my face, and my ears stick on the "we." My heart smiles.

"'Never let yesterday use up too much of today.'" I've always loved this.

"What?" He's confused.

"It's a quote. What happened to me yesterday could be the same thing that happens tomorrow, hypothetically speaking, but I can't let it consume everything I do from day to day. I just can't live that way. I'm always going to have anxiety. Being touched in certain places causes flashbacks and fear. I think of myself being similar to say someone who has a fear of spiders or snakes. Put them in a room with either one of those and what do you think is going to happen?"

"Snakes and the fear of being touched are two completely different things. One is avoidable and one is not." He loosens his bear hug hold on me, and relaxes a little more.

"I know it's irrational, and I've tried to make it better . . . I have. But it's like my mind and my body disconnect from each other and everything goes black. I don't want to feel this way. Believe it or not, I used to be a very huggy person. I would hug friends, family, just about anyone." I pull back and look at his face.

"Well, if you must know, back in the hallway, when you wrapped your arms around me, I was elated. Feel free to hug me as much as you want." He gives me a lopsided smile, complete with one dimple.

"Thank you, Ash, again, for what you did for me last

night, and well, for all the nights. For what it's worth, I am so much better than I used to be, and look at me now. I'm sitting on your lap, with your arms around me." I grin at him.

"I want to kiss you." His eyes drop to my lips.

"Then kiss me," I state brazenly.

Wasting no time, he wraps his hands around my head, licks his lips, and pulls my face to his.

Immediately on contact, both of us let out a sigh, a release of sorts from the tension over the last half hour. His fingers tangle in my hair, his thumbs caress my cheeks, and I lean into him.

This kiss isn't hungry, but filled with a passion that makes me feel treasured, adored. The way his lips move, and the way his tongue dances with mine, it leaves me breathless and still wanting more.

"I love the way you taste," he says against my lips, moving his to the corner of my mouth and then my cheek.

"But I haven't brushed my teeth." I inwardly cringe.

"Can't tell," he says, laying his face next to mine. His eyelashes brush back and forth across my temples as he blinks and wraps his arms around me to hold me.

"Stay with me this weekend," he says in my ear, giving me goosebumps.

"Thought you'd never ask."

He pulls back and smiles at me. The anger and frustration are gone from his eyes, and they've lightened. It's such a beautiful color.

"Hungry yet?" His eyebrows rise while his hands slide down my back to my hips.

"Yes, I think I am." I give him a knowing, almost sultry look.

His eyes widen and his hands tighten on my hips, pulling

me forward slightly.

Leaning to me, his mouth hovering just an inch from mine, his eyes scan over my face and my heart starts pounding. A slow smile stretches across his handsome face, he pops me on the lips with a quick kiss, and then he tosses me off and over to the other side of the bed.

"Soon, Sunshine. But first, food." He chuckles as he makes his way across the room and out the door.

Chapter
TWENTY-EIGHT

WILL ASHTON

GOD, HOW I want her to be mine. Forever.

After spending a week with her in the mountains, talking to her over the last month, seeing her on stage, and hearing her tell her story . . . I'm in complete awe of her, and I'm amazed at how she lives her life, despite everything that happened to her. In fact, all those things that have made her imperfect, have made her the perfect imperfection to me.

"Come to the show tonight." I look at her across the couch.

"What show?" She sits up a little straighter, giving me her full attention.

After lunch, we found ourselves on the couch flipping through the channels, as well as watching the comments about us pop up on Twitter.

"It's a last-minute gig that will be announced at three. The venue isn't large; it'll sell out pretty quickly. According to the label, album sales have dropped, and they think I need to make an appearance. So, I agreed to do this show under duress, but with two conditions. One, it's a small show, and two, we do more songs as a throwback tribute to Blue Horizons. They agreed." I wouldn't do the show otherwise. Some of our current songs I don't ever want to do again.

"I wouldn't be anywhere else" she says, smiling wickedly at me. "It's been a while since I've seen you perform."

"That's right—you're an original groupie." I grin at her, nudging her foot that's closest to me.

She huffs and looks over to the wall with the awards and albums. She grows quiet as she looks at each one.

"How did you come up with the name Blue Horizons?"

It's funny—very few people have ever asked me that question. It's always, "How did you get started?" or "When did you get your big break?" Never much about the meaning of the name. On the opposite wall, there's a large framed photograph of the Smokey Mountains. The image is very similar to the one my grandfather had on the wall. It grounds me when I see it and almost always makes me miss the lake.

"Living a life in the Appalachians isn't all it's cracked up to be. Towns are generally small, the economy tends to drift toward the lower income side, and it can limit your options and make you feel trapped. The mountains are looming giants, and while magnificent, can become stifling. They are all-consuming and inescapable. Even from the highest peak, there's only the rise and fall of the mountains, surrounded by blue horizons, as far as the eye can see. Clay and I used to talk incessantly about what we thought life was like beyond the blue horizons—that was our dream—and naming the band after it just reminded us daily of what we were aiming for." In a way, just talking about it reignites that dream. The dream to create amazing music for the world to hear.

"I think it's a great name." She's watching me and it feels like she's touching me, even though she isn't, which is probably a good thing. Just the thought of last night with her hands on me, and her skin against mine has me adjusting my pants, and I'm not sure if I have the willpower to walk away again. Especially when I don't want to.

"We should probably get dressed. I've got to be at the venue in a little bit," I say dragging my eyes off of her very tempting body and back to her flushed face. Damn, she read my mind.

"Sounds good to me; lead the way."

There's a promise in the suggestive way she speaks those words. A promise that I fully intend to have her keep later tonight.

Walking onstage for the sound check, the entire crew goes silent. Some of them I've met with over the last three weeks to personally apologize. After their years of dedication, I felt they deserved a more personal explanation than the one I'm going to give today. As for the rest, I hope I'll be able to smooth things over today.

I'm not necessarily ashamed of what I did, but I do feel guilty. For a lot of my team, this is their livelihood, and I'm sure I left them all wondering what was going on, and what was going to happen to them.

"Hey, guys, before we get started, I wanna take ten with you." I walk to the middle of the stage, and gradually, everyone comes out from behind the set and from backstage.

Taking a deep breath, it's time to man up. Clay moves to stand behind me in support. The theater is so silent, a pin drop would echo off the walls.

"I'm not going anywhere. We're still here, and we're going to give them one hell of a show. But know that things are going to change—change for the better. I appreciate all of you sticking by us, sticking by me. I truly do believe that what we do on this stage is fucking awesome, and I am super pumped to be back up here tonight." Chuckling rings through the air, and as I smile, they smile. It feels so good.

"Are we all good?" I ask. Murmurs of approval come back at me. "All right! You've seen the new set list, if you have questions, ask. Otherwise, let's do this!"

Whoops and hollers fill the air as everyone moves into place. Pulling my grandfather's guitar from my back to my front, I pop out the pick, and rip off the first chord. My eyes close, shutting everything and everyone out, everything but the sound.

Sparks ignite in my blood and race, chasing after the sound. The sound bounces off the ground around me and reflects off the ceiling and the walls. The sound is warm, the sound is comforting, the sound is *mine*.

Keeping my eyes closed, I strum another one, and a different current runs through my fingers and shocks my heart. Damn, I've missed this feeling.

People who aren't musicians will never understand. I focus on the tonality and how the vibrations feel against my skin. Yes, the sound comes from the instrument, but it also comes from me. It comes from a place so deep in me, I feel it with every fiber of my being. Music is my passion; it's my reality and my escape. I love how intense and free it is at the same time, and I love the places it takes me.

The tinkering of sounds from the crew as they make technical adjustments to the front of the house sound system filters into my auditory periphery, and blends with the chords from my guitar. The many changes in volumes, rhythm, and tone push the acoustics of the venue. To most it would sound like complete cacophony, but to me, it sounds beautiful. I love this sound.

Two hours pass as we run through the changes of the set and rehearse the throwback songs. With each one, the energy of the crew grows, and I know without a doubt that tonight's show will be magical.

Chapter
TWENTY-NINE

Ava Layne

’VE WATCHED A lot of performances over the years, and I've been to more concerts than I could ever remember, but seeing him onstage makes me feel like I'm at my very first one. The excitement and energy of the crowd, listening to him sing, it's all mesmerizing, and not once am I able to stand still. Wow, just wow.

When Ash and Clay walk out onto the stage, the volume of the screaming is so loud, I'm surprised the walls don't crack. Ash doesn't miss a beat though, further charming them with one of his dazzling smiles, and I feel everyone in the venue swoon.

With the band behind him and Clay next to him, I watch in awe as he approaches the mic, leans his mouth against it, and closes his eyes. The lights dim and the music stalls, silencing the instruments. With the only sound being the fade of the echo in the air, it's during this heavy paused moment that everyone knows tonight's show is going to be something else.

Being who he is and doing what he does, it takes a lot out of a person, and the only emotion I could single out through the multitude swirling through me is pride. I am so proud of him.

Clay's guitar rips off the first chord and the vibrations strike every person in the room. A collective gasp sucks the oxygen out of the air, and a rush of adrenaline shoots so fast through me, I feel faint. No, I'm exhilarated.

Back up instrumentals stagger in to accompany Clay, and slowly the lights come back on. The beat, the tone, the draw . . . it's intoxicating.

Hours click by as he sings and performs, and I allow myself to get completely sucked into the energy of the crowd and the allure of the show. I can't tear my eyes away from him; I don't want to miss one single thing. He isn't just a part of the performance, he *is* the performance, and everyone around him is a continuation of him.

Back and forth, he moves across the stage, and the crowd leans with him. At the mic, his right foot taps with the beat, his hips sway between lyrics, and he never puts down the guitar. I know he loves that guitar, but it's as if it's an extension of him. The way he holds it against his chest, the way he moves it from front to back, and how he handles it. More than once, I've found my eyes traveling to his hands. Those same hands that have picked me up, taken care of me, and protected me.

Tonight, Ash is in all black. Black boots, black jeans, a black t-shirt, and his signature black cowboy hat. Standing off to the side, I get a full view of him, front and back. He's already tall, and in these jeans, he's even taller, the strength of his thighs evident, and the perfect shape of his backside too.

Under the lights, it's also easy to see how much he is sweating. His skin is glistening and the back of his t-shirt is soaked through. As I watch him, thoughts of what might happen later drift through my mind, and my heart starts racing in anticipation.

"All right, ladies and gentlemen, I'm going to slow things down a bit. As most of y'all know, I recently took a little vacation, a much needed vacation. It takes a lot to get a man to break, and boy, was I almost there. So, a man's gotta do what a man's gotta do, and I'm sure glad I did. While I was taking a little time off, a few unexpected things happened." His eyes travel over the crowd and past Clay, until they find mine just hidden backstage. He winks at me, gives me a lopsided grin, and then turns his attention back to his fans in front. "For starters, I wrote a few new songs, and Clay, the band, and I would love to debut one of them for you now."

He steps back from the mic, and the crowd goes wild. I'm glued to my spot. Nothing and no one can pry me away.

Clay takes a step forward, a single light hits him, and he solos the opening bars. It's the same melody he played for us at the lake, the day of Ash's birthday, and I know I'm going to love it. My eyes drift back to Ash's. They're on me and heated tingles race across my skin. Listening to Clay, feeling Ash's eyes as they run over the length of me, my heart pounds with the electricity running between us. Ash's foot starts tapping the ground, his hips sway slightly, and he reaches for the mic when it's his cue.

I let out a deep breath I didn't know I was holding in, and my whole body shivers.

"Oh my God," Emma mumbles.

"What?" I say without looking at her, my eyes glued to

Ash.

"I knew y'all had something going, but I didn't know it was like that."

"What do you mean?" I glance at her and she's fanning herself.

"He's got it bad for you, and you've got it bad for him. Just watching the two of you looking at each other . . . wow, I thought your panties had caught fire. I'm happy for you, Av." She squeezes my arm.

"Thanks." Every part of me feels warm and tingly, suffused with a happy glow. I'm hoping that the direction we've been moving in is indicative of our future together.

Ash licks his lips and looks down at his guitar as he works it, just as Clay walks over to stand next to him. Together the two of them play, and the smile they share is one that holds a lifetime of friendship. It's easy to see how fluid they are together, but at the same time, it's easy to see how they're so different. Ash is dark, acoustic, and the melody. Clay is light, electric, and the beat.

The two of them separate and he steps back up to the center of the stage. He closes his eyes, rests his mouth against the mic, and I think it's one of the sexiest things I have ever seen. All thoughts move to his remarkable mouth. A mouth that's been on mine and no one else's in this room. I have beautifully intimate knowledge of how full and warm his lips feel pressed up against mine, the brush of his cheek against mine, what he tastes like, and what it feels like to be devoured by him.

I look at my phone and check the time.

I'm ready for this to be over.

I'm ready to take him home.

Chapter THIRTY

WILL ASHTON

T HE SHOW LASTS exactly three hours, and from start to finish, I give it my all and pour my heart on the stage. In Phoenix, I know that from a technical standpoint, we performed a spectacular show, one of the best ever, but tonight . . . I felt it. Tonight was off the charts! Tonight was one of the most memorable shows I've ever had. Maybe it's because of the break, maybe it's because of the music, or maybe it's because of her, but for the first time in a long time, I feel good. I feel like I'm right where I'm supposed to be, doing what I do best.

Glancing to the right, I see Avery and Emma talking just behind the wall keeping them backstage and out of sight. I've never had someone waiting for me after a show before, at least not one that I've wanted, and it feels so damn good. I've also never wanted anyone as much as I want her. Right now, right this minute . . . no, make that right this second.

She's wearing the same Blue Horizons t-shirt from the night I met her, a tiny little flowy skirt, and this time, black cowboy boots. Her gorgeous legs, her tiny sexy curves, and her wild curly hair all look like perfection to me.

My hands grip the guitar, wishing they were gripping her.

For the last month, I've felt the need to handle her delicately. Knowing what I assumed about her past, I've always approached her as if she's made of glass, but tonight I feel like a Brahman bull that's been let loose in a china shop. Using my hands, fingers, tongue—whatever's necessary—I want to watch as her eyes drift shut, her skin flushes pink, and she breaks into a thousand little pieces. Then, one by one, I'll put her back together, me and only me.

Just thinking about it sends blood roaring through all parts of my body.

It's time to end this show.

Looking back out to the crowd, I smile and the cheering intensifies. "I wanna thank y'all for coming out tonight. I know this show was spontaneous and very last minute, but the best nights usually are, right?" I wink and the crowd explodes, causing me to laugh. "Clay, the band, and myself . . . we've had an amazing time, and I think we should plan on doing this again real soon." I pause and look over to Clay as the cheering continues; he too is smiling from ear to ear. "Y'all be safe traveling home tonight . . . thanks again and take care!" I tip my hat, unstrap the guitar and hold it high as I wave goodbye. The band breaks into our exit ensemble, and relief sets in that it's over.

Walking over to Clay, he gives me a knowing look and smirks at me. He knows I had fun tonight, and we're back to where we used to be. He also knows that I'm headed straight for my girl. Shaking my head, I hug him tight, and hand him my guitar.

Moving more quickly than probably necessary, I walk straight off the stage and straight for Avery. Every part of me feels alive and bursting at the seams. My eyes zero in on her, and nothing else matters. No one stops me; no one even tries.

Anyone who tells you that they haven't thought about their life and what they want out of it is lying. Most at some point will give you the usual, "Sure, one day I plan on getting married and I wouldn't mind having a few kids," but no one really thinks about when this might happen. It's always down the road or later on in life. I too used to have these thoughts, and they were never "if" I was going to get married, they seemed to lean more toward "when." Suddenly, the "when" seems within reach and that excites me more than it frightens me.

With her eyes on me, they grow large as she sees the expression on my face, and she blushes. She knows what's coming, and damn, if I can't get to her fast enough.

Slamming into her, my arms wrap around her and pick her up off the floor as my mouth crashes down, locking us together from head to toe. Her hand lands on my hat to keep it from falling off and her legs wrap around my waist.

Backstage, cheering erupts around us, and I just don't care. She smells clean, like strawberries, and she tastes like candy. Dipping my tongue into her mouth, I just can't get close enough.

"We need to leave," I mumble into her lips.

"You need to shower." She scrunches up her nose.

She giggles and I pull back to stare into her gorgeous face. Damn, she takes my breath away every single time.

"You joining me?" I ask with pure intent in my eyes.

She tips my hat back a little, tightens her legs around me, and leans forward to press a soft kiss against my lips.

"Yes."

Chapter
THIRTY-ONE

Ava Layne

ASH HAD DRIVEN us to the show, so as soon as it ended, we bee-lined for the exit and ran hand in hand to his truck in the parking lot.

"You were amazing tonight," I say as he opens my door and helps me in.

"You think so?" He gives me a lopsided smile, telling me he already knows he was.

"I know so," I grin back at him.

Shutting the door, he jogs around to his side, climbs in, and quickly drives us out the back entrance. His hand reaches over the console, finds mine, and brings it back to his leg. My fingers dig into his thigh and he tenses under my touch. No words are said, and within fifteen minutes, we're at his condo, up the elevator, and walking through the front door. He leans back, slamming it shut, and Whiskey runs over. Both of us ignore him. Both of us know exactly what the other wants.

"I need to touch you, bad," his voice hoarse and filled with yearning.

My eyes drop down and look at his hands. They're tight-fisted next to his sides. So many moments with his hands flash before me: the gentle way he holds my hand, how he tucks my hair behind my ear, and after tonight, how he fingers the strings of the guitar.

I'm not afraid of his hands. I'm infatuated with them.

"I'm not going to hurt you . . . ever," he says, watching me, mistaking my silence for something else.

"I know." And I do, with complete certainty, that I never need to be afraid of him.

"Please, Avery." He takes a step closer to me and ducks his head down so the rim of his hat rests against my forehead. His fingers just barely run over the fabric of my skirt at my hip before he places both of his hands in mine. The heat from his body blankets over me, warming me, and my skin flushes in response.

"Okay," I whisper. A small gasp escapes him and his body stiffens.

"You need to tell me. Tell me where I can touch you and where I can't. Because, Avery, darlin', I want to touch you everywhere." His head tilts and his lips skim over my neck. Goosebumps run across my skin.

"Ava," I whisper, stepping even closer to him.

"What?" he pulls back, confused.

"I want you to call me Ava." Releasing his hand, I grab his hat and toss it onto the hall table. His hair is wet with sweat and sticks up everywhere.

He licks his lips. "Why? I know your real name now."

My hand drifts over the side of his face, down his neck,

and settles on his chest. His heart is pounding through his shirt, and it feels so vibrant, so strong. "Because when I'm with you, I don't feel like the Avery I've become. I really like how I feel with you, I feel like I'm me, and I haven't truly been me for a long time."

He regards me for a few seconds as he thinks about this, his blue eyes searching mine. "Ava it is then."

Bending over, his hand finds my calf and slides up to the back of my knee. He lifts it, grabs the heel of my boot, and pulls it off, dropping it to the floor. Grabbing my other knee, he does the same, and kicks his off next to mine.

Standing in front of me, I look him over from head to toe. The t-shirt pulls just enough across the muscles of his chest to highlight his strength, and it tapers down to show off his narrow hips that just barely hold up these black jeans. Heat rushes up to the edge of my skin.

"Ash is a good name for you," my words barely a whisper. His fingers touch my chin, and he tilts my head back so he can watch my lips. "Whenever I'm near you, I feel like I'm burning up from the inside out . . . only to be left as ashes."

He doesn't say anything, but his eyes darken and drink me in. I suck in a breath of air reminding myself to breathe.

Pulling on my arm, he slips his hand in mine as he walks us past the living room, down the hall, through his bedroom, and into the bathroom.

Dropping my hand, he reaches into the shower and turns the water on. There are two shower heads, and steam quickly floats across the ceiling, making us warmer than we already are.

Facing me, he reaches behind his head and grabs his t-shirt, pulling it off. Golden skin . . . lots of it. Right in front of me. My heart rate picks up.

His eyes drop to the front of my shirt, and he skims his fingers across my breasts and over the band name. "I really like you wearing this, but I'm gonna like it better on the floor." Gently, he grabs the hem and drags it up my body and off. Stepping closer, he reaches around to find the zipper of the skirt, and pulls it down. The skirt drops, leaving me in my bra and panties.

"You are so beautiful." His eyes travel over every inch of me and my body flushes at his appreciation.

Reaching for his pants, my fingertips slide under the waistband as I pop the buttons of the fly. Grabbing the denim on his slim hips, I pull and they slide down his legs. He kicks them off, leaving him in a pair of tight, black boxer briefs.

He's breathing hard, I'm breathing hard, and not one part of me is nervous about what's about to happen. In fact, I'm pretty sure if something doesn't happen soon, I'm going to combust.

Stepping up on my tiptoes, I grab him by the back of the neck, and that's all the invitation he needs. His mouth smashes down on mine and the few pieces of clothing we were wearing instantly disappear.

His hands run up and down and over every part of me, feeling me, memorizing me, branding me, and I do the same to him. Hard lines, lots of muscle, and incredibly delicious, hot skin. Tangling my fingers in his hair, his fingertips pull my hips into his, and I moan at the sensation of his excitement pressed into my stomach. I'm doing this to him, me, and I want more. My mouth falls to his neck, and salt from the sweat reminds me why we're in here in the first place.

Pulling away from him, he groans in protest.

"No." He tightens his hold on me and I giggle.

I reach for the shower door, and he reluctantly lets me go, his hair falling over his forehead and blue eyes tracking my every move.

"You'll feel better once you're clean," I grin at him.

"I'll feel better once I'm buried deep inside of you," he throws back at me.

Oh my.

His words cause an instant visceral reaction and my eyes drop to take him and his impeccable body in. He chuckles and pushes me into the shower.

He steps under one shower head, I step to the other, and both of us stare as we wash away all evidence of tonight's show.

How did I get so lucky to be here, with him, right now? Tears burn my eyes and I close them to hide the emotion. Tilting my head back, the warm water runs over me and washes away the vulnerability. Now is not the time or place for this.

Catching me by surprise, Ash's hands slide over my head, under my chin, and gently, he caresses my throat before wrapping them loosely around the back of my neck and settling them on the tops of my shoulders.

My eyes fly open. He's watching and waiting for my reaction, but my skin burns for him with an inexplicable craze. I know he's worried about me slipping from now to then, but he doesn't need to. I'm here, and I want him. All of him.

With steam whirling around us, and the scent of soap lingering in the air, I look up at him through my wet eyelashes and swallow.

"Ash."

His eyebrows raise just a little in question and he licks his lips.

"More. Lots more. Touch me. Everywhere. I don't just want it, I need it." My words are throaty, laced with a longing that's just for him, and he squeezes my shoulders in response.

Dropping his eyes, he follows his hands as they slide with the water and move over my collar bones, and down to cup my breasts. His thumbs swipe back and forth, causing every muscle in my stomach to constrict. From there, they glide over my ribcage, and onto my hips. One settles on my outer thigh, and the other travels to explore the more intimate parts of me.

My toes curl into the water pooling at our feet in an attempt to grip the travertine. It's been so long since anyone has touched me, and it feels so good to be touched by him.

Him.

Only him.

Reaching up, I cup his face and rub my thumb over his bottom lip. His eyes are hooded and dark, his cheeks are dotted red, and it's obvious what he's doing to me has him as affected as I am.

Bending over, his lips land on mine at the exact moment his fingers sink inside. Grabbing on to his arm for balance, I gasp at the sensation as he begins to make love to me with his fingers and his mouth . . . at the same time.

Sensory overload.

The warmth of the water. The burn of his skin. The taste of his tongue. The determination of his hands. The feel of his heart. The losing of mine. I surrender to him and fall into a trance of complete and utter bliss.

Backing me up against the wall, his hands grab my waist, and he lifts me off the ground. I wrap my legs around him, and he leans forward, bracing me in with his hips. One of his arms falls over my head to support himself, and the other under my butt to hold my weight.

Never breaking eye contact, he gently shifts my body and lowers me to exactly where we both need me to be. My head falls back against the wall and his face falls into my neck. A moan slips out at the pleasure he's giving me, and his fingertips dig in as he begins to rock back and forth.

Back and forth.

Never in my life have I felt anything as moving and earth-shattering as this. He fully imprints himself on me, and I feel ravished, cherished, and loved. From the beginning to the end, the entire experience elicits emotions so raw and so real, I cling to him as tightly as I can as my heart swells and bursts into thousands of tiny sparkling pieces. How I'll ever be able to find them all again, I don't know. I don't even know if I want to.

I am in love with him, and this just cemented his life to mine.

Laying my head on his shoulder, my arms wrapped around him, neither one of us moves. I think if I could stay like this with him forever . . . I would.

Something in his room makes a noise and wakes me.

Cracking my eyes open, I look at the clock and see it's eight thirty. A groan rumbles through me; I've only been sleeping for two hours. I roll over on to my side. Soreness, that's what I feel, and I decide it's a good thing, smiling to myself.

Ash either has a very healthy appetite for sex, or a very healthy appetite for me, or both. Not that I'm complaining. I would repeat the hours we spent together last night any time. The buzz goes off again, and I reach over him, feeling along the nightstand to find it.

It's his phone. No, it's mine. Oh, I don't know, phones all feel the same. Picking it up, a text from Juliet is lit up across the screen.

Juliet: Once she leaves, come back over, we missed you this morning.

Sitting up in bed, I reread the text as my heart starts pounding in my chest. I can't be reading this clearly, but I am. I know it. The screen goes black and I freeze.

Once she leaves. She knows I'm still here. I know there were tweets and photos of me taken at his show last night, but still. How much does she know about me? Did he tell her about us? And if so, how is she okay with him being with another girl? Nausea instantly hits my stomach.

Come back over. This implies that they've been together recently, real recently. Like spent-Thanksgiving-together recently. Tears blur my eyes. I'm so confused.

We missed you this morning. I don't know how to take this. Clearly, he sleeps there, and frequently, if he's missed. *We.* Is she talking about the little boy he has as his wallpaper? Oh, God. Is this even his home, or is it just where he takes girls he meets?

Suddenly, flashbacks of Chris and his spring break affair come to mind. I found out about that too by text, and I can't believe that the past is repeating itself.

Slipping out of bed, I tiptoe over to the closet door and

open it. It's only half full, and not because the other half is meant for someone else, but because he doesn't have a lot of clothes hanging in here. How did I not notice this before?

I feel so stupid.

Who is Juliet?

Looking down, I'm still gripping his phone. Hitting the button, I slide it on; it doesn't have a password. I open the web search and type in "Will Ashton and girlfriend" into the browser, and hit the images tab. There, as I scroll through, are hundreds and hundreds of pictures of him and the girl from the night of the benefit.

Oh my God.

Clicking on a random picture from last year's Country Music Awards, the headline pops up, "Will Ashton, escorted by longtime girlfriend, Juliet Brooks, wins Male Vocalist of the Year."

My heart stops, and tears spill over.

How could he do this me? How could he do this to her? How can she be okay with him being with other women? I know if he was mine, I certainly wouldn't be, but then again, I guess he's not mine and never will be.

With shaking hands, I close the browser and place the phone back on his nightstand. He's lying on his stomach with one arm tucked under his pillow and the blanket has slipped down to his waist.

He's so handsome.

My stomach clenches at the sight of him, and I hate myself for fully trusting him and allowing my heart to so freely become his. Somewhere in the back of my mind, warning bells should have been going off. After all, we started out as a lie; it makes sense that we would end on one.

Sucking up my pride, I quickly move around his room and collect my things. I have to get out of here before he wakes up. I feel humiliated enough without it being shoved in my face any more than it already has.

Glancing at him one more time, my heart feels like it's being ripped from my chest as I force it to silently say good-bye, and tiptoe out the front door.

The elevator comes, the doors slide open, and I step in.

On the back wall, there's a mirror and I gasp at the sight of myself. Swollen lips, color in my cheeks, tired but bright eyes, crazy hair. It's easy to see what kind of night I had, and staring at my refection, I suddenly feel guilty for trying to sneak out versus confronting him.

The doors close and I don't move. If I do, and the elevator leaves this floor, I can't get back.

Regret engulfs me and the weight of it bends me as I collect my wits.

Maybe the media is wrong. This wouldn't be the first time.

Ugh.

What am I doing? This is stupid. I can't leave here without talking to him first.

Running my hand through my hair, I suck in a deep breath, and hit the "open" button.

Taking the walk back to his front door, my heart slams into my chest. I'm nervous, scared even. I feel out of control of this situation and I hate it.

Quietly cracking his door, I'm startled when I hear Ash's voice, my eyes flying up to see Clay standing at the edge of the living room.

"What's wrong?" Ash asks as he approaches him cautiously.

What's wrong? It's eight thirty in the morning and Clay knows I'm here, well, at least he thinks I am. Oh my God. What if there's something wrong with Emma? Prickles break out across my skin; I should just walk in, but something deep inside is warning me not to.

"D-d-did you a-a-ask Juliet to m-m-marry you?"

WHAT?!

No, no, no! This can't be happening.

Ash lets out a rush of air, takes a step back, and tucks his hands into his pockets. He's thinking about how to best answer Clay, when he really doesn't need to—it's written all over his face.

Oh my God.

My hand starts trembling on the door. I so badly want to close it because I know what's coming, but I can't.

"It wasn't like that," he says calmly, shaking his head. The defense in his tone is apparently not what Clay wants to hear and his entire body stiffens.

"That's not what sh-sh-she says. Sh-sh-she says y'all are talking about getting m-m-married." He takes a step closer to Ash and his hands fist and flex at his sides.

Ash's eyes track the movement and his brows furrow.

"We did. If you'll just let me ex-"

Without warning, Clay's fist slams into Ash's jaw knocking him backward and I feel like it was me. I feel sucker punched straight in my stomach and I can't breathe. Ringing fills my ears and tears cover the burn in my eyes.

Forget the text. This is so much worse. He just admitted to his best friend that he talked about marrying that girl. Marrying! And recently!

Why is this happening?

Splintering grief.

Absolute desolation.

Obliteration.

Without even closing the door, my body starts moving on autopilot as tears drip down my face and onto the floor. One foot in front of the other, my feet take me to the elevator . . . which takes me to the lobby . . . and then I'm walking away. Away from the one person I thought was meant for me.

Chapter
THIRTY-TWO

WILL ASHTON

*S**HIT, THAT HURT!***

"What the hell, Clay?" Rubbing my jaw, I lick my lip and taste blood. I can't believe he just punched me. In all the years that we've been friends, we've never fought, and he's never hit me.

Keeping my eyes on him, his nostrils are flared, his face is red, and he's breathing hard. He's really upset over this, whereas I'm silently panicking over Ava.

I don't understand why she left. There was no note, no missed call, and no text—well except one from Juliet—but nothing from Ava.

Ava.

My face hardens as I stare at my best friend. Whatever. I can't deal with this right now. He's not ready to have this conversation with me, and I'm not ready to share. It doesn't concern him anyway.

For almost twenty years, we've been friends, and just like that, a fissure splits into the core of us. He's my family, and yeah, families get upset with each other, but to me, this is more. It's more than that. At least I now know what he really thinks of me. All this time, I thought he'd be happy for Juliet and me. Guess I was wrong.

Without saying another word, I turn, leaving him standing in the living room, and walk back to my bathroom to grab a towel.

The front door slams and the silence resumes.

I've never been one to cry, but damn, if I sure don't feel like it right now. To think I was so happy when I woke up.

Hands down, last night was *the* best night of my life.

Between the show and her, I'm not so sure it could ever get any better. Leaning against the counter and staring into the shower, images of us flash through my mind at a rapid pace.

Her smile, her touch, the willingness, the passion . . . I never expected her to be so responsive. It's been so long since she's allowed anyone to touch her, I was worried I would be too much for her. Nope. She wanted it just as much as I did.

Damn, I adore her.

Blonde hair, blue eyes, full lips, perfect body that fits so well with mine. My heart squeezes in my chest and I slide my hand up to rub it. Between her, Clay, and Juliet, I'm at a loss and just dumbfounded.

Breathing deeply through my nose, it's subtle, but the bathroom still smells like us, smells like her. I want to permanently fuse that smell into everything I own.

Squeezing the edge of the counter, I wrack my brain for what to do. I mean, what do I *do*? Again, I don't understand. The panic I'm feeling turns to worry. My jaw clenches and the muscles across my shoulders and neck tighten. Twisting my head back and forth, I flex them to try and dissolve the tension.

Did I do something or say something to upset her? Did I unknowingly hurt her? Sweat beads across my forehead, so I run the towel across my face. Taking in a few deep breaths, I need to calm my racing heart, pull myself together, and figure out what to do next.

There has to be an explanation. She owes me one after last night, and I'm going to get it, even if I have to track her down.

Walking back to the living room, I drop down on the couch, lean forward, and run my hands through my hair. I just don't understand. She was fully invested in us last night, and I thought we had officially committed ourselves to being something more, something deeper. I know I felt it. And I for damn sure thought she did too.

Shaking my head, the more I think about it, the more I'm certain this doesn't make any sense. Four hours ago, her head was on my chest, her arm was draped across my stomach, and she had completely tangled her legs with mine as she went to sleep. She was content, she was happy, and now suddenly she's gone.

The panic I'm feeling borders a little on fury that she would leave without, one, saying goodbye or, two, confronting me if something happened. She's not the type of girl to have a one-night stand and do the walk of shame. She's also not the type of girl to stir up a bunch of unnecessary drama.

Picking up my phone, I hit her name, and it goes straight to voicemail.

Voicemail.

Dammit!

Chapter

THIRTY-THREE

Ava Layne

I HATE TECHNOLOGY.

If I'd never picked up his phone, I never would have seen her text, I never would have walked out, and I wouldn't be reliving this heartache seven years later.

A stupid text message!

Eleven words that now have more meaning behind them than when I first saw them. Eleven words that have cut open my chest, ripped out my heart, and stomped on it over and over again. Had it been a simple *call me later* or a *I hope you'll come see us soon*, I might have reacted a little differently. But I think it's fair to say after hearing his answer to Clay my knee-jerk reaction to what I read was spot on.

It's been two and a half weeks since I left him in Nashville, and I don't feel even the slightest bit better. Over and over in my mind, I keep hearing him saying, "We did," and each time my heart breaks all over again. I can't believe he asked someone else to marry him and then spent all that time with me.

The front door opens and closes, and Tank launches herself off of the bed to go greet Emma.

"Who's a pretty girl? Who's a pretty girl?" I hear float down the hallway. My mouth turns upward in a smile and it pushes on my cheeks. The feeling is foreign; it's been a long time since I smiled.

Emma wanders into my room and sets down a large Starbucks latte on my desk. Just the smell has my stomach growling and me moaning. I do love coffee.

"Please tell me you are not still in here watching YouTube clips of him," she frowns at me.

"I'm not." I stare up at her guiltily and blink.

Over the last two weeks, I've watched every clip of him performing, giving an interview, and accepting awards. It's like a drug and I can't quit. The way he smiles, laughs, sings . . . I need it and can't get enough.

"Then what are you doing? Because I'm looking at your screen and there's Mancake front and center."

A deep sigh slips between my lips and I glance back at the screen. "I'm scrolling through Google images of him while I wait for the cupcakes to cool so I can frost them." She sits down on the edge of my bed and looks at the photo of him walking with Juliet, holding a tiny brown-haired baby. She frowns and then flips to another one.

Looking at these photos of him, he looks so different from the guy I've grown to know. In the pictures where he's by himself, he's smiling, but there's an apparent brooding and a ruggedness to him that comes across as standoffish. In the pictures where she's with him, he looks relaxed, there are permanent laugh lines around his eyes, and those sexy dimples are present more than they're not.

"You do realize how pathetic this is, right? You need to stop wondering and ask him about her. Clearly he wants to talk to you, so answer his texts! And you need to stop baking. If it's there I'm gonna eat it, I can't help it, and today my pants were tighter." She glares at me, and then her eyes turn sad as she takes in my appearance. I had accidentally thrown his t-shirt I'd worn after the benefit into my bag, and upon discovering it, I haven't really taken it off except to shower and wash it.

"Yeah, I know, pathetic, and next batch, I'll drop off at the studio." The thought of her not wanting anymore baked goods makes me frown. She's always loved them, but I guess I have gone overboard.

And pathetic doesn't even describe the person I've become. Work doesn't pick up again until this weekend, so I haven't been needed anywhere, Instead, I've been sitting in the apartment wondering how he's spending his days. Is he with that little boy, is he with Juliet, is he really even disappointed that things ended?

On the way back to the hotel, I opened Pandora's Box. I never should have typed his name into the search bar on my phone. Photo after photo, page after page, article after article. There are so many of him. In hindsight, I feel extremely stupid for not recognizing him sooner. Especially the first night at Smokey's. He even had his signature black hat on then. Everyone knows him, regardless if they like country music or not. But what broke my heart and continues to break it into a thousand pieces are all of the pictures of him and her together.

Not once did he mention her.

I would feel differently if she was some girl passing in the wind, but she's not. There are years of photos of them together, and after hearing his confession, I'm just sad.

Torturing myself, I did scroll through the pages, hoping to see him in photos with lots of women, and sure, there were a few here and there, but it was obvious they were with fans. All of the promotional and awards photos, *she* was in them. She is the one he spends his time with, and as far back as these photos go, she is the one his heart must belong to. Juliet Brooks.

But the images that took the pieces of my heart and pulverized them were the ones of him, her, and the little boy. Most of the boy's pictures are censored, but Ash is in them from the very beginning: from stroller walks to playing on the playground. If my guess is accurate, he must be around four or five now.

"Has *he* texted you yet today?" she asks, pulling me from my thoughts of squashed dreams of him, me, children, and a playground.

He's texted me every day since I walked out. Multiple times. At first they were urgent, then they were short and pleading, now they are determined.

"Yes. Early this morning he asked again if I would come spend Christmas with him at the lake house." Why he wants me there, I don't know. Shouldn't he be with her? After all, from the way that text sounded at his condo, he'd spent Thanksgiving with her.

Emma even tried to play detective for me, slipping Juliet into one of her conversations with Clay, but he refused to talk about Ash, Juliet, or me. He said it wasn't his story to tell, and that Ash and I needed to work it out on our own.

Maturity points there for Clay. And even though we didn't find anything out, it endears me to know that he won't gossip about his friend.

"Did you respond?" Emma asks, taking a sip of her latte.

"Not once, although that hasn't stopped him." And as much as I don't want to admit it, I'll be even more crushed the day it does.

I don't even know why I'm not texting him back. Me! I'm probably the real problem here, not him. He's been nothing but a complete gentleman to me. A simple question asking him to explain who she is to him would be sufficient, but I just can't bring myself to do it. What if he really is planning on marrying her? She obviously means enough for him to broach the subject. I'm just not sure if I can handle the truth when he means so much to me. I do feel horrible though, and that makes me the worst friend in the world to him.

Emma stands up and turns to face me. "Well, heads up, a little birdie told me the guys are headed to New York."

"What?!" I jerk toward her in the desk chair, almost knocking the coffee over.

Right then my phone dings and lights up with an incoming text. I grab it, and read it.

Ash: I'll be at your apartment in thirty minutes. You better be there and make sure you tell your doorman to let me up.

Oh my God!
Nerves. Excitement. Worry. Anticipation.
He's on his way here.

Sitting on the couch, my heart races as I stare at the clock. My knee is bouncing up and down and my fingers are working overtime as they tap a rhythm on my leg. I wasn't prepared to see him today. It's like I need to be in a certain mental state, and I'm just not there yet.

And of course Emma sprinted out of here, leaving me alone. She claimed she had to meet someone, and now here I am, feeling like I'm sitting in the lion's den.

How does he even know where I live? I don't remember telling him. Maybe Emma did. Ugh . . .

Twenty-nine minutes.

The doorbell rings.

My heart leaps into my throat, I gasp, and my eyes dart to the door. It startles me even though I knew it was coming.

He's on the other side of the door!

Taking a deep breath, I wipe my hands across my thighs to dry them off and calm them, and I get up to answer the door.

As I open it, my eyes drop to his feet. I'm so nervous.

Blood is pounding through my ears and I feel instantly sucked into his orbit. I'm in love with this guy, and it's been two weeks of complete heartache. I want nothing more than to walk into his arms and have him make it all better.

Slowly dragging my eyes up, I soak him in. He's wearing chunky, black, retro boots, well-worn designer jeans, he's wrapped in a navy pea coat with a navy and green plaid scarf tied around his neck, and topped off with a navy beanie.

His height, the lines of his arms, the thickness of his legs—all of him—my body hums with familiarity for his.

Settling my eyes on his, he's watching me closely with those gorgeous blue eyes of his that seem to pop out amongst all the navy. Brown pieces of hair are sticking out from under the hat, his face is clean-shaven, and his lips are red from the bitter cold outside.

Just the sight of him causes an ache way down deep in the pit of my stomach. He's just so much more than anything I have ever seen. I can't breathe.

With his eyes locked onto mine, he pinches his lips together, and rocks back on his heels.

"Do you want to come in?" I fumble, opening the door a little wider and hanging on to it for support. Tank runs around my feet, growls at him, and wags her tail at the same time.

"No," he says quietly, but firmly.

My heart sinks with disappointment.

Taking in a deep breath, his cheeks flush and his eyes brighten with an unspoken emotion. "I just wanted to come and drop this off. I know I could have mailed it, but it was important for me to give to you." He pulls a box from behind his back and holds it out to me. It's the size of a shirt box, and I'm confused.

"You bought me a Christmas present?" I look back up to his face.

He looks off to the side and swallows. "No, not really. But it is something that I wanted to give to you, and only you." He frowns through his words, and my heart sinks knowing I'm the one who's made him this unhappy.

Carefully, I take the box from him and hug it to my chest. He's wrapped it in silver paper and tied it with a red bow. A lump forms in my throat along with the inevitable sting of tears.

"Thank you," I whisper, trying to hold it together.

Did he really travel here just to give me this? My arms tighten around the box. I know he's not going to take it back, but I feel the need to grip on to it just in case. It's something tangible from him, and even though I have no idea what's in it, it doesn't even matter. This present means more to me than he'll ever understand.

Chapter
THIRTY-FOUR
WILL ASHTON

THERE ARE TEARS in her eyes.

Why are there tears in her eyes?

Is she crying because she feels guilty for leaving me? Is she crying because her heart aches just as much as mine does? Or is she crying because she feels awkward and doesn't want to deal with me at all?

I don't understand, and her shutting me out has made me feel terrible.

Shit!

Needing to put some space between us, I take a step back from the doorway and shove my hands in my front pockets. I don't trust them enough to not reach for her, and there's a good possibility if I touch her, I might never let go. Looking at the ground, I suck in another deep breath and then allow my eyes to drift up the length of her.

I wasn't going to—take her in with my eyes, that is—but

I can't help it.

I was only going to focus on her face, give her the gift, and leave. Looking at her affects me. It affects every nerve, every cell, and every atom in me. Can't she see what she does to me? I feel like a starved man that can only be nourished by her, and two weeks is a long time to go without food.

She looks like my Ava, and my heart breaks. I want this girl, and I want her for forever.

Her hair is super curly, her lips are glossy, she's wearing an off-the-shoulder pink sweater, skinny jeans, and her toenails are painted bright red.

Damn, she is so beautiful.

On top of all of that, she's baked something. She looks like home and smells like home, but yet she's not my home. My broken heart sinks to my stomach and is immediately consumed by something so much deeper than despair.

"Avery . . ." my voice is hoarse and my words trail off. It's not lost on her that I used her given name, and not our nickname, as her eyebrows rise slightly.

I have so much I want to say to her and so many questions to ask. I thought I knew how this conversation was going to go down, but now that I'm here standing in front of her, my mind is racing and it won't stop long enough to make a coherent thought.

"At any point—since I've known you—have I been un-kind to you?"

Her eyes widen, she looks away from me, and swallows. "No," she whispers.

"Have I ever lied to you?" I ask. I need her to tell me something—anything—as to why she left.

She tilts her head, a shadow crosses over her face, and she

pauses, contemplating her answer. "You lied about your name and who you are."

That can't be what she was thinking, and that's not fair. My eyes narrow and a streak of frustration pulses through me. My hands fist in my pockets.

"No, I didn't." I need a few seconds to calm my emotions, and her eyes on me are making it worse. I love her eyes. "The two people who mean the most to me in the whole world, my grandfather and Clay, both call me Ash. That's my name. I never led you to believe it was something different. And we both agreed to set our professional lives to the side."

I want to point out that it was actually her who lied about her name, but that won't do us any good. I'm not here to get into a pissing match with her; I'm here to give her the gift and try and get some answers.

She doesn't say anything, she really can't. In all honesty, we've moved past the name thing, so I'm not sure why she brought it up.

"Why won't you text me back?"

The shadow returns and her features darken. Whoa, I didn't think my texting her would make her angry. With every one that I've sent, I've spent an unhealthy amount of time staring at my phone just hoping she would respond.

Her eyes lock onto mine, blue to blue, and I hold my breath waiting to hear her response.

"What about Juliet?" she asks, punctuating the syllables of her name.

Juliet!

Is this the reason for all of the miscommunication and the silent treatment? No, it can't be. Juliet is . . . Juliet. Anyone who knows the band, knows her. She's been with us step-by-step since the very beginning, and there's no secret to our relationship. Her mentioning Juliet is just another diversion to avoid telling me what the real problem is.

"What about her?" I ask, suddenly angry.

She sees the shift in my mood and she pales. I'm confused. What's happening here?

"You know what? It doesn't even matter," she says with a resigned tone, dropping her gaze.

What?

Anger and disappointment swirl through me. Why won't this girl talk to me? It's been weeks and I've tried, I really have. Whatever. No more.

"You're right, I guess it doesn't matter." A defeated sigh escapes me. "I thought you and I were . . . something more. Apparently not." My lips press into a thin line and my head shakes.

Her eyes flash up to mine and tears linger at the edge. I hate those tears, but I hate how I feel even more—pathetic. I shouldn't have come here. I thought this would be easier; I thought I'd get some answers. I thought wrong.

I take another step back and memorize her beautiful face, one last time.

"Ash . . ." she says taking a step closer to me.

"Merry Christmas, Avery."

With my head down, I turn and walk down the hall, away from her, and to the elevator. How is it possible to be completely in love with a girl, yet so angry at her at the same time? Never in my life did I think I would ever be in a situation like this—and because of Juliet. That's what this is all about, right?

This just sucks. I'm thirty years old and pining over a girl that's made it crystal clear over the last two weeks that she doesn't want me.

Leaving her building, flurries drift through the air, and I look for Clay. He was going to come up with me to see Emma, but he got distracted on the way in and changed his mind. I don't know what it was, but it didn't matter, I just needed to see her.

And I did.

I saw her and she saw me.

It's funny, because over the last couple of years, I've felt like something was missing from my life, from me, and I always thought, "How do you miss something you've never had?" Because if I'd known what it was I was missing, I would've found it. Well, now I know, only it didn't want to be found. And now here I am, walking down the cold street by myself wishing I was anywhere but here.

Chapter
THIRTY-FIVE

Ava Layne

ATCHING ASH WALK away is probably one of the most soul wrenching things I've ever had to do. His hands are tucked into his coat pockets pulling it tight across his back. His head is dropped down just a little as his shoulders slouch forward, and his walk, which usually holds a swagger looks more stiff than relaxed. Every part of me aches to run after him and beg him to stay.

But I had to do it.

His reaction when I asked about Juliet told me everything I needed to know. The muscles in his jaw ticked as he grit his teeth, his brow furrowed, and he immediately grew angry when I brought her up. He made me feel like I wasn't allowed to talk about her. At all. How am I supposed to open myself up even more than I already have when he's keeping secrets? Why didn't he tell me about her? He should have over six weeks ago.

The elevator dings and Ash steps in. Not once does he glance back in my direction. As the door closes and it whisks him away, the silence in the hall surrounds me, mocking me.

He's gone.

I'm alone.

And with him, he took my heart.

My teeth start chattering as the cold draft in the hallway settles in under my clothes, and big, fat tears roll down my cheeks as devastation sinks in. I wish it didn't have to be this way. I wish it wasn't ending. I clench my hands and feel the gift. A gift he took the time to bring to me. Looking down, my heart leaps in my chest. It's wrapped so prettily. I hug it to my chest, clinging to it as if it were him. Turning around, I walk back into the apartment and quietly close the door.

I didn't think seeing him would feel like this, and I feel ruined. I mean, I hadn't forgotten how handsome he is—I've been staring at his photos for weeks now—but seeing him in person, being sucked into his magnetism, no photo will ever do him justice. A hollowness moves into my chest and it makes me feel like I can't breathe.

Tank circles my legs as we make our way back to my room. Even she was happy to see him, standing there wagging her tail. Traitor.

Sitting down on my bed, I hold the gift up to my nose and smell it. I know it's irrational, but just to get a whiff of his cologne, something, would make me feel better. Only there's nothing, just the smell of paper, so I lower it back to my lap.

Staring at the present, part of me doesn't want to open it. I know that's crazy, but if I leave it unopened, it's like there is still unfinished business between the two of us . . . but deep down, I know I'm not ready for us to be over. The other part of me, however, is really excited to see what's in the box. After all, he hand-delivered it. Maybe he was already in town, or maybe not, either way, he took the time to come here, and I do find that very, *very* endearing.

Gently shaking it, something hard hits the edges, and as curiosity wins out, I carefully slide the bow off as to not disrupt its shape and set it on the bed. My finger carefully slips under the edge of the paper to pull the tape free, but not rip it. The silver paper is thick, perfectly cut, and it's beautiful.

I officially love silver because he picked this out for me.

Setting the paper next to the bow with trembling fingers, I grip the lid of the white box and my heart begins to pound. I can't pinpoint why I'm so anxious to open this, but I am.

Lifting the lid, there sitting on top of red tissue paper is a letter folded in half with my name scribbled in his handwriting. My stomach squeezes. I wasn't expecting a letter too.

Dear Ava,

I had hoped to be giving you this next week at the lake, but when I was honest with myself, I realized you were never going to come.

I've thought about all the different ways to give you this, I even tried to change my mind, but in the end, I really want you to have it.

Next to my family and my grandfather's guitar, this is the only other thing in this world that holds any value to me. You shared parts of your inner world with me, and I want to share mine with you. This is the story of my life.

My grandfather brought this cheap notebook home one day just before he died. He said, "Every great musician has a place where they keep their thoughts and write their songs, and I thought this could be yours. Create the magic, kid, and show me what you've got." He always did believe in me.

I've been writing in this notebook since I was thirteen. Every phase of my life has inspired different songs, from his death to meeting you, it's all in here. Some we went on to record, and others we didn't.

You once mentioned how the lyrics of the songs from the days of Blue Horizons meant something to you, and I'm hoping as you read between the verses and lines, you'll find the heart of me, because I want to give it to you.

I'm not sure why you left, I wish you'd tell me why. For what it's worth, I really wanted things to turn out differently.

Merry Christmas.

Love,

Ash

Oh my.

Staring at the letter, I read it again, taking in each word, and more tears swell and fall. This letter is perfect, this letter is for me, this letter is him. The guy I just let walk out of my life.

Biting my lip, I look at the wrapped book. I know what he's giving me, and he's right—as a musician and songwriter, that one place where you pour your heart out is one of the most important things in the world. It's priceless and not something easily shared.

Tearing off the tissue paper, there in the middle of the box, is an old composition book that looks worn and full. It's tied shut with a string, and under the string is a picture of us. It was taken at the benefit when we were dancing.

Untying the string, I lift up the 5x7 photo and absorb every detail. We look stunning, dressed in formal attire, but it's more than that. It's the way we're standing so close together, looking at each other. It's the way he's kissing the back of my hand, so affectionately. It's the love pouring out of his eyes as he regards me. It's easy to see how the world latched on to the idea of us being a couple. We look enchanting and it's hopeful.

Hope.

Not long after I moved to New York, I was walking down the street and as I passed a stationary store, there was a canvas print in the window that said, "Hope shines brightest in the darkest moments," and I felt that was written just for me. I bought it and it hangs on the wall in my room.

Hopeful—that's how Ash's made me feel over the last six weeks.

Up until that weekend at the lake, I was fine with my life. I was content with my friends, the success of our career, and to me, it was pretty much perfect. But he came roaring in and showed me what was missing.

I'm not sure if I ever thought I could be with someone again. No one wants a damaged girl, or a girl they can't touch. But Ash, he saw past all of it, and in those darkest moments, he was the light.

Doubt slips in under my skin and my stomach starts to ache. Maybe I've read him and this entire situation wrong. Maybe I jumped to conclusions when I should have been asking for an explanation. Maybe I made a mistake.

Pushing the uncertainty from my mind, I crawl under my covers with his black and white notebook and open the cover. There on the inside is a short inscription from his grandfather, and I run my fingers over the three little words that must have meant the world to him.

Page after page is filled with ideas, lyrics, musical notes, and songs. Some are complete, and some are fragments, but he's right—it all tells the story of him. His handwriting, the depth of his words, the talent, it's easy to see his personal as well as professional growth as the pages turn.

In many ways, people might think this is more like a diary or a journal, but really it's so much more than that. These aren't just words; they are his inner feelings all tied to a sound. A sound that isn't just heard, but felt. Felt in the very soul of him and then shared with the world.

I love this book. Coffee stains, tears, and laughter, it's all in here, and it's all him.

I'm beyond speechless that he would give me this. Something so dear and irreplaceable. It speaks volumes about him, and it speaks volumes about how he truly feels about me.

Hope again blooms in my chest, whereas just a few minutes ago I thought it was withering and dying. Hope that maybe I'm not in this alone—that he feels what I feel—and hope that maybe everything will turn out all right.

Flipping to the end, I read over the last couple of pages. His words go from screaming desperation, which I assume was his mindset last summer, to finding peace, which I'd like to think is because of me. There are bits about soulmates, love, and even the beginnings of a song called "Blue to Blue."

But it's the last page that causes me to tremble. It's the last page that takes my breath away. It's the last page that finally tells me everything I need to know.

It's a page titled "Be."

And there in the middle are two words, and only two words . . .

Be mine.

Chapter
THIRTY-SIX

Ava Layne

HE NIGHT AFTER Ash dropped off his amazing gift, I sent him a text to tell him thank you and that I loved it. He didn't respond, but the message did show it was received and read. It hurt that he was distancing himself and cutting me off, but I knew I'd done it to myself.

Not that I blame him. He'd tried to talk to me, but I never responded.

I decided to make a grand gesture and surprise him at the lake, but the holiday season had us so swamped with holiday party gigs, I couldn't break away until so much later than I wanted, every minute ticking by so excruciatingly slowly. So here it is, Christmas Eve, and I'm finally landing in Asheville.

Winding my way through the mountains, the sun has just started to rise. Not that it can be seen—the sky is dark and gray. Flurries swirl around the car, and I'm grateful the roads have been cleared. I didn't expect this much snow, but then again we are at a higher elevation.

Turning onto his driveway, I slow the car to take in a few deep breaths. Butterflies are awake and have apparently called in for reinforcements. They are fluttering through my stomach and causing it to ache. I don't even know if he's here, but several of his last texts had been inviting me, so I'd like to think he is.

Pulling up to the house, the first thing I notice is there are three vehicles. Warning bells start going off, but I put them aside and chalk it up to anticipatory anxiety. It's a holiday, and he must have invited several people, not just me. I will not be afraid. I can do this.

His words . . . *Be mine.*

Climbing out of the car, I walk across the driveway toward the front door. The snow has picked up, becoming denser, making it hard to see through, and the ground is a mixture of gravel and ice.

I know it's early and I probably shouldn't ring the doorbell in fear of waking up the whole house, but if he's sleeping, he might not hear me otherwise. I push the button and my heart starts racing.

Is he going to be happy to see me, or is he still mad? Maybe I shouldn't have come. Maybe I should have called him first. With my stomach aching and my hands sweating, the front door opens, and on eye level, brown eyes stare back at me.

Death of my heart.

There in the doorway, standing three feet away from me, is the girl who's haunted my every dream, or I should say starred in every nightmare.

Juliet.

And she's standing in slippers, little pajama shorts, and a guy's button down pajama top. Her hair looks like she's just crawled out of bed, and she has no makeup on. She's beautiful and sexy. I couldn't look like her if I tried. No wonder he asked her to marry him.

I am such an idiot.

My heart slams into my chest, and it's so fierce it hurts. I don't know why, but when I put this little scenario together in my mind, it never occurred to me she would be here.

I can't breathe.

I think I'm going to be sick and my eyes blur.

Why is this happening to me?

"Hi," she says, smiling timidly at me, pushing her brown hair off of her face.

Why is she smiling at me? Why isn't she yelling at me?

And then her eyes drop and run over the length of me. I feel pushed, and I take a step back.

This was such a bad, *bad* idea.

I swallow to try and hold down the utter and complete humiliation I feel.

Her eyes come back to mine and her eyebrows raise in question. Yeah, I'd be questioning me too.

I need to get out of here—immediately.

Why won't my feet move?!

Three seconds later, a little brown-haired boy peeks out from around her legs and I gasp at the sight of him. I knew he existed, but actually seeing him in the flesh just makes this so much more real and so much worse.

Am I the other woman? Why isn't she trying to hide this from him? Is he going to remember me showing up at their door?

Oh my God.

"Who's this, mama?" he asks. His voice is so sweet and so innocent.

She wraps her arm around his shoulders and with her eyes locked on mine, she quietly says, "This is Avery."

She knows my name. *Of course she knows my name.* But if she knows my name, she must know other things too. My face burns with embarrassment.

I can't be here.

I can't be a part of this.

Turning around, I wrap my coat around me more tightly and start walking quickly to my car. My chin quivers, and cold, wet flakes hit my face as my eyes flood with tears. My body feels numb from a lack of oxygen, so I suck in air through my nose to try and catch my breath.

This is horrible.

I'm devastated and drowning on the inside.

"Avery, wait!" I hear her call after me.

No way.

I am not going to stand here and subject myself to her questioning and judgment.

Why would he do this? Why would he ask me to be his and then bring her here?

I feel naïve and stupid. I feel tricked and used. I feel like succumbing to the grief that's weighing me down, and it's then I feel the footsteps behind me.

Is she coming after me? My heart starts racing even more.

No, he's coming after me and my vision tunnels and darkens.

No! No! No!

This is not happening to me. Not here and not in front of her.

Looking down, I focus on the snow, on my boots, and the dark purple color of my coat. I need to stay in the present and not slip into the past.

Breathe in. Breathe out. Breathe in. Breathe out.

The crunching of footsteps behind me increases and grows louder. The driveway begins to disappear, and in an instant, it flashes to the hallway. The whiteness of the snow fades to darkness and tears drip down my face.

Wet snow on my face . . . cold rain soaking my skin.

The crunch of gravel . . . the roll of thunder.

Pounding footsteps . . . chasing footsteps.

Light . . . dark.

It's going to happen.

It is happening.

Conscious chaos.

It's like it doesn't matter where I am, who I'm with, or what we're doing. It's so sudden and so quick that I can't even catch the transition into the vortex of complete and utter bedlam.

Panic swirls through me and I'm back there, in the dark, in the hallway, and as hard as I try, I know I'm not going to be able to escape him.

"Juliet, no!" I hear a guy's voice behind me, and it's then I feel the hand.

The pressure . . . the grip.

The restraint.

The pain.

Chapter
THIRTY-SEVEN

WILL ASHTON

P ULLING THE KAYAK in, I hear Clay's voice, and then I hear the scream. Whiskey and I both turn toward the house, and he takes off.

What the hell is going on?

Following closely behind him, I round the corner just as Clay bends over and picks someone up off the driveway. Blonde curly hair drapes over his arm and I think my heart stops.

She came!

She actually came. I don't know why I didn't think she would, but here she is, and it's then I realize she's hurt. Hysteria shoots through me, and then complete agony.

"What happened?" I yell, running to them and taking Ava from him. Her eyes are closed and blood is dripping down the side of her face. Clutching her to my chest, I gasp for air to keep myself from losing it.

"I don't know." There are tears in Juliet's eyes as she sweeps Ava's hair off of her face. "I tried to stop her, but when I touched her, she kind of freaked out, slipped, and hit the ground."

Glancing at Clay, I know he knows, but Juliet doesn't.

The thought of her having another panic attack and me not being here to protect her is almost too much to handle. She got scared and had to experience that asshole in her mind all over again. I desperately want those memories diminished, not enhanced. Sucking in my irritation, I push past them both, and head straight to my room. Bryce is in the corner by the couch—I hate that this is scaring him.

"Clay, grab a washcloth and let's see if we can get the bleeding to stop," I toss over my shoulder.

Ava groans in my arms, her face scrunches up in pain, and she turns, snuggling into my chest.

Lying her down on my bed, her eyes open and she blinks at me.

Blue to blue.

My heart stops as I fall into the ocean of her eyes.

Seconds pass as we stare at each other, and Clay runs in with a towel. Her eyes cut from me to him, and then to Juliet who is on the other side of me. Ava's eyes widen and panic streaks across her face.

"Here," Clay shoves it at me. I take it and press it gently to her head. She winces and tries to pull away from me. Yeah no, I hate to break it to her, but I am done with her pulling away. She's here, which means she's mine, and despite everything at the moment, I am so happy.

Holding the towel to her head, it quickly fills with red.

"Shit." I know head wounds have a tendency to bleed a

lot, but this seems excessive. I pull the towel away to get a better look. There at her hairline, the skin is split open, and it's too much. She's going to need stitches.

Replacing the towel, my eyes find hers just as they start to water. Looking away from me, she closes her eyes and her chin starts to quiver.

"Ava." She squeezes them tight. "Please keep your eyes on me." The demand in my tone is soft, but it can't be missed. She opens her eyes and I fall all over again.

I would be lying if I said I'm calm and under control. Because I'm not.

This time when we go into the urgent care, two things happen. One, we are recognized, and two, every person working there remembers us and eyes me suspiciously.

Yes, I understand that us showing up with injuries twice in two months doesn't look the greatest, but I would never lay a hand on her and they make me feel like the bad guy I'm not. Sideways glances, whispering, frowning, I'd bet just about anything that tomorrow's headlines call me abusive.

On top of that, Ava does what Ava does, and she closes in on herself. The entire drive there, she keeps her head on the window with her eyes shut. In the examining room, she talks to the nurses and doctors, but never me. And on the way back, the only thing she mumbles is that she wants to go home. By the time we pull up to the house, my nerves feel like they're about to explode.

Cutting the engine, I look over to Ava and she is studying her car. Her car is the only one in the driveway, both Juliet's and Clay's are gone. I briefly wonder where they've gone, and then decide I don't care.

"Thank you for taking me," she says quietly, before looking over at me.

She looks tired. She looks sad. She looks small all tucked into her coat.

Desperate to talk to her, I ask the first question that comes to mind.

"Did you just fly in this morning?"

She frowns and drops her eyes to her hands. Both of them are sitting in her lap, and her left hand starts tapping on her leg.

"Yes," she answers, as I reach across the truck and lay my hand over hers. She links her fingers through mine and lets out a sigh.

"You must be exhausted. Let's get you inside so you can rest for a bit."

She looks around the driveway again, and her right hand reaches up to touch the bandage on her head. I wish I could understand what she's thinking; I hate that she's not talking to me.

"Okay." She slides out of the truck and I do the same, quickly catching up to her to help her across the driveway.

Whiskey bolts out the door and I yell, "Heel." Clay and I have been trying to train him and I'm praying the newly learned command will work.

He stops midstride, and cocks his head at us. I know him, she knows him, and he is five feet away from ramming his head into her leg. I'm certain she has bruises from falling; I just don't know where yet.

He follows us into the house, and it's very quiet. Ava pulls away from me and wraps her arms around her stomach.

"Actually, Ash, I think I'm going to go ahead and go." She looks around the living room and then to the front door.

"What? Why? You just got here." I walk into the kitchen and stare at her from across the island.

No girl has ever confused me before like this one. Yes, she's been a mystery from the beginning, and yes, she's been a puzzle that took me a while to put together, but she let me. She let me in, and I am not letting her go. She came all this way because of me, because of us, and once and for all, we're gonna talk. There's no way I'm letting her leave until she tells me exactly what happened.

"You have company, and I don't think I should be here." Her eyes fall to Bryce's plastic plate sitting on the counter. Does she not like children?

Next to the plate, there's a note. I pick it up and see it's from Jules.

Hey,

Thanks so much for letting us crash this week. I do still love coming here, and it was much needed. Sorry for the hasty departure, but given the situation, I'm thinking you probably want the house to yourselves. I also think you're right, it's time to stop hiding and give myself a chance. Please tell Avery that I can't wait to meet her and I'm sorry if I played any part in her confusion. Good luck, big brother! Hopefully, I'll be hearing good news from you . . .

Oh, Clay spoke to his friend, Emma, so the three of us are headed to her house. We'll see you tomorrow.

Love, Jules

Well, there you go. I no longer have any company, so there's no reason for her to leave. Not wanting there to be any more barriers, secrets, miscommunication, or anything between us, I walk the letter over and hand it to her to read.

Her eyes scan over the words twice as she bites on her bottom lip. I lean backward against the island, cross my arms over my chest, and watch for any clue of what she's thinking.

"Brother," she says quietly to herself.

"Yeah, she loves to call me that, even though I'm only older than her by two weeks."

Ava's eyes flash up to mine and her fingers clench the letter. Her forehead wrinkles in confusion and she shakes her head like she has no idea what I'm talking about.

Turning away from me, she walks into the living room and slowly sits down on the couch. I follow her, pick up the remote to turn on the electric fireplace, and then sit down next to her. Her back is straight and every muscle is tight. I want her warm, and comfortable. I want her to stay.

"But?" She leaves the question lingering in the air, and turns to look at me.

I lean back against the cushions and toss my arm across the back of the couch. "I thought you understood. She's not just my friend, she's my family." I really thought she understood how much my family meant to me.

Her eyes scan my face, she starts breathing harder, and her hand moves to rub the bandage on her head. "So, you two aren't . . . ?"

She can't be serious, especially after that weekend in Nashville. "Aren't what?" I ask, feeling slightly annoyed, but amused at the same time.

"Together?" Her eyebrows raise in question.

I bust out laughing and she flinches. "No, but it's nice to know what you really think of me." My tone is sarcastic, and if I'm honest with myself, I'm hurt.

"But, that morning, I heard you and Clay . . ." She drops her head, looking at her lap.

That morning! In my condo!

"Wait. I thought you left?" I sit up and turn to face her.

"I did. But as I got in the elevator, I felt stupid for jumping to conclusions over a text, so I went back to talk to you. I heard you tell Clay that you had asked her to marry you." She looks so sad.

Running my hand over my face, I let out a deep sigh. "Ava, Juliet and I made a stupid pact back when we were twenty. You know the one, if neither of us is married at thirty we would get married. Last summer when she brought it up again, I seriously entertained the idea. Clay didn't know."

Her eyes widen and she crosses her arms over her chest. "So, you were planning to marry her?" she asks biting down on her bottom lip.

"No. I never would have gone through with it, but I understood why she brought it up. Both of us were in a really dark place. Her ex hurt her badly, and after the divorce, she kind of changed, decided that finding someone new to love wasn't worth the risk. Whereas I was looking for something, anything that could drag me out of my downward spiral. Ava, I love her, but not like that. Not at all. She's my family."

"She's divorced?" Her hands grip the couch next to her legs.

"Yes."

She gets up and starts pacing around the room. Back and forth, I watch her and think how this conversation is pretty similar to the one I had with Clay. As I was making plans to head to New York to drop off the book, he came over, and with a six-pack, we hashed it out. I still can't believe he hit me, but it's nice to know it wasn't because he thought I wasn't good enough for her, but more along the lines of, "You're going to ruin her life by not allowing her to find someone who truly loves her." He was right, and I knew it all along. I just hadn't pulled my head out of my ass yet to tell her. I left her wondering for way too long.

Juliet's a smart girl. She's pretty, genuine, and has a lot to offer someone—someone else. She does agree with me, and maybe by me finding someone to love, it'll give her more courage to try again. That guy was a dick, but not all of us are.

Stopping right in front of me, Ava looks me in the eyes and asks, "You two never . . ."

"No. Never have been, never will. I did kiss her once when I was fourteen, but that was more out of a curiosity of kissing than a desire to kiss her."

"How long have you known her?"

"Since I was thirteen." I'll never forget that day. It's bittersweet really.

"What?" She's still confused.

"I told you, after my grandfather died, I moved in with Clay and his family. She's his sister. I thought you knew that."

Her jaw drops open and then snaps shut.

"His sister. Ash, how would I have known that?" Her voice is slightly raised.

"Because I've talked about that time of my life with you and told you they became my family. Juliet and Clay are all I have now. Well, and Bryce too." Bryce was an unexpected, but very welcome, addition.

"Who's Bryce?"

"Her son."

"Oh. You never mentioned he had a sister. What was I supposed to think? At the blue grass concert she called you, at the benefit she was with you, her text after the morning of your show is what woke me, you admit to Clay you proposed, you were mad when I asked about her in my hallway, and there are so many photos of the two of you together online and half the time she's listed as your girlfriend."

Shit. That's a lot, and I had no idea.

Other than my profession, I never tried to hide anything from her. In fact, I've been more open with her than I have with anyone, ever. It never even occurred to me that she might think differently about my relationship with Juliet than what it actually is. Yes, the media always liked to romanticize her and I, but they all know she's Clay's sister. She's been around from day one.

"What do you mean I got mad at you in the hallway?" Leaning forward, I reach for her leg, but she steps back and my hand drops. I don't like the space or the tension between us— at all.

"You did. I asked you about her and you scowled at me."

Getting up off the couch, I move to stand in front of her. "I wasn't angry at you. I was irritated because I was trying to figure out why you walked out, what had happened to *us*, and you brought her up. At the time, to me, she was an irrelevant topic of conversation and I didn't understand why you were bringing her up."

"Oh." She looks away from me and touches the bandage again on her head. Her eyes squeeze shut; it must be hurting her.

Wandering back into the kitchen, I grab her some pain medicine and a bottle of water. She appreciatively takes it from me and swallows it down.

"Thanks," she mumbles, and then looks at me in confusion. "Ash . . ."

"Yeah?" My eyebrows raise.

"Where do you keep all of your clothes?"

"What?" I ask, chuckling.

"It's just, the closet at the condo in Nashville is really empty. It looks more like a place you crash at, versus live."

My gaze on her grows serious as I think about how this might look from her point of view. Taking the bottle, I toss it on the couch, and move to sit on the armrest closest to her. "Ava, my clothes are spread out between the tour bus, the lake house, and the condo. I'm a pretty simple guy and don't need a whole lot."

"Oh," she pauses thinking about my answer. "Now I feel kind of stupid." She drops her head and looks away from me.

"Don't, I can see how everything combined might be misleading or confusing. You know, after the benefit, you didn't ask me about her; I just assumed you knew who she was."

"Well, I didn't," she says, frowning.

"I'm sorry," and I really am. She should have asked me and I should have pushed harder in New York City.

"So, Bryce isn't yours?" She looks up at me with a very blank expression.

My hands squeeze the fabric of the armrest. "No. I told you we've never been together. Why would you assume that?" Not that I'd mind, I love the kid immensely and would take him in a heartbeat should the unthinkable happen.

She pulls her phone from her pocket and moves to sit next to me. I watch her type in my name along with "son." Image after image pops up of me with him over the years. Everything from him being a newborn, to recently when we were spotted in the park.

Shit. Well, that explains how she came to that conclusion.

Covering the phone with my hand, I push it down to her lap to gain her attention. "Ava, he's not mine."

She lets out a breath and then stands back up to put some distance between us. I really hate the distance.

Ava regards me for a minute before finally nodding her head in understanding. Breaking eye contact, she turns and walks out of the living room and toward the windows that overlook the lake.

Midstride, she freezes, and so do I.

She's spotted her real Christmas gift.

"You have a piano," she says without turning to look at me.

"I do."

"I don't remember this. Have you always, or did you recently get it?" She walks over and runs her hands over the glossy black lid—hands that when they touch me make me feel like the most important person in the world.

I swallow and try to push down my emotions. "I just got it . . . for you. Merry Christmas." I didn't realize I would be so nervous about her reaction, but I am. I'm worried it might be too much for her. A month ago, I was pretty sure which direction we were headed, now I'm just waiting for her lead.

"When did you get it?" She turns to look at me, leaving her hand on the top. She looks perfect next to it, just like I knew she would.

"Before Thanksgiving." It was a little presumptuous of me to purchase it for her so far in advance, but I knew then what I wanted, and it's her.

"Why?" Little wrinkles form between her eyes and her

fingers lightly tap across the top. She's nervous, and I don't know why. It's me sitting in front of her. Me and her. I like the way that sounds.

"Because I meant it when I said I wanted you to be mine. You once told me that you wanted to buy a place here on the lake. Well, I don't want you to do that. I want you to share my home with me. I want this one to be yours."

Her eyes widen a little and her lips part as she gasps.

"Ash . . ." her voice trails off as I push up off the armrest and approach her, her eyes never breaking from mine.

Stopping to stand directly in front of her, I place my hands on the piano, caging her in. Leaning down so we're on the same level, and with no uncertainty, I tell her the one thing I've wanted to tell her for weeks. "I am in love with you."

Her eyes fill with tears. "And I love you."

My heart jumps and dives in my chest. I thought she did, but hearing it from her just means so much more. She's made me the happiest man in the world, and instantly, I feel guilty for the part I played in her confusion. If I had just told her, things over the last couple of weeks would have been so different.

"I'm sorry I didn't tell you sooner. I guess I thought you knew." Picking up her right hand, I kiss the piano tattoo on the inside of her wrist. Her heartbeat pulses underneath her skin and I love how it feels on my lips. "You are the only one I have ever loved like this. You, just you. Since the very first time my eyes met yours, you've been it. That's all it took, just one look."

Blonde curls fall across her face and I gently tuck them behind her ear, trailing my finger down her cheek. "Blue to blue," she murmurs, watching me.

"Ah, so you did read the notebook." I crack a smile at her, lowering my hand and linking our fingers together.

"I did." She smiles back, blushing just a little.

Wrapping my other hand around the side of her head, I gently tilt it back and stare down at her mouth. Her bottom lip is swollen from her biting on it, and damn, if it doesn't look inviting. Bending over, I gently brush my lips to hers. It's been too long since I've kissed her.

"Please say you'll stay." I rest my mouth against the corner of hers.

"I'll stay," she says, with a deep sigh, the roughness of her coat brushing against me.

"Here let me help you out of that," I say, taking a small step back, releasing the top button.

"Always trying to help me out of my clothes," she giggles and the sound pierces my heart. God, I love that sound.

"If you only knew," I smirk at her and she gives me the biggest smile.

Damn, she's beautiful.

Removing the coat, I toss it onto the couch and step back into her personal space. I want to be as near to her as possible because I'm never letting her go.

Reaching up, she places her hand over my heart, and I cover it with mine.

Taking in a deep breath, my eyes travel up her arm, over her chin and lips, and find her eyes. Eyes that make me feel at home. Eyes that are shining back at me with pure love. A comfortable silence falls between us as she feels for the beating against my chest. A beating that is for her.

Soulmates are supposed to connect with ease, maybe that was our moment—that very first night, standing in the driveway, she found and connected with the beat of my heart. In return we found a comfort and a simplicity that allowed us both to reveal our true selves. She relaxed into me, and I to her, and together we found an inner calm.

I understand her, and she understands me.

My hand skims across her hip and around to her lower back. Her eyes flick up through her lashes and she licks her lips. Needing no more temptation, I take what she is freely giving, and fall into her mouth, her body, her heart, and her soul.

Love's like that though, right? A free falling. When you know, you know, and there's no turning back.

When I think back to the night I walked off the stage in Phoenix, I was lost. I spent years chasing a dream and trying desperately to find my way, but what I didn't realize is I had to go through all of that to get to her, and I do believe timing is everything.

All I ever wanted was to be somebody. Somebody to someone and somebody to myself. Ten years later with the brush of her hair across my arm, and the flash of blue under the lights of the bar, I knew, just like that . . . I'd finally been found. Without her, I am nothing. With her, I am finally something. And together that makes us everything.

The End

From the Author

Thank you for reading *Blue Horizons*.
If you enjoyed this book,
please consider leaving a spoiler free review on Amazon.

About the Author

OVER TEN YEARS ago my husband and I were driving from Chicago to Tampa and somewhere in Kentucky I remember seeing a billboard that was all black with five white words, "I do, therefore I am!" I'm certain that it was a Nike ad, but for me I found this to be completely profound.

Take running for example. Most will say that a runner is someone who runs five days a week and runs under a ten minute mile pace. Well, I can tell you that I never run five days a week and on my best days my pace is an eleven minute mile. I have run quite a few half marathons and one full marathon. No matter what anyone says . . . I run, therefore I am a runner.

I've taken this same thought and applied it to so many areas of my life: cooking, gardening, quilting, and yes . . . writing.

I may not be culinary trained, but I love to cook and my family and friends loves to eat my food. I cook, therefore I am a chef!

My thumb is not black. I love to grow herbs, tomatoes, roses, and lavender. I garden, therefore I am a gardener!

I love beautiful fabrics and I can follow a pattern. My triangles may not line up perfectly . . . but who cares, my quilts are still beautiful when they are finished. I quilt, therefore I am a quilter.

I have been writing my entire life. It is my husband who finally said, "Who cares if people like your books or not? If you enjoy writing them and you love your stories…then write them." He has always been my biggest fan and he was right. Being a writer has always been my dream and what I said I wanted to be when I grew up.

So, I've told you who I am and what I love to do . . . now I'm going to tell you the why.

I have two boys that are three years a part. My husband and I want to instill in them adventure, courage, and passion. We don't expect them to be perfect at things, we just want them to try and do. It's not about winning the race; it's about showing up in the first place. We don't want them to be discouraged by society stereotypes, we want them to embrace who they are and what they love. After all, we only get one life.

In the end, they won't care how many books I actually sell . . . all that matters to them is that I said I was going to do it, I did it, and I have loved every minute of it.

Find something that you love and tell yourself, "I do, therefore I am."

Ways to Connect

www.kandrewsauthor.com
https://www.facebook.com/kathryn.andrews.1428
https://twitter.com/kandrewsauthor
Monthly Newsletter: http://eepurl.com/9qAqr

Other Books

The Hale Brothers Series

Drops of Rain
(Book 1)

Starless Nights
(Book 2)

Unforgettable Sun
(Book 3)

Acknowledgements

TO MY THREE guys, thank you for having patience with me and for giving me the time to dream up and write another beautiful story. I love each of you immensely and cannot imagine a life without you.

Kelly and Michelle, not a day goes by that doesn't include the two of you, and I am so blessed. Thank you for your generous hearts and for being there for me, no matter what. I love you both.

Author Elle Brooks, my book bestie, we did it! Number four! This book isn't complete without a toast, so cheers to us with our pink Moet Champagne!

Author E.k. Blair, thank you for your friendship and all of the professional guidance you continue to give me. You have taught me so much and I will forever be grateful.

To my dear friend Megan C., I can't say thank you enough for all of the weeks, days, and hours you have spent going line by line with me to make Ash and Ava's story come to life. Your continued encouragement and love of these characters kept me going. Thank you for being you, and thank you for being my person . . . xoxo

Ry, thank you for sharing your line with me. The words are beautiful and they sum up Ash perfectly. xoxo

Lisa, from Adept Edits, thank you so much for the time and countless suggestions made to make this manuscript so fantastic. I love this story, and it's because of you it is polished and perfect. Drink some wine for me, and *grazie di cuore*!

To the KiSS Sisters, words cannot express how amazed I am by each of you. Your friendships, your time, and the way you love my stories means the world to me. You gals are wonderful and I can't say thank you enough . . . Love y'all! xoxo

Elle, Rachel, and Lexi, thank you so much for being my final set of eyes, and the best proofreaders ever!

Murphy, from Indie Solutions, I love the cover for Blue Horizons and I love how you took the vision I had and made it come to life. Thank you for always being available, I appreciate it more than you know. I look forward to working with you more in the future and I can't wait to see what you come up with next!

Julie, from JT Formatting, thank you for being my formatter and for creating the inside look to all of my paperbacks. Every time I open one of them, I think of you and smile. Thank you for what you do . . .

To the book bloggers: Thank you! The book community on a daily basis still awes me. I am indebted to each of you. Thank you for the endless amount of support and interest you have shown for my stories. It's through you that my dreams continue to come true. I hope to meet so many of you over the next year at signings. Look for me, because I'll be looking for you.

And finally . . . to the readers: I am humbled daily by your kind words and love. Every review, every inbox message, and every comment means so much to me. Keep writing them and keep sending them, I read them all! I hope you enjoyed **Blue Horizons**, and be on the lookout because I've got more headed your way real soon! Always remember—never let yesterday use up too much of today and be yourself, because that is the best person to be. Take care . . . Kathryn xoxo.

Made in the USA
Lexington, KY
18 September 2018